Praise for

HE WHO FEARS THE WOLF

"In spare, incisive prose, Fossum turns a conventional police procedural into a sensitive examination of troubled minds and a disturbing look at the way society views them...A superb writer of psychological suspense."   —*The New York Times*

"With sharp psychological insight and a fine grasp on police procedure, Fossum is easily one of the best new imports the genre has to offer."   —*The Baltimore Sun*

"Fortunately, we can now transfer our affection onto Norway's Karin Fossum, whose books about Chief Inspector Konrad Sejer are finally reaching the U.S."   —*Time Out New York*

"Throughout [*He Who Fears the Wolf*] Ms. Fossum raises interesting questions...That [she] doesn't pretend to have all the answers only adds to the force of her story."

—*The Wall Street Journal*

"Fossum's second novel is convincing, subtle and logically plotted, and Inspector Sejer is a great addition to the detectives' league."   —*The Dallas Morning News*

"Fossum not only explores the psyches of three wounded souls but delves into Sejer's inner life, revealing a lonely, no-longer-young cop still grieving over the death of his wife. This dark and moody psychological thriller will especially appeal to fans of Henning Mankell."   —*Library Journal*

"*Any* novel that opens with someone who first feels his face sliding off his skull and then his body splitting open, spilling out entrails that he frantically gathers back inside, pretty much has your attention."   —*Houston Chronicle*

HE WHO FEARS THE WOLF

Karin Fossum

HE WHO FEARS
THE WOLF

*Translated from the Norwegian
by Felicity David*

A HARVEST BOOK

HARCOURT, INC.

ORLANDO AUSTIN NEW YORK
SAN DIEGO TORONTO LONDON

www.HarcourtBooks.com

This is a translation of *Den som frykter ulven.*

First published in English in Great Britain by the Harvill Press.

The Library of Congress has cataloged the hardcover edition as follows:
Fossum, Karin, 1954–
[Den som frykter ulven. English]
He who fears the wolf/Karin Fossum; translated
from the Norwegian by Felicity David.—1st U.S. ed.
p.   cm.
I. David, Felicity. II. Title.
PT8951.16.O735D4613 2005b
839.8'238—dc22   2004025584
ISBN-13: 978-0-15-101091-2   ISBN-10: 0-15-101091-9
ISBN-13: 978-0-15-603049-6 (pbk.)   ISBN-10: 0-15-603049-7 (pbk.)

Text set in Minion
Designed by Scott Piehl

Printed in the United States of America

First Harvest edition 2006
C E G I K J H F D

To Kari

I hate people for the simple reason that they exist
and envy them intensely when I see them moving
around in their own country.
Inside my block of ice I sit, the lunatic,
taking meticulous notes on all the hostile deeds
that people direct specifically at me.
And from inside the dark space of revenge
emerges a master of the world.

—Elgard Jonsson

CHAPTER 1

A dazzling ray of light slanted in through the trees.

The shock brought him up short. He wasn't ready. He got out of bed, made his way slowly through the dark house, still half-asleep, and came out onto the front steps. And there he encountered the sun.

It struck his eyes like an awl. He raised his hands to his eyes, but the light kept coming, penetrating cartilage and bone, all the way into the dark of his skull. Everything turned blindingly white inside. His thoughts fled in all directions, shattered into atoms. He wanted to scream, but he never screamed because to do so was beneath his dignity. Instead he clenched his teeth and stood as still as he could on the steps. Something was happening. The skin on his head began to tighten; a tingling sensation that was getting stronger. Trembling, he stood with his hands on his face. He felt his eyes being pulled apart as his nostrils flared, growing as big as keyholes. He whimpered faintly and tried to resist, but he couldn't stop the violent force. Bit by bit his features were erased. All that remained was a naked skull covered with translucent, white skin.

He struggled frantically, moaning as he tried to feel his face, to be sure it was still there. His nose had turned soft and disgusting. He took his hand away—he had ruined what little was left, could feel it sliding off, losing its shape like a rotten plum.

And then it released him. Anxiously he took a breath, and then he felt his face slip back into place. He blinked several times, and opened and shut his mouth. But as he was about to move forward he felt a deep pain in his chest, the sharp claws of an invisible monster. He doubled over, wrapping his arms around his torso to restrain the force that was yanking the skin of his breast tighter and tighter. His nipples vanished into his armpits. The skin on his bare chest grew thinner, the veins stood out like knotty cables, pulsing with black blood. He was bent nearly double, and knew that he was no longer able to resist it.

Suddenly he split open like a troll in the sunlight. His guts and intestines poured out. He tried to keep everything in by seizing hold of the edges of the wound and pulling them together, but it seeped out and ran through his fingers, collecting at his feet like the entrails of a slaughtered animal. His heart was still beating, trapped behind his ribs, terrified, pounding. He stood like that for a long time, bent double and gasping. He opened one eye and cast an anxious glance down his body. His abdominal cavity was empty. The outpour had stopped. He clumsily began to gather up what had come out, stuffing it back in with one hand while he held on to his skin with the other, to prevent it from sliding out again. Nothing was in the right place; there were strange bulges everywhere, but if he could get the wound closed, no one would know. He wasn't made like other people, though this wasn't plain to see. He held on to the skin with his left hand, continuing to shove with his right. At last he got most of it inside again. Only a small spattering of blood was left on the steps. He pressed hard on the wound and felt it starting to close up, breathing cautiously so it would not open again. The sun was still shining through the trees, its white beams as sharp as swords. But he was whole again. Everything had happened too fast. He shouldn't have gone straight from bed out into the sunlight. He had always moved in a different space, seeing the world through a murky veil that took the sting out of the light and the sounds coming from outside. He held the veil in place by concentrating hard. A moment ago he had slipped up, had run out into the new day without taking stock, like a child.

His punishment seemed unreasonably harsh. Because as he slept on the dark bed, he had dreamed about something that made him sit bolt upright and then rush outside without thinking. He closed his eyes and recalled some images. He was looking at his mother at the bottom of the stairs. Out of her mouth gushed warm red blood. Fat and round, wearing a white apron with big flowers, she reminded him of a toppled jug, emptying red gravy. He remembered her voice, always accompanied by a dark velvety tone.

Then he went back inside the house.

———

This is a story about Errki.

It began like this: at 3 A.M. he left the asylum. We don't refer to it as the asylum, Errki, and even though you sure have the right to call it whatever you like in private, you ought to take other people into consideration and give it a different name. It's a matter of courtesy. Or tact, if you will. Have you ever heard of that?

She was so eloquent, God help her, that her words seemed to seep out of her like oil. After the words came her sound, a shrill electric organ.

"It's called the Beacon," he said, and gave an acid smile. "Those of us here in the Beacon are all one big family. The telephone rings, may I speak to the Beacon please? Could someone get the mail for the Beacon?"

"Precisely. It's all a matter of habit. Everyone has to show a little consideration."

3

"Not me," he replied in a sullen voice. "I was committed against my will, per Paragraph 5. Dangerous to myself and possibly to others."

He leaned forward and whispered in her ear.

"Thanks to me you can moon around on pay grade 27."

The night nurse shivered. This was the time of day when she felt most vulnerable. This no-man's-land between night and morning, a gray void when the birds stopped singing and you couldn't be sure that they'd ever sing again. When anything might have happened and she didn't yet know about it. She slumped a little, feeling faint. She didn't have the strength to see his pain, to remember who he was, that he was her charge. She simply found him repulsive, self-absorbed, and nasty.

"I realize that," she snapped. "But you've been here for four months now, and as far as I can tell, you seem to like it well enough."

As she said this her lips pursed like the beak of a hen. The organ struck a strident chord.

And so he left. It wasn't hard. The night was warm, and the window was nearly a foot open. It was locked with a steel bar, but he managed to remove the whole bar, using his belt buckle. The building was more than a hundred years old, and the screws came smoothly out of the rotting wood. His room was on the second floor. He jumped out the window as light as a bird and landed on the lawn.

He didn't cross the parking lot but instead headed through the woods toward the small lake, which they called the Well. It didn't matter which route he took. The point was that he didn't want to stay in the Beacon any more.

The lake was beautiful. It didn't put on airs, just lay there without a ripple, resting in the landscape, open and still. Didn't push him away, didn't lure him forward. Didn't touch him. Was simply there. The asylum was only a stone's throw away but invisible because of the trees. Nestor asked him to stop for a moment, and he did. He stared down into the black Well, and thought of Tormod, who was found floating face down in the water, wearing rubber gloves, as always, with his blond hair waving in the greenish black water. He didn't look very good, but then he never had. He was fat and sluggish with colorless eyes, and besides he was stupid. A disgusting, puddinglike fellow who went around asking people to excuse him, afraid of infecting them or of being in the way, afraid that someone would notice his contaminated breath. Now the poor man was with God. Maybe he was sloshing around on a cloud, freed at last from his clammy gloves. Maybe he'd met Errki's mother up there, maybe she was floating on the cloud next to his. Errki loved his mother. The thought of Tormod's fluttering eyes with the blond eyelashes made him swallow hard. He gave a couple of irritated shrugs of his thin shoulders and kept walking.

The dark figure was quite visible against all that light green foliage, but no one saw him. The others were asleep. After his suicide, Tormod was reduced to a practical phenomenon for which they had need: an empty bed. An astonishing transformation. Tormod was no longer Tormod, he was an empty bed. And he, too, would become an empty bed, with the sheets tucked in tight. He listened to the voice and gave a brisk nod. Then he walked on, sauntering through the dense woods. By the time the night nurse arrived to peek into his room, he had been walking for more than two hours. She didn't dare repeat their conversation. "No, I didn't notice anything unusual, he was as he always is." The sun had come up and shone in her face through the window of the staff room where they held their morning meetings. The words burned her throat like acid.

He passed the riding center. Heard the big dark animals restlessly scraping their hooves. One of them saw him and gave a loud snort. He looked at them out of the corner of his eye and felt a deep longing to stay with them, to be like them. No one would go up to a horse and ask: who are you? A horse had to bear whatever burden it was given, and afterward it was allowed to rest. And the horse that was incapable of doing anything got a bullet in its forehead. One day at a time. Walk around the enclosure with a child on its back. Take a drink from the old bathtub. Sleep standing up with its head drooping. Shake off a few insects. Until the end of its days.

Now he was walking along the road. People would soon be crawling out from under sheets and quilts. Tumbling out of holes and anthills. He could feel it approaching, like a vibration in the air. Before long the traffic would be on the move. Errki picked up his pace. It would be better to go back into the woods. Occasionally he raised his head. He liked the quivering trees, the light shimmering through the leaves, and the smell of grass in his nostrils. The sound of twigs and heather crunching under his feet. Trees, gray and dry, that stood there, anchored in the earth. He snatched at a fern and pulled it up, roots and all, held it to his eyes and muttered, "Root, stem, and leaf. Root, stem, and leaf."

After a while he grew tired. In the distance he saw a crag and beneath it a dark shadow. When he reached it he curled up in the grass, listening all the while to the voice. It hummed inside him, steady and peaceful, like a power station. In his pocket he had a little pillbox with a screw-on lid. Sleep is Death's brother, he thought, as he closed his eyes.

———

He was at the edge of a plain.

Only Errki could walk like that, his tread heavy, limping like a crow with clipped wings, but moving fast. Everything hung from him, his long hair, his open jacket, and the baggy trousers that he hadn't taken off in a long time—old polyester trousers

6

with a rank smell of sweat and urine. His head was tilted, as if a tendon were pulling his neck. He seldom looked up; instead he kept his gaze mostly fixed on the ground, so that what he saw was his feet trudging along. They moved by themselves. He didn't need a destination, he could keep going for hours without getting tired. He walked as tenaciously as a windup toy with a key in its back.

He was a man of twenty-four with narrow shoulders but surprisingly wide hips. He had inherited bad hip joints, and had to swing his hips in a special way to make his legs cooperate. An annoying swing, as if he had something hideous on his back that he wanted to shake off. It made people think that he walked like a woman. His neck was also thinner and longer than usual for a man, almost too thin to bear the weight of his head. Not that his head was particularly large, but the contents were definitely heavier than was common for most people.

He weighed only 130 pounds and ate little. It was hard to decide what he wanted to eat. Bread or cornflakes? Sausage or a hamburger? An apple or a banana? How did people actually go about making all the choices that life required? *How did they know if they'd made the right choice?*

In his pocket he had a little pillbox with a screw-on lid that contained all he needed to arrange his thoughts in acceptable order, and to make his legs obey him, up and down the corridors of the Beacon, on the bus, on the train, or wandering along the road.

When he wasn't on the move he would lie still and rest. His hair was long and black and wiry. It hung over his face like a filthy tassel. His skin was scarred with acne. The pimples had appeared in his thirteenth year, fermenting like tiny volcanoes. He stopped washing. They looked much worse if he rubbed them with soap and water. They weren't quite so noticeable with dirt and grease caked on his skin in a thick layer. Beneath the wiry hair a long, narrow face could be glimpsed, with sharp cheekbones and narrow black brows. His eyes were deep set and strange, usually downcast, avoiding anyone's glance. But if someone did make contact, they shone with a pale light. Because of his long hair and all the clothes he wore, his skin was white even in the summer. His trousers rode low on his hips, held in place by a leather belt. The buckle was a brass eagle with outspread wings and a crooked beak. It had tiny enamel eyes that stared down at an invisible prey, perhaps at Errki's modest genitals within the filthy trousers. His penis was small for a man his age, and it had never been inside a woman. No one knew this, and even he ignored the fact, focusing on more important matters. Besides, the eagle was impressive enough as it swayed in time with the rotation of Errki's hips. Maybe it fooled people into thinking that the equipment below might actually be a beast of prey.

It was quiet and hot along the road, and there were yellow fields on both sides for as far as the eye could see. A girl with a baby carriage was approaching. She saw the dark, lumbering figure from far off and realized that she would have to pass him. He looked odd, and as he got closer she could feel her body tense, and her steps grew stiffer. The figure was jolting and twisting along; there was something both timid and aggressive about him, and it occurred to her that she should not look into his eyes but move quickly past, with an indifferent and superior look on her face. She must not show that she was afraid because she had the feeling that if he smelled her fear, he would attack, just like an untrustworthy dog.

The girl was as fair and pretty as Errki was dark and ugly. Even through the veil her approach was like a sharp light. She was clutching the handle of the carriage, pushing it brusquely ahead of her like a shield, as if she were willing to sacrifice whatever it contained to save her own skin. Or so Errki thought. He had been walking for a long time, lost in thought. Now he was aware of the figure mincing toward him on the periphery of his vision. It looked insignificant, like a piece of fluttering white paper. He did not raise his head. He had long ago registered the contours that were approaching. Of all the things in Errki's world of perceptions, a girl with a carriage was the most pitiful. That producing a child should give a woman that stupid expression of bliss was something he couldn't understand. In spite of the billions of wailing inhabitants on earth, having a child changed their whole view of life. It was beyond his comprehension. Yet he did cast a glance at her and asked the question: evil intentions or none at all? He had no experience of good intentions. But he never let himself be fooled. It was impossible to recognize an enemy by outward, superficial appearances. Under the baby blanket she might have hidden a knife. He imagined something with a barbed point and jagged edge. One never knew.

They passed each other. At that instant Errki heard the brittle sound of tinkling glass. The girl tightened her grip on the handle of the carriage. For a brief moment she looked up. To her horror she saw the strange light in his eyes and inside his open jacket she read the words on his T-shirt: KILL THE OTHERS.

It was something she wouldn't forget. And so she became one of many who would later report to the police that she had seen the man they were looking for on that day at that particular spot.

The others were always after him. Not just his ravaged body with its organs all jumbled together, or his hard-as-stone heart that trembled behind the grating of bones. *They wanted to get inside him.* Into the secret space with the dazzling lamps. They wrapped their evil intentions in fine words, nagged him about the blessing of reality and the exciting challenge of community. He couldn't bear it.

What if he didn't want to?

He shook his head in confusion. His thoughts had wandered out of control, disturbing his sense of time. He tottered back into the room and sank down on the filthy mattress. He was glad that he had run away from the suffocating asylum, glad that he had found the abandoned cabin. He curled up on his side with his knees bent, his hands between his legs, his cheek pressed against the moldy mattress. He was staring deep inside himself, down into the dark, dusty cellar where a narrow hole in the ceiling opened, letting in a ray of pale light. It formed a circular patch on the stone floor. There sat Nestor. Beside him a ragged coat. The coat looked quite innocent, like something discarded, but Errki knew better. He lay still for a long time, waiting, and then fell asleep again. The wound needed time to grow together. While it grew he dreamed. After the punishment he was always given comfort, and he accepted it. It was part of the agreement. It was 6:03 A.M. on July 4th, and a fierce heat was already seeping in.

───────

The cabin had come as a surprise, hidden in a dense grove of trees. It was an old place where no one had lived for decades, yet it was in good repair, although most of the furnishings had been ruined long ago by drifters. Over the years quite a few such people had made themselves at home for a brief period, setting their mark on the worn rooms, leaving empty bottles behind.

He had stood in the grove for a while and stared. It was a wooden house, and in front was a little yard with a lush lawn. He put his hand tentatively on the door and pushed it open, then stood for a moment, sniffing the air. Inside he found a kitchen, living room, and two bedrooms. On one of the beds lay an old striped mattress. He tiptoed from room to room, looking around, breathing in the smell of old timber. In this house Errki was closer to his ancestors than he knew. It was an old summer cabin, constructed on the ancient site of one of the many Finnish dwellings built in the 1600s. As he walked around he listened to the mute walls. It looked as if something had happened. A rage had settled in the walls. Many of the thick beams had splinters sticking out of deep gashes, as if someone had attacked them with an ax. Not a single windowpane was intact; only a few shards of glass remained in the shattered frames. He thought of three or four things at once. It was impossible to get here by car, and as far as he knew no one had seen him when he turned off the road and began clambering through the undergrowth. He didn't have a watch, but he knew he had walked for precisely thirty minutes after leaving the roadway. The fact that he had no food or extra clothes didn't bother him, but he was thirsty. He ground his jaws together to create some saliva and began chewing on his tongue.

He went into the room that had been the kitchen and started opening the drawers. The knobs were gone, so he had to pry them open with his long fingernails. He found a fork with missing tines and a box of candles. Crumbs and cobwebs. Bottle caps. An empty matchbox. Under the broken kitchen window lay the remnants of a net curtain, but when he picked it up, the fabric dissolved in his fingers. He went back to the living room. The room had one window facing out the front and one on the opposite wall, looking out at a pond. Against one wall stood an old couch with rough green upholstery. Across from it stood a large wardrobe. He opened it and peered inside. It was empty. The wooden floor was stained and rough under his feet. He let himself sink onto the couch. The springs screeched and a cloud of dust rose up from the threadbare fabric. He changed his mind and went into the bedroom with the bed and mattress. He pulled off his jacket and T-shirt and lay down. He was gone for an eternity. When he woke up he had forgotten where he was, and besides, he had been dreaming. That was why he made the big mistake, stepping straight out

into the sunshine without stopping to think. It was humiliating
to scrape up his own guts from the step, listening to Nestor's
spiteful laughter, as his intestines slid through his fingers like
baby snakes.

He woke for a second time, sat up very slowly, and stared
around the room, running his hand over his chest to make sure
it was whole. Only a jagged red scar remained. It ran from between his nipples all the way down to his navel. He got up from
the bed. The sun was higher now. The room was empty except
for a rough bedside table that was really no more than a crate.
Slowly he straightened his back and walked over to the table and
pulled out the drawer. While he stood there staring down at the
drawer, he rubbed absentmindedly at a tender spot on his hip.
He had been lying on something hard. He went back to the bed
and looked down at the mattress, and felt around with his fingers. Something narrow and hard was there. He lifted up the
mattress with difficulty and rolled it back. Underneath was a big
hole in the striped cover where some of the foam had been removed. He stuck his hand inside and dug around, until he felt
something cold. He pulled it out and stared in amazement, not
believing his eyes. Of all the things to find in this dilapidated
place, inside a moldy old mattress: a pistol. He held it gingerly
in both hands and looked down the barrel. In Errki's hands it
was a foreign object, but when he gripped it in his right hand
with a finger on the trigger, it felt good. What power it had. All
the power of heaven and earth. Breeze, gale, and storm. Out of
curiosity he turned a lever and opened it. There was one bullet
in the chamber. Eagerly he pulled it out and examined it. It was
long and shiny and surprisingly round at the tip. He pressed the
round back into the chamber, pleased at how well it fitted. The
discovery made him look around. Someone had spent the night
here and left the pistol behind. That was odd. Maybe the person

had been caught by surprise and didn't have time to take it with him. Maybe he was waiting somewhere until he could come back and get it. It was a fine gun. Errki didn't know much about firearms, but he thought it was a large-caliber revolver of an expensive kind. He read the tiny letters on the stock: Colt.

"What do you think, Nestor?" he murmured softly as he turned the weapon this way and that. Then he stopped abruptly and tossed it away. The gun crashed onto the floor. He ran out to the kitchen and stood there for a moment, clinging to the bench. He should have thought of that. Nestor would come up with some disgusting suggestion. He could hear them down there in the dark cellar, laughing so the dust flew. He went back and stood looking at the gun for a long time. After a while he put it back inside the mattress. He didn't need it; he had other weapons. He wandered around the house, from the kitchen to the living room and back again, keeping his eyes on the stained floorboards. They creaked and carried on, the pitch varying. Soon he had created a whole melody from his route from room to room. His black hair and his jacket and trousers shook frenetically. His arms stuck out woodenly from his body, and he moved his fingers in time with the creaking boards. He was sucked into the rhythm; he walked and walked, unable to stop, not wanting to. In the repetition he found peace. He had no other aim than to walk, back and forth, taking even steps, his fingers splayed. Creak, creak, Errki goes, to and fro, over and over, from room to room, bumpety-bump.

He didn't know how long he had been walking, but eventually he gathered his courage and went to stand in the doorway. He opened the door hesitantly. Bright sunlight flooded the clearing. He lowered his eyes and took a cautious step out onto the stone steps, then made his way through the deep grass. He stopped and sniffed up at the pinecones and down at the thicket of ferns and bracken. Root, stem, and leaf. At last he was in motion again, though he didn't know where he was going or what he would do. Nestor was guiding his steps down through the undergrowth toward civilization.

It was still early morning. Only the early risers had got out of bed. They had opened their curtains and looked out at the radiant day. Hot. Bright. Shimmering green. They made optimistic plans for the day, wanting to take advantage of the all-too-briefly beautiful summer weather. One of them was Halldis Horn. She lived alone on a little farm not far from the old Finnish cabin. As Errki took his first steps through the grass, she was pulling her nightgown over her head.

CHAPTER 2

Both the first and the second bloom of youth had long since passed, and she was much too heavy, but for a few unprejudiced souls, she was definitely still a looker. Tall and plump and full breasted, with a gray braid that hung like a thick iron rope down her back. She had a round face with good coloring, cheeks like red roses, and her eyes had retained their flashing brightness even though she was old.

She went through her living room and kitchen and opened the door to the courtyard. She lifted her face to the sun, squinting, and stood on the steps for a moment in her checked apron and wooden clogs. She wore brown knee-high stockings, not because it was cold, but because she thought women of her age shouldn't show too much flesh, and even though no one ever came to her house except for the grocer once a week, there was always Our Lord and His eternally present gaze. For better or worse, to put it bluntly, because although she was a believer, she did send Him angry thoughts sometimes, and she never asked for His forgiveness. It was the invasion of dandelions that she was looking at now. The whole yard was full of them. They seemed to spread like a rash, polluting the entire garden, which she tended so carefully. Twice each summer she would root out the weeds with a hoe, hacking at one plant after the other with furious blows. She liked to work, but once in a while she would complain, just to remind her blessed husband what kind of mess he had left her in by dropping dead at the wheel of his tractor, the result of a clot the size of a grain of rice in his artery. That her tough and solid husband, a mountain of muscles, could be felled in such a way was beyond her understanding, even though the doctor had tried to explain it. She found it as impossible to believe as the fact that a plane could fly, or that she could ring her sister, Helga, in Hammerfest way up north and hear her plaintive voice so clearly.

She had better start before it got too hot. She found the hoe and carried it out to the yard. Shaded her eyes with her hand and scanned the area to plan her route. Decided to start near the steps and work her way in a fan formation past the well and over to the shed. In the hall she found a bucket and rake. She established a swift rhythm, hacking steadily at the weeds until she was tired, giving each plant two or three chops, then slowing the tempo, filling the bucket and emptying it on the compost heap behind the house. Ashes to ashes, she thought, giving the bottom of the bucket a hard thump. Then she went back to hacking. Her wide behind pointed toward the sky and swayed in time with the rhythm of her hoe. The red and green checks of her apron fluttered gently in the sun. Her brow was damp with sweat, and her braid kept swinging forward over her shoulder. She usually wore it pinned up, coiled around like a shiny snake, but not until after morning chores.

She liked the sound she made, hacking through the grass. The hoe was as sharp as an axe; she had sharpened it herself. Now and then she hit a stone, and winced at the thought of the shiny blade with its razor-thin edge. The weeds lay like fallen soldiers on a battlefield as she worked her way forward. She didn't sing or hum. She had enough to do just carrying out her task, and besides, the Creator might end up thinking that life was going too well, and for Halldis that would be an exaggeration. In her mind she set the table. Home-baked bread and her own brown whey cheese made from goat's milk.

She straightened up. Several birds shrieked high above the trees, and she thought she heard a swishing sound and then something falling through the leaves. Then silence. She paused for a while and stared, stealing a few moments of rest and letting her eyes glide over the woods, where she knew every single tree. In the familiar pattern of black trunks she thought she saw something dark. Something that had not been there before. An irregularity.

She narrowed her eyes and stared intently, but since it didn't move, she dismissed it as an illusion. Her eyes stopped on the well. The grass around the pump was tall and untidy; maybe she should cut it later. She bent to the work again, this time with her back to her front door. The sun was getting hot, even though it was early. Her wide backside was baking in the sun, and the sweat tickled as it ran down the inside of her thighs. This was Halldis Horn's life. Solving one problem, then another, as they appeared, without grumbling. She was the type of person who never questioned the Creation or the meaning of life. That wasn't proper. And besides, she was afraid of what the answer might be. She kept on hacking, making her bottom shake. Up the slope, hidden behind a tree, watching, stood Errki.

———

The woman fascinated him. Like heavy spruce trees, she grew out of the earth. Behind her he could hear her sound, a lonely, majestic trombone. For a long time he stood and devoured her with his eyes: her round shoulders, the fluttering dress. He had seen her before. This was someone who lived alone, he knew that. Someone who seldom spoke and listened only to the wind, or the screeching of the magpies. He took a

17

couple of steps, making a few twigs crack. The sound of the hoe grew sharper. He fixed his eyes on her hands, thick fingers, and wrists. The force of the blade as it sliced through the grass was fearsome and had nothing feminine about it. As he moved, without a sound now, he could tell that the woman gradually became aware of something alive approaching her. People who live alone develop an acute awareness of their surroundings. Her rhythm changed, becoming first slower, then faster, as if to deny that something was about to happen. She stopped and straightened up. Suddenly she caught sight of him. Her body stiffened. She stood as taut as a bow, her chest heaving. A cord of fear trembled between them. Her hands wrapped tighter around the hoe. Her eyes immediately widened, then turned narrow and hard. There was not much she was afraid of in the world, but just at that instant she felt uneasy.

He came to an abrupt halt, wanting her to keep on working. The only thing he wanted was to watch her as she carried out the simple task, to observe her rhythm and her wriggling backside. But Halldis was alarmed. Errki recognized all the sharp signals she was sending out and stopped short, his fists clenched, incapable of moving. Her gaze struck him like a rain of arrows.

The sun continued to climb, relentlessly blazing down on man and beast and the crackling dry forest. Police Officer Robert Gurvin sat alone, lost in thought. He opened a button on his shirt and blew at his chest. Sweat trickled down his neck. He tried to push back a lock of hair from his forehead, but it refused to stay put. He gave up and tried instead to slow his heart rate by focusing his thoughts. He had heard that old Indians could do this, but all the concentrating just made him sweat more.

Someone was shuffling outside. The door opened, and a fat boy of about twelve entered breathlessly. He stopped in the middle of the room, panting hard. In one hand he held a gray container that resembled an oddly shaped suitcase. Maybe it contained a musical instrument, like a lyre. Although the boy didn't look much like a lyre player, Gurvin thought. He studied him closely. The boy was astonishingly fat. His arms and legs stuck out from his body as if someone had pumped him full of helium and he was about to take off. His hair was brown and greasy, plastered to his skull in thin strips. He was barefoot and dressed in pale cutoff jeans and a dirty T-shirt. His mouth was agape with excitement.

"Yes?"

Officer Gurvin shoved his papers aside. He didn't have much to do that day, and he enjoyed having visitors. Right now he couldn't get enough of the incredible sight standing before him.

"Can I help you, son?"

The boy took a step forward. He was still panting; it was clear that he had something he needed to get off his chest in a hurry. It was presumably something along the lines of a stolen bicycle. His eyes were glittering, and he was shaking so much that Gurvin couldn't help but think of a warm soufflé in the oven, just before it caves in.

"Halldis Horn is dead!"

His voice teetered somewhere between the bright sounds of a child and the darker tones of the man he would become. He started low, but when he came to the word "dead" his voice rose to a falsetto.

Gurvin was no longer smiling. He looked at the creature in front of him in amazement, not sure that he had heard him correctly. He blinked and pressed a hand to the back of his neck.

"What did you say?"

"Halldis is dead. She's lying on her front steps!"

He looked like a brave soldier who had come back to camp alone to report on the terrible loss of his whole platoon. Shaken to his soul, but with a sort of acquired dignity all the same. Standing before his commander, he had completed his mission.

"Sit down, young man!" said Gurvin with authority, nodding toward a chair. The boy stayed where he was.

"You mean the woman who has the small farm up in Finnemarka?"

"Yes."

"Have you come straight from there?"

"I was walking past. She's lying on the steps."

"Are you sure that she's dead?"

"Yes."

Gurvin frowned. This heat could have an effect on anyone.

"Did you examine her?"

The boy looked at him in disbelief, as if the mere thought made him feel like fainting. He shook his head. The movement caused his heavy body to ripple.

"You didn't touch her at all?"

"No."

"How can you be so sure that she's dead?"

"I'm sure," he panted.

Gurvin took a pen out of his shirt pocket and made a note.

"Could I have your name?"

"Snellingen. Kannick Snellingen."

The officer blinked. The name was just as peculiar as the boy, but it suited him. He wrote it down on a pad, not letting his face show what he thought of the parents' choice of name.

"So you were baptized Kannick? It's not a nickname? Short for Karl Henrik, for example?"

"No, it's Kannick. Spelled with a c-k."

Gurvin wrote the name down with a flourish.

"You'll have to forgive me for my surprise," he said politely. "It's an unusual name. Age?"

"Twelve."

"So you say that Halldis Horn is dead?"

The boy nodded, still breathing hard and shifting his bare feet unhappily. He had set his suitcase on the floor beside him. It was covered with stickers. Gurvin noticed a heart and an apple and a couple of names.

"You're not trying to pull my leg, are you?"

"No!"

"In any case, I think I'll give her a call, just to see if she answers," said Gurvin.

"Go ahead and call. Nobody's going to answer!"

"Sit down in the meantime," Gurvin said. For the second time he nodded at the chair, but the boy remained standing. It struck Gurvin that he might not be able to stand up again if he set his rump down. He found the number in the phone book under the name Thorvald Horn. It rang and rang. Halldis was an old woman but still quite quick on her feet. Just to be sure, he waited for a long time. The weather was magnificent. Maybe she was out in the garden. The boy kept his eyes fixed on him, licking his lips. Gurvin could see that the boy's forehead was whiter than his cheeks because his wispy shock of hair shaded it from the sun. His T-shirt was a little too short, and some of his huge belly bulged over his shorts.

"Now that I've told you," he said, out of breath, "can I go?"

"No, I'm afraid not," said the officer as he put down the phone. "No one is answering. I need to know what time you were at her farm. I'll have to write up a report. This could be important."

"Important? But she's dead!"

"I need an approximate time," Gurvin said gently.

"I don't have a watch. And I don't know how long it takes to get here from her farm."

"Would you say about thirty minutes?"

"I ran almost all the way."

"Then we'll say twenty-five."

Officer Gurvin looked at his watch and made another note on his pad. He couldn't imagine that so fat a boy could move at any great speed, especially carrying something. He picked up the receiver and tried Halldis's number again. He let it ring for a long time before he put down the phone. He was pleased. This was a break in his routine, and he needed it.

"Can I go home now?"

"Let me write down your home number."

The boy began to squeak in a shrill voice. His double chin quivered on his plump face, and his lower lip trembled. The officer began to feel sorry for him. It began to look as if something had happened.

"Shall I call your mother?" he asked gently. "Can she come and pick you up?"

Kannick sniffled. "I live at Guttebakken."

This piece of information made the officer look at him with new interest. A film seemed to slide over his eyes, and Kannick instantly saw how the adult had put him into a new file labeled "unreliable."

"Is that so?"

Gurvin took his time cracking the knuckles of each finger, one by one.

"Should I call them and ask someone to come and get you?"

"They don't have enough staff. Margunn is the only one on duty."

The boy shifted his feet again and kept on sniffling.

The officer softened his tone. "Halldis Horn was old," he said. "Old people die. That's how life is. You've never seen a dead person before, have you?"

"I just saw one!"

Gurvin smiled. "Usually they pass away in their sleep, sitting in a rocking chair, for instance. There's nothing to be afraid of. No reason for you to lie awake at night thinking about it. Promise me that?"

"There was someone up there," the boy blurted out.

"Up at the farm?"

"Errki Johrma."

He whispered the name like a swear word.

Gurvin looked at him in surprise.

"He was standing behind a tree, by the shed, but I saw him clearly. And then he took off into the woods."

"Errki Johrma? That can't be right." Gurvin shook his head. "He's in the asylum—has been for months."

"In that case, he's escaped."

"I can easily check on that," said the officer calmly, but he bit his lip. "Did you talk to him?"

"Are you crazy?!"

"I'll look into it. But first I have to check on Halldis."

He let the news of Errki sink in. He wasn't superstitious, but he began to understand why some people were. Errki Johrma sneaking around in the woods nearby, and Halldis dead. Or at least unconscious. He felt as though he'd heard this before. A story that was repeating itself.

Something occurred to him. "Why are you dragging that case around with you? You don't have orchestra practice in the middle of the woods, do you?"

"No," the boy replied, planting one foot on either side of the case, as if he were afraid it would be confiscated. "It's just a few things that I always take with me. I like to walk in the woods."

The officer gave him a penetrating look. The boy was apparently defiant, but underneath lay fear, as if someone had frightened him to the bone. Gurvin called Guttebakken—the home for boys with behavioral problems—and talked to the superintendent. He explained the situation succinctly.

"Halldis Horn? Dead on her front steps?"

Her voice grew strident with doubt and concern. "It's impossible to say whether he's lying," the woman said. "They all lie when it suits them, but in between there might be a scrap of truth. At any rate, he's already deceived me once today, since he obviously took the bow with him, knowing perfectly well he's only supposed to use it with adult supervision."

"Bow?"

Gurvin didn't understand.

"Doesn't he have a case with him?"

The officer cast a glance at the boy and at what lay between his feet.

"Yes, he does."

Kannick understood what they were discussing, and pressed his fat legs closer together.

"It's a fiberglass bow with nine arrows. He roams in the woods, shooting crows."

She didn't sound angry, more worried. Gurvin made another call, this time to the hospital where Errki Johrma was committed. Or should have been, since it turned out that he had in fact escaped. He tried to play down the episode. The rumors about Errki were already bad enough. He didn't mention Halldis.

Kannick was growing more and more uneasy. He glanced at the door. What had happened? Gurvin wondered. He hadn't hit her with one of those arrows, for God's sake, had he?

"Well, at least Halldis died on a beautiful day," he said, giving the boy an encouraging look. "And she was old, after all. That's the way we all dream of dying. Those of us who are no longer spring chickens."

Kannick Snellingen didn't reply. He shook his head and stood there motionless with the case between his legs. Grown-ups always thought they knew everything. But Officer Gurvin would soon think otherwise.

CHAPTER 3

He drove slowly up toward the farm. It was a long time since he had last been there, maybe a year. In his chest a jagged stone was frantically spinning. Now that he was alone in the car, he felt a churning inside. *What had the boy seen?*

Kannick had insisted on walking the mile or so home to Guttebakken. Margunn had promised to come out to meet him. If Gurvin knew the superintendent, there would be juice and sweet rolls and a brisk scolding, followed by a tender caress of his hair. Never mind what the others might say. Margunn was smart enough to know what he needed. The boy had calmed down a bit and wore a brave expression as he left.

The Subaru moved up the wooded slope with the eagerness of a terrier. Everyone around here had a four-wheel drive, and it was needed in winter because of the snow and in the spring because of the mud. The slopes were steep, and driving was difficult enough even on this dry paved road. As he drove he thought about Errki Johrma. At the hospital they had confirmed that he made an easy escape through an open window, then set out for this area, where everybody knew him. And why shouldn't he? This was where he felt at home. The boy did not appear to be lying. Like most people, Gurvin was wary of the man because of all the rumors, which were as ugly as Errki himself. Misfortune followed him everywhere. He was like a bad omen that left fear and dread in his wake. It wasn't until he was involuntarily committed that people began to have a little sympathy for him. The poor man is sick, after all, they said; it's best for him to get some help. It was rumored that he had tried to starve himself to death, that he'd been found in the locked ward, as feeble as a prisoner of war. He lay on his back and stared at the ceiling, chanting monotonously, "Peas, beef, and pork, peas, beef, and pork." Over and over.

Gurvin remembered what had happened long ago. As he drove he glanced out of the side windows. In some way he was hoping that Errki wouldn't turn up. He was so impossibly strange. Dark and repulsive and unkempt. His eyes were two narrow slits that he never fully opened, making one wonder sometimes whether he actually had two eyes in there at all, or whether there was merely a raw abyss through which you could look right into his twisted brain.

And Gurvin was finding it hard to believe that Halldis was dead. He had known Halldis and Thorvald since he was a child, and she had always seemed immortal. He couldn't imagine the little farm without them. It had been there forever. Kannick must have seen something else, something he didn't understand that had frightened him. Errki Johrma, perhaps, scowling from behind a tree. That alone would be enough to startle anyone and prevent them from seeing clearly. Especially a high-strung boy with one foot on the path to trouble. Both front windows of his vehicle were open, but even so he was sweating profusely. He was almost there now and could see the shed at Halldis's place. He found it extraordinary that such an old woman kept everything so neat; she must be forever tidying the yard with her rake and scythe. Then the garden appeared, lush and green in spite of the drought. Everywhere else the lawns had turned yellow. Only Halldis could defy the forces of nature. Or water the grass illegally, perhaps. He turned at once to look at the house. A low white building with red trim. The front door stood open. He had his first shock: a head and arm were visible on the front steps. Horrified, he stopped the car and turned off the engine. Although he could see only her head and arm, he knew immediately that Halldis was dead. Damn it, the boy was telling the truth! Reluctantly he opened the car door. Everyone was headed down the same road in life, and Halldis was an old woman, after all, but he was suddenly alone with death.

Gurvin had discovered dead bodies before, but he had forgotten how strange it was, this unfathomable feeling of being alone, more alone than at any other time. To be the *only one*. He got out of the car and approached slowly, as if wanting to postpone the moment for as long as possible. He looked over his shoulder, he couldn't help himself. There wasn't much for him to do. Just go over and bend down, place one finger at her throat and confirm that she was indeed dead. Not that he had any doubts. There was something about the angle of the head in relation to the white arm, and something about the way the fingers were spread out. But it had to be confirmed. Then he could just sit in the car, call for an ambulance, roll a cigarette, and wait with a little music on the radio. It wouldn't serve any purpose to examine anything indoors. This was a death by natural causes, and he saw no reason to do anything else. He had almost reached her when he stopped short. Something gray and milky had run down the steps. Maybe she was carrying something and dropped it when she fell. He walked the last few paces with a pounding heart.

The sight completely overpowered him. He could only stand and stare breathlessly for several seconds before he was able to decipher what he was looking at. She lay on her back with her legs spread. In the center of her plump face, buried deep in the left eye socket, was a hoe. A small section of the shiny blade was visible. Her mouth was open, and her top dentures had come out, making the face he knew so well take on an ugly grimace. He lurched back and gasped. He wanted to pull the hoe from her face at once, but he couldn't. He turned on his heel and managed to get as far as the lawn before the contents of his stomach came pouring out. As he vomited he thought about Errki. Halldis dead, Errki nearby. Maybe he was still up in the woods, hiding behind a tree and watching him. Gurvin heard his own voice ringing in his ears. *That's the way we all dream of dying. Those of us who are no longer spring chickens.*

———

Less than an hour later the place was swarming with people.

Chief Inspector Konrad Sejer stared at the other eye, which was still intact. His face was expressionless. Hers was discolored from internal bleeding. He went into the house, astonished at how neat everything was. How quiet it was. Nothing in the tiny kitchen shouted back at him when he peeked inside. He went through her mail, pulled out a letter, and scribbled a note. Stood for a long time, using his eyes. Nothing seemed out of place.

Most of those present had clearly defined tasks, and they made it through the day by doing their best to concentrate on the job at hand. But each person knew that it would come back to them, later, on bad days. The few who couldn't immediately set about their duties, turned their backs to the stairs and lit cigarettes. Afterward they made sure to put the extinguished butts back in the packets. Be careful where you step and what you touch. Stay calm, make room for the photographer, it's just another case, there will be others, you didn't know her. There are other people who will grieve. Let's hope so.

Gurvin stood by the well, smoking. He had been chain-smoking since the vehicles arrived. Now he turned around and looked at the men. He heard their voices: low, brisk, serious, with a degree of respect in their tone, for her, for Halldis. He wondered if she had ever pictured herself in her mind, the way he imagined old people did when they were approaching eighty and the end of their life. Lying in an open coffin, wearing a lovely dress, her hands folded. Maybe a discreet touch of rouge on her cheeks, put there by a considerate person whose job it was to make her as beautiful as possible before she met her Maker. But that wasn't how things had turned out. She wasn't the least bit beautiful. Half of her head had been destroyed, and no man on earth would be able to hide that fact. He lit another cigarette, and caught himself staring up at the woods, as if he thought Errki was still watching them with his burning eyes. *Why?* Gurvin thought. An old woman like her? Could she have seemed threatening to him, or was it just that every single person he met was his enemy? What could she have said or done that aroused such terror in him that she had to be slaughtered? He could make sense of most things, at least when he tried hard to. He understood sixteen-year-old boys who roamed the streets at night, in search of excitement. Who hot-wired cars and tore through the town sharing a bottle. The speed. The rush. The idea that someone was after them, that someone had at last noticed them. He understood how a man could commit rape. The rage, the impotence when confronted by the female sex, the fact that a woman remained an incomprehensible mystery that a man had to break. And in dark moments he could even understand men who beat women. But he could not understand this. How something could sprout and grow inside someone, spreading slowly, like poison. Erasing all normal inhibitions and turning that person into a wild animal. Often they remembered nothing afterward. The murder would be like a bad dream, never entirely real. Not even if, contrary to all expectations, they recovered from their illness and reached a certain level of clarity, and were told: you did something horrific. But you were sick.

Gurvin stared at the chief inspector, who revealed nothing of what he was feeling—although every once in a while he ran his hand over his hair, as if to keep everything in order. At regular intervals he issued an order or asked a question, all with a natural authority that seemed to come from within, speaking in an impressively deep voice from a height of more than six feet. Gurvin looked up just as Halldis's body disappeared into the rubber body bag. Now all that remained was the house, with its windows and doors wide open. Most likely it would be sold to some foolish fellow from town who dreamed of owning a small farm up in the woods. Maybe for the first time children would come up here, and they would set up a swing and a sandbox. Colorful plastic toys would spread all over the lawn. Young people wearing shockingly skimpy clothes—it was a good thing that Halldis would never see them. All of that would be fine. But something was gnawing at him inside, something he couldn't ignore.

———

July 5th, and still hot.

Chief Inspector Konrad Sejer was struck by a strange impulse. He turned and sauntered into the Park Hotel bar. He never went to bars. He realized that he hadn't been inside this place since before Elise died. Inside, the lighting was comfortably dim, and it was a great deal cooler than out on the street. The thick carpets muted his footsteps, and the semidark room made it possible for him to open his eyes wide.

The place was almost deserted, but at the bar a woman was sitting alone. She stood out in part because she was alone and also because she was wearing a striking red dress. He could see her in profile. She was looking for something in her bag. Her dress was very beautiful. Soft, slinky, poppy red. She had blond hair that tumbled around her ears. When she looked up and smiled, he was unprepared and nodded back stiffly. There was something familiar about her. She looked like the young officer at the station, the one whose name he could never remember. There was no drink in front of her on the bar. Apparently she hadn't got that far yet. Perhaps she was looking for her money.

"Hello," he said, making his way to the bar. "It's hot today. Can I buy you a drink?"

The words just popped out of his mouth. He leaned confidently on the bar, a little surprised at his boldness. Maybe it was because of the heat. Or his age, which at times oppressed him. He was fifty now, and from here on it was downhill all the way, toward the mysterious darkness.

But she nodded and smiled. He could see down the front of her dress. Her breasts took his breath away. As did her collarbone, straight and slender, sharply defined under her skin. He felt embarrassed. It wasn't the young officer after all, but Astrid Brenningen, who was a receptionist at the justice department. How could he be such an idiot?! She was twenty years older than the officer and didn't look a bit like her. It must have been the dim lighting.

"I'll have a Campari, thanks." She gave him a teasing smile, and he fumbled in his back pocket for his wallet while trying to appear calm. He wouldn't have expected to find her here, without an escort. But for heaven's sake, why shouldn't Astrid go out on the town and have a drink, and why shouldn't he buy it for her? They were more or less colleagues, after all. They didn't talk much, but that was because he never had time to stop and chat. He was always on his way to do something that was more important than pausing to gossip in the lobby. Besides, he never flirted. He couldn't imagine what had come over him.

She sipped elegantly at her Campari, and then smiled in an oddly familiar way. He felt something prick at the back of his neck, and had to lean over the bar so as not to fall. His knees buckled, his heart raced and pounded violently. It wasn't Astrid Brenningen at all. It was his own Elise!

He began to sweat. He didn't understand how on earth she could be sitting here, right there in front of him, after all these years, smiling as if nothing had happened.

"How have you been?" he stammered, wiping the sweat from his brow with the back of his hand. At that instant he noticed the naked underside of his own arm. Again he almost fainted. He wasn't wearing a shirt! He was standing at the bar in the Park Hotel, bare chested! Desperately he rolled over onto his side and pulled up the quilt. Then he opened his eyes, blinking in confusion at the light for a moment. His dog, Kollberg, was sitting next to the bed, staring at him. It was 6 A.M.

Kollberg's eyes were big and glistening, like polished chestnuts. Now the animal tilted his head in a completely endearing way. His heavy tail wagged twice, optimistically. Sejer tried to pull himself together after his dream.

"You're starting to go gray," he said brusquely, looking at the dog's snout where the fur had taken on the same shade as his own hair.

"Stay home today. Watch the house."

The words sounded sterner than he had intended, as if to hide his embarrassment after the dream. He climbed out of bed. Offended, Kollberg whined and flopped down heavily on the floor. The dog gave his master a wounded look. Sejer never ceased to be amazed by that heartbreaking look or by how an animal weighing 150 pounds and with a brain the size of a meatball could prompt such emotion in him.

He showered, feeling dejected, taking longer than usual. He kept his back to the door, to emphasize who was the boss.

He didn't care for days this hot. He much preferred somewhat cloudy weather with no wind, about sixty degrees Fahrenheit in August or September, with comfortable, dark evenings and nights.

This morning he took his time. He read the newspaper through from start to finish. The murder in Finnemarka was on page one and the first story on the radio news. This was a tragedy that would fill his next few weeks. As he ate breakfast he listened to the interview with Officer Gurvin. Then he took the dog out for a walk. Next he opened the kitchen window a crack, lowered the shutters, and checked that there was a spare key in the vase outside his door. If he had to be away for a long time, he would ask a neighbor to walk his dog.

By the time he set off down the street on his way to work it was 8 A.M. He was still upset by his dream. A hand had seized hold of his heart and shaken it; he could still feel a soreness inside. Elise was gone. No, more than gone, she no longer existed at all. And here he was, dragging on alone for the ninth year. His legs carried him along, steadily and evenly. He washed and dressed, ate and worked, he was even thriving. As a matter of fact, he felt good most of the time. Was it an exaggeration to say that? The feeling of powerlessness popped up only every now and then, like this morning. Or when he sat alone in the evenings and listened to music. The music that she liked, that they had listened to together. Eartha Kitt. Billie Holiday.

A steady stream of people was moving along the street, dressed in summer clothes. It was Friday. Ahead of them lay a long weekend, and the dream of what it would bring was evident in all of their faces. Sejer had no such plans. His vacation wasn't until the middle of August, and it was quiet during the summer months, provided it didn't get so hot that people went completely berserk. So far the heat had lasted for three weeks, and already, at 8:13 A.M., the thermometer on the roof of the department store showed eighty degrees.

Because the justice department was located beyond the center of town, he felt a bit like a fish heading upstream, dodging pedestrians in the crowded street. It seemed as if everyone else were going the opposite way, heading for the offices and shops that were situated around the square. He looked at the cloudless sky. It was a bright, pastel color that assailed his eyes. Behind that thin veil of light was a vast, cold darkness. Why was he thinking that now of all times?

Sejer cast swift glances at the faces in the throng. For a split second he met their eyes, one by one. They all did the same thing: stared for an instant and then looked down. What they saw was a tall, wiry, gray-haired man with long legs. If asked they would say that he held a high-level position. Handsome but rather conservatively dressed. Putty-colored trousers, a bluish gray shirt, and a narrow dark blue tie with tiny red dots on it.

In one hand he was carrying his dark leather briefcase with a brass lock and the initials K.S. on the top. His shoes were black and well polished. His eyes were inquisitive and uncommonly dark beneath his silvery hair. But most things about him they couldn't see. He was born and raised in lovely Denmark, and the day of his birth was a difficult ordeal for both him and his mother. Even today, after fifty years, he still had a small hollow at his hairline from the forceps. He often scratched that spot, as if prompted by a vague memory. Those who might see him on the street would not see that he had psoriasis, that under his newly ironed shirt were several patches of scaly skin. Or that he had a restlessness in his body that came and went. Deep inside his private universe there was a weak spot. He had never recovered from his grief at the loss of Elise; it had grown bigger and bigger and then imploded to form a black hole that sucked him in every once in a while.

He refocused on the swarm of people walking toward him. In the midst of all the bright, airy, summer attire one figure stood out. A man in his early twenties was walking close to the building walls, moving swiftly. He was in heavy clothes in spite of the heat, in dark trousers and a black sweater. On his feet he wore brown leather shoes with laces, and around his neck he had, of all things in the intense July heat, a ribbed scarf. Yet his clothes weren't the main thing that distinguished him from the rest of the people on the busy street. It was the fact that he didn't raise his head to look up, not once for a moment. His rapid and determined gait, as well as the way he kept his eyes fixed on the pavement, forced everyone else to step aside to let him pass. Sejer caught sight of the man when he was fifteen or twenty yards away and fast approaching. The man's swift pace and tense air, in addition to his odd expression, triggered something in the chief inspector. The scarf was long and loosely coiled several times around his neck. Sejer had just passed Fokus Bank and heard the little electronic click that told him the bank was now open. The scarf might be a hood that the man could pull over his head with one motion, leaving only a slit for his eyes. He was also carrying a shoulder bag. And what was more: the bag was open and the man's right hand was slipped inside. He had his left hand in his pocket. If he was wearing gloves, no one would know.

Sejer kept on walking. In a matter of seconds the man was only a few feet away. A sudden impulse made the inspector move closer to the walls and walk in the same manner, with his eyes on the pavement. He wanted to continue in this way, to see if the man would move aside or if they would collide. He was even mildly amused by his whim, and it occurred to him that maybe he had spent too many years on the police force. At the same time, there was something about the man that made him uneasy. He quickened his pace and sensed rather than saw the dark figure looming before him. Just as he thought, they did not collide. At the last moment the man veered to one side and raced past him. So he wasn't walking along completely lost in his own thoughts. He was paying attention. Maybe he was walking like that so no one would see his face and remember it. But Sejer would. A broad, fleshy face with a round chin framed by curly blond hair. Straight eyebrows. A short, wide nose.

The man passed Sejer, moved back over to the wall, and started walking even faster. The inspector narrowed his eyes to watch him as he headed down the street, and felt his skin prickle as he slipped through the doors of Fokus Bank. No more than thirty seconds had passed since he had heard the click of the lock. In his mind Sejer reviewed the inside of the bank. He had his own savings account there. The customers first had to go in through the glass doors, then walk down a narrow corridor that swung to the left. This meant that the interior was not visible from the street. Inside, the tellers' windows were on the left, the counter with deposit slips and other forms was next to the exit, and on the right were chairs for four or five people. There was room for five tellers behind the windows, when the bank was busy. Right now there was most likely only one teller. After the customer completed his transaction, it was possible for him to go out by a door that opened onto the square. A robber might, for instance, park a getaway car there, leave the key in the ignition, and walk around the block, through the glass doors; then rob the bank and vanish in seconds. It wasn't possible to park a car on the street without attracting attention. But the bank had four metered parking spots allocated for customers at the entrance to the square.

Sejer was still standing there, staring. He couldn't quell his unease. With a resigned heave of his shoulders and firm steps he walked back. He didn't have to tell anyone about this. He opened the door, trudged down the narrow corridor, and emerged near the tellers' windows. There were two customers there. The man with the bag and a young girl. A woman employee had just put on her glasses and was bending over the keyboard of her computer. The man with the bag stood with his back turned, filling out a form. He didn't look up as Sejer came in. It looked as if he was in a hurry.

Sejer looked around in confusion. For the sake of appearances, he plucked a brochure about retirement funds from a rack on the wall, and then left. There has to be a limit, he told himself sternly. And besides, he was now several minutes late, and he wasn't in the habit of being the last one to arrive at work. He made his way back out to the pedestrian street and walked off at a faster pace toward the justice department. He passed the jewelry store advertising a sale, Brunner's Florist, and Pino Pino, where Elise used to buy her clothes. Including that red dress. A few minutes later he could see the top floors of Headquarters, and at that moment a shot was fired. Some distance away, but still quite clear. Then someone started screaming.

CHAPTER 4

Almost everyone stopped in their tracks. Only a few people heard it and kept walking, casting a quick glance over their shoulders. Others were pressed up against the walls of the buildings across from the bank. A mother put her arms protectively around her child. An old man who seemed to be hard of hearing looked around in bewilderment, wondering why everyone else had stopped. He stared open-mouthed at Sejer, who came rushing up, his briefcase swinging wildly. He was a good runner, but the briefcase interfered with his rhythm, making him look clumsy. A woman staggered out of the bank. She leaned against the wall of the building and hid her face in her hands. He recognized her as the teller. The next moment she collapsed, sliding down to a sitting position on the pavement.

"Police," he said, out of breath. "What happened? Is anyone hurt?"

"Police?" She looked up at him in astonishment. "He robbed me," she gasped. "He robbed me and then ran out to the square. He's gone, drove off in a white car."

Sejer's eyes widened when he heard the rest of her story.

"He took a girl with him."

"What did you say?"

"He took her with him. Took her out of the bank and put her in his car."

"A hostage?"

"He stuck his gun in her ear!"

Sejer turned to look at the square. A thin stream of water was streaming out of the fountain, and the pigeons were calmly pecking at breadcrumbs. He left the teller and went over to two youths who were talking excitedly. They were standing near the fountain and had a good view of the bank and the main street.

"Did you see which way he went?"

They stopped talking and stared at him.

"Police," he added as he set down his briefcase.

"That was damned fast work!" exclaimed one of the young men, who seemed as thin as a beanpole. His sunglasses were perched on top of his head, and his hair was black with a bleached streak in the middle. He turned around and pointed toward the main street, which wound past the fire station and the Diamond restaurant before heading out of town.

"He was shoving a girl in front of him. Threw her into the car."

"What kind of car was it?" he asked quickly as he fumbled with his belt to unfasten his cell phone.

"A little white car. Maybe a Renault."

"Stay here," he said.

"We're supposed to be at work by now," said the other youth. "And besides, it wasn't a Renault if you ask me, it looked more like a Peugeot."

"Today you're going to be a little late for work," Sejer said curtly. "It can happen to the best of us. Was he wearing a ski mask?"

"Yes."

"Black jumper and corduroy trousers?"

"Do you know who he is?"

"No."

"Can we come down to the station?"

"Probably."

It might have been staged, he thought suddenly. They might have been in on it together. Maybe she was his girlfriend. A fake hostage. Two people inside the bank thirty seconds after opening, how likely was that? Criminals were getting so damned inventive.

The small groups of pedestrians were gradually dispersing, but a few people were lingering, perhaps hoping they would be asked to give statements. There was nothing more to see. The man was gone. It was all over in seconds. A few people couldn't help but think how easy it was. With a fast car and knowledge of the area, someone could cover a lot of territory in only half an hour.

The boy with the badger hair put on his sunglasses. "You've got the whole thing on video, haven't you?"

"Let's hope so," Sejer muttered. He'd had mixed experiences with video surveillance. He turned around just as a squad car drove into the square. Gøren Soot jumped out, bringing a frown to Sejer's face, and right after him came Karlsen, which caused him to breathe a sigh of relief.

"We've got a hostage situation. A young woman. And the gun is loaded. He fired a shot inside the bank."

Karlsen stared openly at the boy's badger hair.

"Take these two in so they can give a statement. They saw the robber and the car. And have a look at the videotape as fast as you can. We've got to find out who the hostage is. Set up a roadblock at E18 and E76. Use our private radio band. It's a small white car, possibly French."

"Did he get much?" Karlsen peered in through the bank door.

"Don't know yet. How many men can we scrape together?"

"Not many. I sent Skarre to talk to Officer Gurvin, four officers are away taking a course, and another four are on vacation."

"We'll have to ask for reinforcements. The only thing we can focus on right now is the hostage."

"Let's hope he opens the car door and dumps her on the road."

"We can always hope," Sejer said grimly. "Let's have a talk with the teller."

The two young men had to wait in the backseat of the squad car, and they didn't mind in the least. Sejer and Karlsen went into the bank, where the teller was sitting on one of the chairs near the window. With her was the bank manager, who had been inside the vault and had no idea what was going on until he'd heard the shot, and then he didn't dare venture out until he heard the sirens.

Sejer quietly observed the young woman who had just been robbed. She was as white as a sheet, with beads of sweat on her forehead, but she wasn't hurt. All she had done was raise her hand to pick up several bundles of notes from a shelf and place them on the counter. Yet it was obvious that from now on her life would never be the same. She might think about making her will. Not that she had much to bequeath in all likelihood, but it was the kind of thing she'd think should be taken care of while there was still time. He sat down next to her and spoke gently.

"Are you all right?"

She began to sob.

"Yes," she said as firmly as she could manage. "I'm OK. But when I think about that girl he took with him...you should have heard what he said. I don't dare think about what he's going to do with her."

"Now, now," Sejer said. "Let's not jump ahead of ourselves. He took her along to gain free passage out to the car. Have you ever seen her before?"

"Never."

"Can you tell me what he said when he was standing at the counter?"

"I can tell you exactly what he said," she replied. "I'll never forget it. He went up to her from behind. First he put his arm around her neck and pulled her away from the counter, then he shoved her to the floor and put his foot on her head. And then he screamed at me, 'If you hesitate for one second I'm going to blow her brains out!' Then he fired a shot. At the ceiling, I mean. The ceiling tiles exploded and flew in all directions. My hair is full of plaster."

She wiped the sweat from her forehead on the sleeve of her blouse, and he paused for a moment to watch Karlsen, who was unfastening the camera from the ceiling and taking out the videotape.

"He spoke Norwegian?"

"Yes."

"Without an accent?"

"That's right. He had a high voice. Maybe a little hoarse."

"The girl, did she say anything at all?"

"Not a word. She was scared to death. And he was the type of man who knew what he was doing. Full of contempt for everybody. I'm sure he's committed a robbery before."

"We'll see," Sejer interrupted her as he took the tape. "I hope you won't mind coming down to the station to have a look at the tape."

"I need to make a phone call."

"We can arrange that."

Karlsen looked at her. "Can you estimate how much money you gave him?"

"Gave him?" she cried, staring at him as if he were crazy. "What kind of thing is that to say? I didn't *give* him anything— he robbed me!"

Sejer blinked and looked up at the ceiling.

"I'm sorry," Karlsen said. "Do you have any idea how much he got away with?"

"Today is Friday," she said, still sounding insulted. "I had put about a hundred thousand in the till."

Sejer stared out the open door. "Let's talk to the people outside who saw them. There were several witnesses. We might at least get a usable description."

He sighed heavily as he said this. He had seen the man himself, from a distance of only a few feet. How much would he be able to remember?

"The car was white, and it looked new. It was really small," she added. "I didn't see anything else special about it. It was unlocked, and the keys must have been inside because he drove off almost before the door was closed. Right across the square, between two flower boxes and out on to the road."

"Chances are it was stolen, and he has his own car parked elsewhere. He could be dangerous. It must have been sheer impulse to take a hostage. If that's what he did, that is. He probably wasn't counting on a customer coming in here so soon after opening. And... did she enter the bank from the other door?"

"Yes."

Sejer looked up at the gaping hole in the ceiling and frowned. "He's a fast thinker. Or desperate."

Another squad car pulled up in front of the bank, and two forensic technicians in overalls came inside. The first thing they did was to squint up at the hole made by the bullet in the ceiling.

"I wonder how many rounds he has," said one of the technicians.

"I don't dare think about that," said Sejer gloomily. "But no question he's a tough character. First he takes a hostage, and then he fires his gun in the middle of the morning rush hour."

"Very effective," said the technician. "Everybody freezes. He was only thinking about one thing—doing the robbery fast. No dawdling, full speed ahead. Was he wearing gloves?"

The teller nodded. "Thin gloves."

Sejer cursed himself for not lingering inside the bank and foiling the robber's plans. But the man would only have waited and come back another day. He took another look at the teller. Her eyes had taken on that particular gleam that meant she'd been shaken out of the life she'd taken for granted. He understood, and yet he didn't.

"OK," he said. "We've got a lot to do. Let's get moving."

He was breathing hard. He leaned forward in his seat, as if wanting to urge the car out of the city. He had been planning this for a long time, had run through the robbery in his mind over and over, picturing all the details and how it would go. But he had been wrong. Everything had gone at such a dizzying speed. He had the money, that's what was supposed to happen, and yet things weren't right. There was someone sitting in the passenger seat next to him.

The streets were full of people. They didn't even glance at the white car. He rode the clutch and glided through the intersection, staring with suppressed rage at the road ahead and letting the hot air out of his lungs. After fifteen minutes he pulled off his hood, although he instantly felt naked. He didn't turn to look at the hostage. He had no choice, he couldn't keep driving with the hood on. The oncoming drivers would see it and take note of his direction, the car, and his license plate. The hostage sat next to him, her head drooping, motionless. They drove by a bridal shop. He reduced his speed to let a Mercedes pass, and focused on keeping his eyes straight ahead. Only now, after a few minutes, as his pulse slowed down, did it occur to him how strangely silent it was in the car. He looked at his passenger out of the corner of his eye. Something wasn't right. He felt sick to his stomach. And with the nausea came fear, and with the fear came terror at the thought of doing something wrong, worse than he'd already done.

What the hell was he going to do with the hostage?

He hadn't thought that far. The only thing he had concentrated on was getting away as fast as possible, making sure no one tackled him and knocked him to the ground. He'd read about things like that in the newspapers. People who tried to play hero.

"You've seen my face," he said roughly. His voice was thin for such a strong body. "What do you think we should do about that?"

At that moment they were passing a funeral parlor, and his eyes took note of a white coffin on display in the window. Brass handles. A wreath of red and white flowers on top of it. It had been there for years and was probably made of plastic. It looked as though it was about to melt in the heat, just as he was. His sweater was sticking to his body, and his corduroys were practically steaming. He changed gears and braked for a truck on his right. The hostage didn't reply, but her shoulders had started to shake, as if she were at last about to react. It would be a relief. He felt the need for some kind of outlet himself, after all the stress. Some goddamned outlet, like bellowing out of the half-open window. His body shook as he fought for control.

"I said, what do you think we should do about it?"

It sounded so pathetic. He could hear his own fear and the way it was forcing his voice up into a screechy, shrill tone. He felt an overwhelming need to be alone, but it was too soon to stop. First they had to get out of town, to an isolated spot where he could shove this unwanted person out of the car. This witness.

She remained silent. He was getting more nervous. He was feeling the effects of it all, the weeks of planning, the sleepless nights, the anxiety and doubt. Normally he was just the driver, with no responsibility for any of the planning. Other people took care of that. He would wait outside with the engine running. And then he wasn't even armed. He had made a promise, and now he had kept it. But he had a hostage. It had seemed a smart move at the time. Outside the bank, people stood paralyzed, not lifting so

45

much as a finger, afraid his gun would go off and the hostage would be blown to bits right before their eyes. Now he had no idea what to do. And there was no one to help him, either. The silence was total. "There are only two options, of course," he said, clearing his throat.

He couldn't stand this any longer. "You either stay with me or I dump you somewhere along the way, in a condition that will make it impossible for you to talk."

The passenger still didn't speak.

"What the hell were you doing in the bank so early in the morning, anyway? Huh?"

When he still got no answer, he rolled the window down farther and felt the wind blow across his burning face. Cars passed. He shouldn't be showing his face, shouldn't even be talking, but he hadn't expected the flood of emotions welling up inside him. This sensation of boiling over. He had been waiting so long, had been alone for an eternity, he was nothing but a thin cord threatening to snap. Now, on top of everything, there was someone sitting next to him, watching the whole thing.

He drove past the hospital, veered sharp left at the Orthopedic Institute, crossed the main street, and entered Øvre Storgate, then drove past the abandoned pharmacy and the central garage. He turned left again and drove across the old bridge, continuing along the south bank, through the industrial area. He approached the railway tracks just as the light turned red. For a moment he considered racing across, but changed his mind. It would attract attention. He snarled between clenched teeth, "Sit still and keep your mouth shut. I've got my gun on you."

His words were wasted. The hostage did not utter a sound. In his rearview mirror he saw a red Volvo pull up and stop right behind him. The driver drummed his fingers on the steering wheel. Their eyes met in the mirror. He turned to look along the tracks for the train and heard it roaring in the distance; for a brief moment it drowned out the sound of his heart. The hostage remained motionless, staring out the window. The train thundered past, but the barrier remained down, not moving. He put the car in gear and waited. The car behind him rolled a little closer, almost touching his bumper. On the other side was a green Citroën. Sweat ran into his eyes, but the barrier stayed down. For a wild moment he thought the police had put it there to block his way, that any second they would pull up alongside with loaded guns and take him in. He was trapped. There was no room to turn around and head back. Why the hell wasn't the barrier going up?! The train was long gone. The Volvo behind him started revving its engine. He raised his hand, the one holding the pistol, and wiped his brow. At that moment he remembered the green Citroën on the other side, certain that the driver had noticed the gun. At last the barrier rose, slowly and painfully. Looking straight ahead he drove over the tracks. The Volvo turned right and disappeared. He had planned to go across the river, passing the square on the way down, and the police and the throngs of people outside. While they were busy interviewing witnesses, he would drive right past, only a hundred feet away. He was impressed with his plan. The problem was the hostage. Without warning, he slammed on the brakes, stopped. The car was parked behind a dumpster near the bus station. He pulled on the handbrake. "What I was wondering," he said, clearing his throat, "was what the hell you were doing in the bank so early?"

Silence.

"You're deaf, aren't you? You can't hear a damn thing."

The hostage raised her head. For the first time the robber stared into her flickering green eyes. It was quiet in the car, and it was getting hotter. He tried to read the expression on her pale face. Far away he heard a siren. It started out faint, grew louder, and then stopped with a little gurgle. An odd feeling came over him—that he hadn't robbed the bank at all, that it was all a

47

dream without logic, in which peculiar figures came and went and he couldn't understand what role they were playing.

"All right," he said, jabbing at the hostage with the muzzle of his gun. "A deaf person can hear, too, if you tap her on the shoulder."

He put the car in gear, drove across the bridge, and passed the bank. He had decided not even to glance in that direction, but he couldn't help himself. He looked swiftly to the left. A small crowd was huddled around the entrance. One person towered above all the rest. A tall man with short, silver hair.

CHAPTER 5

He should have been working on the murder in Finnemarka. Instead he sat at his desk, staring at a blank piece of paper. By closing his eyes he could see the robber's face before him, almost like a photograph. The problem was trying to describe it to the man sitting across from him.

Many other people had sat in the same place, sweating and struggling to remember everything: a distinguishing characteristic, eye color, whether the nose was long or short. He was confident that he had a good memory, and he thought he was an observant person. But now he started to have doubts. He was certain that the man's hair was blond, but it occurred to him that the sun flooding the street might have given it a golden sheen. And besides, the man was wearing dark clothing, which could have made his hair seem lighter than it was. His mouth was small, he was certain about that. He seemed to have quite a tan, maybe with a tinge of sunburn. And he remembered his clothes. He was quite muscular, undoubtedly in good shape, but not as tall as he was, actually not tall at all for a man.

Sejer stared at the police artist. He was a newspaper illustrator who had landed in this job by accident and had proved to be pretty talented, especially from a psychological point of view.

"First you're going to get me to relax," Sejer said with a smile. "You want to establish a sense of trust first, don't you? Demonstrate that you're listening to me and believe in me."

The artist gave him a wry smile. "Don't be so afraid of losing control, Konrad," he said. "Right now, you're not the boss. You're only a witness."

Sejer raised his hand in apology.

"The first thing I want you to do," said the artist, "is to forget the man's face."

Sejer looked at him in surprise.

"Forget the details. Close your eyes. Try to see his figure in front of you and concentrate on what kind of impression he makes. What kind of signals is this person sending? He comes walking toward you down the street in broad daylight, and for some reason you notice him. Why?"

"He seemed so tense. So full of something."

Sejer shut his eyes as requested and visualized the man. Now the face was merely a bright, hazy patch in his memory. "His steps were quick and firm. His shoulders hunched. A mixture of fear and determination. Panic lurking just below the surface. So afraid that he didn't dare glance up and look at anyone, even for an instant. Not exactly a professional robber. He was too desperate."

The artist nodded and made a note at the bottom of the page.

"Try to describe his body, the way he moved as he walked along."

"His body hardly moved at all. Tiny, choppy movements. No swinging of his arms, no swaying or limping. Straight ahead. Stiff-legged. Stiff across the shoulders."

"Think about the proportions," the artist continued. "His arms and legs in relation to his torso. The size of his head. The length of his neck. The size of his feet."

"His arms and legs weren't out of the ordinary. Rather on

the short side. He had one hand inside his bag, and the other in his pocket. A short, thick neck. Not very big feet. Smaller than mine, and I take a size 10. He was wearing loose clothing, but his body gave the impression of being muscular in a bulging sort of way."

More nods. The pencil touched the paper for the first time, and Sejer heard the stroke of graphite on the page. It was a loose sketch that gave the figure a trembling, lifelike quality, something in motion.

"His shoulders? Wide or narrow?"

"Wide. Rounded. The kind you get from lifting weights. Not like mine," he added.

"Oh, yours are very wide."

"But they don't bulge like his. They're more flat and bony, you know."

They both laughed at this. The artist, whose name was Riste but who went by the nickname Sketches, was short and pudgy and bald, with small oval glasses and long thin fingers.

"His head?"

"Big. Round. Big cheeks but not exactly dumpling shaped. A rounded chin. Not sharp or firm. No cleft or anything like that."

"How did his head sit on his body? If you understand what I mean by that."

"Kind of sunk between his shoulders. His head jutted forward from his body. Like a sulking child."

"Excellent. That's significant," he said. "What about his hairline?"

"Is that important?"

"Yes, it is. A person's hairline establishes a lot about his face. Take a look at your own face. You have a nearly perfect hairline. Straight and even across your forehead, with a nice arc at the temples. And your hair is of the same thickness all along it. That's quite rare."

"Really?" He shook his head. Vanity was not one of his sins, not anymore at any rate, and the last thing he paid attention to was his hairline. He paused to think.

"Curving, not straight. Maybe a little pointed toward the middle of his forehead. His hair was cut short, that's why I saw it so clearly."

This slow method of approaching the actual facial features made the man's appearance clearer than ever. The police artist certainly knew his job. Fascinated, Sejer stared at the piece of paper and saw a figure gradually emerge, like a print in a darkroom.

"Now his hair."

He kept on sketching lightly so that new strokes were constantly added on top or on the sides. He didn't use an eraser. The dozens of thin lines gave substance to the figure.

"Thick and curly, almost like an Afro. It grew straight up from his skull, but it was cut very short. Like mine."

He ran his hand over his hair, which was short and bristly, like a brush.

"The color?"

"Blond. Possibly very light colored, but I'm not entirely sure about that. Some hair looks extremely fair in certain situations, you know, but it can look dark when it's wet. It all depends on the amount of light. I'm not quite sure. Maybe close to your hair color."

"Mine?" Sketches looked up. "But I don't have any hair."

"No, but the way your hair used to look."

"How would you know what my hair was like?"

Sejer hesitated. He didn't know if he had offended the man or simply sounded stupid.

"I don't know," he replied. "I'm just guessing."

"Well, you guessed right. My hair is—I mean was—light blond. You're very observant."

"The sketch is starting to look like him."

"Now we come to the eyes."

"That will be harder. I didn't see them. He was walking along with his eyes fixed on the ground, and inside the bank he stood with his back partly turned."

"That's a shame. But the teller saw them, and it's her turn next."

"It's worse than a shame. It's a disaster that I didn't stay in that bank a little longer. I'm old enough to take my intuitions seriously."

"Well, you can't do everything right all the time. What about his nose?"

"Short, and quite wide. Also a little African-looking."

"His mouth?"

"A small, pouting mouth."

"Eyebrows?"

"Darker than his hair. Straight. Wide. Almost joined in the middle."

"Cheekbones?"

"They didn't stand out. His face was too full."

"Any distinguishing marks on his skin?"

"Nothing at all. Nice smooth complexion. No beard or stubble that I could see. No shadow on his upper lip. Freshly shaven."

"Or not much of a beard to start with. Anything distinctive about his clothes?"

"Not that I remember. Well, yes, there was one thing."

"What's that?"

"His clothes didn't look as though they belonged to him. It wasn't the way he would normally dress. They seemed old-fashioned."

"Most likely he's changed clothes by now. His shoes?"

"Brown shoes with laces."

"And his hands?"

"I didn't see them, as I told you. If they match the rest of his body, they would be stubby and round."

"And his age, Konrad?"

"Between nineteen and ... twenty-five."

He had to close his eyes again in order to block out the artist.

"Height?"

"Quite a bit shorter than me."

"Everybody is shorter than you," Sketches said dryly.

"Maybe five foot five or six."

"Weight?"

"He was powerfully built. Over 170, I'd say. You haven't asked me about his ears," Sejer said.

"What were his ears like?"

"Small and well formed. Round lobes. No earrings or studs." Sejer leaned back in his chair and smiled with satisfaction. "Now all that's left is to figure out what political party he votes for."

The artist chuckled. "What would be your guess?"

"I doubt that he votes at all."

"What did you see of the hostage?"

"Virtually nothing. She was standing with her back to me. . . . You'll have to talk to the teller," he added. "Let's hope she can handle the pressure."

———

Gurvin had been expecting the chief inspector, but because of an armed robbery in town early that morning, they sent over an officer to take his statement.

Jacob Skarre looked like a young choirboy, with fair curls and delicate features. His uniform suited him, and seemed to have been tailored for his slight form. Gurvin, on the other hand, never felt happy in his official attire. Maybe it was because of the shape of his body. At any rate, the uniform just didn't feel comfortable on him.

The confident air of the young man made him feel ill at ease, prompting him to think back over his own life. He did that at regular intervals anyway, but he liked to decide on the appropriate time.

The worst of the shock at discovering Halldis dead had begun to wear off. Gurvin was now the subject of attention, the likes of which he hadn't experienced for a long time, and he was obviously enjoying it. But still, he had known Halldis for years. He remembered something she used to say when he and his friends were children, and stood at her door asking for something.

There are too many of you! When I was a child only the toughest little brats survived!

"What do you think?" Gurvin said tentatively, catching sight of the pack of cigarettes sticking out of Skarre's shirt pocket. "Shall we risk breaking the no-smoking law?"

Skarre nodded and plucked the cigarettes out of his pocket.

"I've known Halldis and Thorvald ever since I was a child," Gurvin began, taking a drag on his cigarette. "As children we were allowed to pick raspberries and rhubarb behind their shed. And she wasn't that old, either. Only seventy-six. She was in good shape. Thorvald was, too, but he died of a heart attack seven years ago."

"So she lived alone?" Skarre blew smoke up toward the ceiling.

"They didn't have any children. Her only family is a younger sister in Hammerfest."

"You've written up a report?" said Skarre. "May I see it?"

Gurvin took a plastic folder out of his desk drawer and handed it to Skarre, who read it line by line.

"It says, 'Still unclear whether anything was removed from the house.' Did you check the drawers and cupboards?"

"Well, you see," Gurvin said, "Halldis had quite a lot of silver, but everything was still in the cupboard in the living room. The same is true of the few pieces of jewelry that she kept in the bedroom."

"What about cash?"

"We don't know whether she had any there."

"But did you find her handbag?"

"It was hanging on a hook in the bedroom."

"What about her wallet?"

"We didn't find a wallet, that's true."

"Some thieves only want cash," Skarre said. "Someone without contacts, who might have trouble disposing of valuables. He might not have intended to kill her. Maybe he was caught by surprise. Maybe she was outside, and he sneaked in through the kitchen."

"And then she appeared in the doorway? Is that what you mean?"

"Yes, something like that. We must find out if any money was taken. Did she do her own shopping?"

"She went to town once in a while, by taxi. But she had her groceries brought up to the farm by the shopkeeper here. Once a week."

"So the shopkeeper delivered her groceries, and she paid with cash? Or did she have an account?"

"I don't know."

"Call him up," Skarre said. "Maybe he knows where she kept her money, if he's someone she trusted."

"I'm sure she did," said Gurvin, reaching for the phone. He got through to the shopkeeper and spent a few minutes mumbling into the receiver.

"He says she kept her wallet in the bread box. A metal bread box on the kitchen counter. I actually opened it. There was half a loaf of bread inside, nothing else. He said it was red, with a pattern in the leather. Imitation alligator hide, with a brass clasp."

Skarre read through the report again. "Someone by the name of Errki Johrma was supposedly seen near her farm. Tell me about him. Is the boy who saw him a reliable witness?"

"Well, that's an interesting question." The officer smiled at the memory of Kannick. "But if he's telling the truth, it creates a staggering possibility. Errki had been committed to the psychiatric ward, you see, but he escaped. He grew up here. So it's not unlikely that he would come back to the area and roam around in the woods."

"But was he capable of killing someone?"

"He's not all there."

"Tell me more. What's he like?"

"A young man, about your age. Born in Valtimo, Finland. Grew up with his parents and a younger sister. Has always been different. I don't know what kind of diagnosis he's been given, but at any rate he's long gone. Has been for years."

"But is he dangerous?"

"We don't know. There are lots of stories about him, but I doubt they're all true. He's become almost a mythic figure, someone parents mention to scare the children into coming home in the evening. I do it myself."

"But he was committed. Does that mean he's regarded as dangerous?"

"I would reckon that the greatest danger he poses is to himself. It's just that whenever anything bad happens around here, Errki gets the blame. It's always been that way, ever since he was a boy. Even if something is not directly his fault, he seems to invite the blame. Who knows what he hopes to achieve by that. And he talks to himself."

"He's psychotic?"

"I'm sure he is. It's typical that Errki would show up in the vicinity of Halldis's farm on the day she's murdered. Similar things have happened before, but he's never been connected to a crime. He floats around like a bad omen. Like the blackbird in fairy tales, foretelling death. Forgive me for not sounding more objective," Gurvin sighed. "I'm just trying to describe him as people around here think of him."

"How long has he been ill?" Skarre tapped the ash from his cigarette into the officer's coffee cup.

"I don't know exactly, but it feels like forever. He's always been different. Peculiar and afraid of people. Never had any friends. I don't think he wanted any. His mother died when he was eight, and that's probably when it all started. After her death Errki's father took him and his sister to the States, and they lived in New York for seven years. There are rumors that Errki became an apprentice over there, to a conjurer."

"A conjurer?" Skarre smiled. "You mean a magician?"

"I'm not sure. More like some kind of sorcerer. And when they came back to Norway the rumors began to fly that Errki could make things happen. You know, by using his willpower."

"Good God," said Skarre, shaking his head.

"Go ahead and laugh, but I know people who are much more levelheaded than you or I who can tell you some strange things about Errki Johrma. For instance, Thorvald Horn told me once that his dog laid back his ears and growled when Errki came by. Long before Errki made an appearance, as if the dog could smell him from far off. Errki generally doesn't smell very good; he's always so messy. But there are also stories about horses running away when he came walking down the road. Clocks stop ticking. Lightbulbs go out. Doors slam. He's like a sudden gust of wind that makes the leaves on the ground swirl up. And he's got that look in his eyes. Sorry," Gurvin said abruptly. "I'm not saying very nice things about him, but it's hard to find anything positive to say. He's dirty and disgusting and unattractive in every respect."

"That doesn't make him a murderer, even if he's a clever illusionist or suffers from some illness," Skarre said. "We'll have to contact the hospital and talk to his doctor. I'm sure he can tell us a great deal. We're going to have to find Errki so we can see what he was doing up there. Did we get any good prints from the hoe?"

"Only two faint prints, in addition to Halldis's own. Which is strange. The hoe had a fiberglass handle, and her prints were very clear. He couldn't have wiped off the hoe without erasing her prints as well. We found lots of prints inside the house, several footprints in the blood on the front steps, and several in the hall and the kitchen. Might have been running shoes. The pattern on the sole is quite clear, and that ought to tell us what we need to know. The forensic technicians will make drawings of them. The murder took place in the hall. Halldis stood with her back to the front steps, and he came toward her from inside the house. Maybe she was the one originally holding the hoe, and he had to yank it out of her hands. He should have left behind some decent fingerprints. I don't really see why he had to kill her. If he had found the money, he could have just taken it and run away. She never would have caught up with him. I know Halldis, though. She was stubborn. I bet she stood in the doorway and refused to move. I can just picture it," he said softly. "A furious Halldis, full of righteous indignation."

"The fact that he killed her could mean that he was someone she knew, someone she might have identified to the police."

"Yes," Gurvin said thoughtfully. "And she definitely knew Errki. He had just escaped from the hospital, so he presumably didn't have any money."

Skarre nodded.

"But he wouldn't have found much there," the officer continued. "I doubt she kept large sums in the house. She lived alone, after all."

"Yes, but in an isolated spot. Being robbed couldn't have been much of a worry for her. Has she ever been robbed before?"

"No. And besides, she was tough. It wouldn't surprise me if she went after him with the hoe."

"In that case he might have suffered an injury."

"You've seen the photos of the body?"

"Yes, I've had a look at them."

"Not very pretty, is it?"

Skarre felt weak for a moment at the memory of what had been presented to him early that morning. "Where does Errki Johrma's father live?"

"He went back to the States."

"What about his sister?"

"She did too."

"Do they have any contact with him?"

"No. Not because they don't want to, but because Errki refuses to see them."

"Do you know why?"

"He feels he's above them."

"Is that right?"

"He feels he's above everyone. He lives in his own world, and he has his own laws. In his universe he's the ruler. It's not easy to explain. You have to meet him to understand."

"But surely he must feel some despair, if he's so ill?"

"Despair?" Gurvin uttered the word as though the thought had never occurred to him. "If he does, he hides it well."

Skarre nodded toward the road. "We've put out an APB on him. Do you want to go up there with me? I'd like to have a look at the house."

Gurvin grabbed his jacket from the back of his chair. "Let's take the Subaru," he said in a low voice. "The road up to Halldis's place is steep as hell."

CHAPTER 6

The woods surrounding the farm appeared denser than usual, as if the trees had drawn together out of respect for the woman, now gone, who had taken such good care of everything. And even though she had never allowed anything to clutter her garden, not tools or a wheelbarrow or clothes forgotten on the bench against the sunny wall, the place seemed totally abandoned. It no longer breathed. The flowers under the kitchen window were already drooping; in less than one day their lives had become threatened by the blazing sun. The front steps had been rinsed, but a dark patch remained.

Skarre turned to look at the woods. "What was the boy doing up here?"

"Shooting crows with a bow and arrow."

"Does he have permission to do that?"

"Of course not. He does what he likes. He lives at Guttebakken."

This last comment was intended to explain everything, and Skarre understood.

"And he definitely knows who Errki is?"

"Yes, he does. Errki's easy enough to recognize. I sympathize with the boy. First he finds Halldis dead. Then he catches sight of Errki in the woods. His lungs were practically bursting by the time he reached my office. He must have thought he would be the next victim."

"Did Errki know that the boy had spotted him?"

"He thought so, yes."

"But Errki didn't try to stop him?"

"Evidently not. He disappeared into the woods."

"Let's go inside."

Gurvin led the way, unlocking the door and heading down the little hall and into the kitchen. Halldis Horn was beginning to take shape for Jacob Skarre as he stepped onto the linoleum and looked at the tidy kitchen. Copper pots, shiny and clean. An old-fashioned sink with green rubber around the edge. An old refrigerator from Evalet. And an old paper, folded up on the windowsill. Skarre lifted the lid of the bread box.

"Where did you find the fingerprints?"

"On the kitchen doorknob and door frame. No prints on the bread box except for Halldis's. If the fingerprints belong to the killer, why were they so indistinct on the hoe? And why were there none on the bread box? How could he take out the wallet without leaving any prints, even though he left prints elsewhere in the house? I don't understand it."

Skarre narrowed his eyes. "But surely other people came here once in a while?"

"Almost never, but we did find a letter," Gurvin said. "Posted this week, in Oslo. It says, 'I'll come to visit. Greetings, Kristoffer.'"

"One of her relatives?"

"We don't know, but I think she was killed by someone she knew. Statistics will support the theory. He obviously panicked."

"Human beings are strange that way."

Skarre went into the living room. There was her rocking chair, with a shaggy blanket. He picked it up and sniffed cautiously, recognizing the smell of soap and camphor. A strand of hair tickled his nose. He plucked it up between two fingers. It was almost two feet long and silver in color.

"Did she have long hair?" he asked in amazement.

Gurvin nodded. "She was a beauty when she was young. As kids we didn't know that; we just thought she was fat and friendly. Her wedding picture is on the wall over there."

Skarre went to look at it. The image of Halldis Horn as a bride was breathtaking.

"Her dress was made from parachute silk," Gurvin said. "And the veil is an old English lace curtain. She told us all about it. And we listened politely, the way children do, because we had to repay her in some way for the raspberries and rhubarb."

He turned abruptly and went back to the kitchen.

"Where is the bedroom?" Skarre called.

"Behind the green curtains."

He pulled them aside and opened the door. The room was small and narrow. From the bedroom window Skarre looked out at the woods and one side of the shed. Thorvald's side of the high-posted bed was neatly made up. A framed verse hung over the bed.

> You have seen him among the falcons.
> He comes from the south, all ablaze.
> Carries everything out, leaves nothing behind.
> For the gnat you forget in a crack,
> He will call you to account.

Underneath someone, possibly Halldis, had written in blue ink: *How horrid!*

Skarre smiled faintly. He noticed that Gurvin had gone outside, and followed him out. They began combing through the grass, hoping to find a clue, something the others might have overlooked. A cigarette butt, a match, anything at all. He glanced back at the house. Just below the kitchen window there was a gash in the timber, repaired, but still visible.

"That's from the day Thorvald died," Gurvin said, pointing. "Halldis was standing in the kitchen, about to call him in for dinner. She thought he was driving unusually fast, as if he had turned reckless in his old age and wanted to show off. The tractor came rolling up the road with a terrific roar. The next second it crashed right into the wall. Halldis stood at the window and looked straight into the cab. She saw that Thorvald had collapsed over the wheel. He was dead before the tractor came to a stop there."

Skarre glanced up toward the woods again. "Where do you think we should look for Errki?"

Gurvin squinted at the sun. "He's almost certainly roaming around, sleeping rough. He hasn't been back to his apartment, at least not yet. Maybe he's still in the woods."

"And beyond this point it's all wilderness?"

"Yes, it's mostly wilderness. An area of 270 square miles. There are a few cottages on the other side of the river, and the sites of some old Finnish dwellings. A few people have summer cabins there. Hunters often use them in the autumn, or berry pickers sometimes slip inside to rest. Errki is a good hiker. Going into the woods and searching at random would be hopeless. He could be hiding in the basement of the hospital, or maybe someone has given him a lift and he's on his way to Sweden. Or home to Finland. He's always on the move."

"If he's as odd as you say, he should be easy to spot."

"I don't know about that. He sneaks around. All of a sudden he's standing there and nobody has heard him coming."

"We have an excellent canine unit," Skarre said optimistically. "Do you know whether he's on any medication?"

"Ask the hospital. Why do you want to know?"

Skarre shrugged. "I'm just wondering what would happen if he suddenly stopped taking his drugs."

"Maybe his inner voices take over."

"We all have inner voices of one kind or another," Skarre said, smiling.

"Good heavens, yes," Gurvin said. "But not all of them order us around."

Gurvin coaxed his car through the trees. A cloud of dust swirled up behind them.

"Whenever Errki turns up, something nasty happens," he said, his voice tense. "His mother died when he was eight, did I tell you that?"

"You did, but how did she die?"

"She fell down the stairs. Errki took the blame for it."

"Took the blame?"

"He frightened the other children by saying that he did it. They were terrified and stayed away from him. I think that's what he wanted. Several years later the body of an old farmer was found up by the church. He had fallen off a ladder, but Errki was seen running away from the scene. So maybe you can understand that even if he had nothing to do with Halldis's death, people around here will have made up their minds by now. And if you ask me, I'd very likely be of the same opinion. Take a look around. This is a remote area. People don't come poking around here unless they're familiar with the place. Errki is familiar with the place; he grew up here."

"But it's a fact," said Skarre slowly, trying not to sound pedantic, "that the violent tendencies of psychiatric patients are enormously exaggerated. Because of prejudices, or fear and ignorance. You need to remain objective, since you're right in the thick of things, and because you know him, and you knew Halldis too. When the newspapers get wind of this, he's going to be made to seem like a monster."

Gurvin looked at him. "That's what's so difficult. Because he always keeps to himself and avoids other people. He almost never talks to anyone, so we really don't know who he is. What he is."

"He's ill," Skarre said.

"That's what they say. But I don't really understand it." He shook his head. "I don't understand how voices could invade a man's mind and make him do things that he can't remember afterward."

"We don't know what he has done."

"We have fingerprints and several footprints. He can be as crazy as he likes and forget things from one second to the next, but he can't run away from the forensic evidence. This time we have forensic evidence."

"It sounds as if you'd like to nail him for this."

Skarre's voice had an innocent ring. Gurvin couldn't read him. "It would be good. It would be better for all of us if they put him away for good, in accordance with Paragraph 5. Right now he's wandering around out there somewhere, talking to himself. God help me, but my children are going to have to come home early at night as long as he's on the loose."

"Errki may be more frightened than your children are," said Skarre.

Gurvin pursed his lips and accelerated. "You're not from around here. You don't know him."

"No," Skarre said ruefully. "But I have to admit that you've aroused my curiosity."

"It's a fine thing that you're blessed with an unwavering faith in human beings," Gurvin said. "But don't forget that Halldis is dead. Somebody killed her. Somebody came here and lifted that hoe and hurled it right at her eye. Whether it was Errki or someone else, it makes me shudder to think that the murderer has the right to be defended for an act that can't be justified in any way."

"The act can't be defended. Just the person who committed

it," Skarre corrected him. "And we don't know why she died. Can I smoke in your car?"

Gurvin nodded and fumbled for his own cigarettes. "What's your boss like? Tell me about him."

Skarre smiled. This was a common reaction when someone came across Konrad Sejer.

"Stern and gray. Slightly authoritarian. Reserved. Smart. Sharp as a scythe. Thorough, patient, dependable, and persistent. With a soft spot for little children and old ladies."

"Not anyone in between?"

"He's a widower." Skarre gazed out the window. "He has forgotten that the only promise he made was to remain true to her until death separated them. He thinks that means his own death."

———

Sejer stared intently at the gray screen.

The bank interior. The teller windows. The windows facing the square, with light slanting in, making the picture blurry. He had the whole thing, from beginning to end, but it wasn't a clear tape. It was hard to identify any of them.

The car was long gone. They had blocked off all the escape routes, but the small white car hadn't been found. Maybe it had been abandoned long ago, maybe the robber had driven across one of the bridges and continued along the south bank, hiding in the center of town. Sejer suspected that the hostage had been released, but he had no way to be certain. He leaned back in his chair and stretched out his long legs. He had loosened his tie and rolled up his sleeves. His shirt was wrinkled. The teller and bank manager and a number of witnesses had been interviewed, one after another. He had made his own notes of what he had seen, had turned his memory inside out to try to remember all the details he could. The police artist had listened and nodded and produced an excellent sketch. And he himself had acknowledged the likeness, at least initially, although afterward he began having doubts. Now he straightened up in his chair as someone knocked on the door. Skarre came in with Gurvin.

The community officer stared at Sejer with interest. "I hear you have a hostage situation."

He fumbled a little with his sunglasses and sat down. The roles were reversed now. He was here with the big boys who had every conceivable type of equipment available to them.

"I'm sitting here staring at this wretched video," Sejer said gloomily. "The quality is so poor."

"Can we see it?" Skarre asked eagerly.

"Of course. Put your glasses on, if you need them."

He started up the tape again, waiting for their surprise. There were the teller windows. The young girl appeared first from the entrance leading to the square. She looked around a bit uncertainly and went over to the brochure rack. No more than fifteen seconds later the bank robber came in. He stopped short at the sight of the customer who had arrived before him. Hurriedly he reached for a form and began filling it out. Then the door opened a third time, and that's when the exclamation came.

"What on earth!" Skarre cried. "Isn't that you, Konrad?"

He gave his boss a bewildered look. Sejer had decided to take the whole thing in stride. He started laughing. Gurvin stared at the two of them in astonishment.

"Damn right it's me. I was walking down the street on my way to work and out of the blue I had the feeling that a person I passed looked like a bank robber. So I turned around to see where he was going, saw him go into the bank, and decided to follow."

"And? What happened?"

"As you can see on the video, I peeked inside, noticed the young girl, saw that everything was nice and calm. And I left."

He looked at them both, and gave an eloquent shrug. "I just left."

Skarre started laughing. Gurvin felt an immense regret that he himself had no colleagues.

"As soon as I was out of the bank, the robber struck. Take a look now."

There he was, striding across the bank, then he took his hostage. A moment later the shot was fired. Gurvin gasped, blinked several times, and stared in disbelief.

"We have to find that girl," Sejer said. "If we don't get her out of this situation in one piece, we run the risk that hostage-taking will become fashionable, which is just about the worst thing that could happen. And because of this awful video, it's more or less impossible to identify her, even if someone reports her missing today. And yet . . ." He rewound the tape and played it over again. "There's something that doesn't seem right."

"What's that?" asked Skarre.

"Something about the way she reacts. Or rather, her lack of reaction. She doesn't scream or wave her arms around. It almost looks as if she's in a trance. Or, to put it another way, as if she's not surprised. As if the attack is something she was expecting. Maybe it was a setup."

Skarre looked at him in surprise.

"Let's say it was all prearranged, that they were in on it together. That she was actually his girlfriend."

"I doubt she's his girlfriend," Gurvin broke in. His eyes were fixed rigidly on the flickering screen. "That hostage is a man. And his name is Errki Johrma."

———

He suddenly realized what had happened. It rose up through his consciousness like a great shock. He had taken a madman hostage!

He drove as fast as he dared go without attracting attention, keeping a watchful eye on the traffic in his rearview mirror. His pulse was still racing, his body taut and tense, and he was hyperventilating. It made him dizzy. He scowled at the man sitting next to him.

"I'm asking you again: what were you doing in the bank so early in the morning?"

Errki heard the snare drums. They were playing a drum roll that was seriously off tempo. He didn't answer, just opened and closed his fists, and stared down at the floor of the car as if he were looking for something. The words were drowned out by the drums. Don't move, don't say anything. He rocked back and forth in his seat and closed his eyes.

"I said, what the hell were you doing in the bank so early in the morning?!"

This time Errki heard the angry voice. The man was scared. He stored this away in his mind and began silently to shape an answer. Nestor listened to his thoughts; he had to approve of the words before they were released. That's why it took time. Nestor was meticulous. Nestor was—

"Are you deaf, man?"

Am I deaf? thought Errki. That was a new question that required a new answer. He shoved the first one aside and started working on the second. Nestor was still listening. The Coat was silent. No, he thought. I can hear perfectly. I can hear his pulse pounding in his veins because his blood pressure is too high, and he's expending a huge amount of energy on something as simple as trying to communicate. But does he really want an answer that hasn't been properly thought through? Isn't it a mark of respect to take your time finding an answer? On the other hand—does he deserve respect? Of any kind?

Demanding money from a young teller was no great feat, at least not in Errki's opinion. And besides, he had a gun. But the man was plainly excited by his exploits. It was making his cheeks bulge. Now he needed to let off steam.

"Is it possible to get some kind of answer around here?"

His voice, a nice tenor, was ruined by the drums, which scrambled the words and gave him a shrill sound. Too bad, thought Errki. Men were more concerned with other things than their voices. Muscles. Bravado. Having the right jeans to wear. Such pitiful things. Errki had discovered that he had the ability to drive a grown man almost mad without even trying, just by keeping silent. It was tough for the man not to get an answer. Not to find out who you were. What you were. Errki still didn't say a word.

The robber was breathing hard next to him, his curly hair damp with exertion. He looked in the rearview mirror and reduced his speed, then turned off the road and stopped. The engine was still running. He threw a quick glance at Errki and snarled between clenched teeth, "I have to take off some of these clothes. Don't try to escape!"

Errki didn't have any intention of escaping. The pistol bothered him. He could feel it piercing his body like a ray of light. Now the robber placed the gun on the dashboard, above the steering wheel. He struggled to pull off his sweater and then the corduroy trousers, keeping his gloves on. It wasn't easy because the car was so small. He groaned and cursed and tugged at the trousers, but at last he was done, and more sweaty than ever. Now he was sitting there dressed in what must be a form of disguise, Errki thought. Nestor chuckled softly from the cellar. Under the clothes he had removed, the robber was wearing a pair of gaudy Bermuda shorts covered with fruit and palm trees, and a blue sleeveless shirt with Donald Duck on the chest. He reached across Errki and opened the glove compartment. He took out a pair of sunglasses and put them on. His outfit was perfect. Errki couldn't help staring. The muscular man looked so odd in the colorful shorts. He was fighting to control his voice.

"You don't understand any of this, so keep your mouth shut! Just shut up unless someone speaks to you!"

Errki hadn't said a word. In spite of his leather jacket and black trousers he wasn't sweating. He concentrated on not moving. If he remained motionless, he would be almost invisible.

"Damn, you smell terrible!" The robber sniffed loudly to show his disgust and opened the window even farther. Errki wondered whether he expected a reply to this or whether he was just slinging a little shit. To be on the safe side, he kept quiet. Besides, Nestor was singing a beautiful hymn in a low voice, and it would be best to take advantage of his good mood. Errki didn't think much about where they were headed or what might happen later on. He was using all his strength to close himself up and hold everything else out. This man. This moment. The gun. But he couldn't stop his hands. They kept on opening and closing, faster and faster.

"Can't you stop doing that with your hands?" the robber said, his eyes wide. "It looks so creepy. It's driving me crazy!"

Errki began rocking back and forth instead. It was impossible to make himself invisible here, with the storm in the seat next to him that wasn't going to let up. He tried to turn away from the man. Stared out the window. The drums were making his ears hurt. He gave a little wave of his hand to make them stop.

"I suppose you're not interested in money," the robber said, a little calmer now. "Maybe you don't know what it's good for."

Errki listened. The man had lowered his voice. Now he was suddenly extremely alert: the question was filled with curiosity. *Interested in money?* Well, yes, up to a point. But he already had a few kroner in his pocket, so the answer was both yes and no. Is that what he should say?

"It looks as though you've escaped from some kind of institution. That's a tough game to play. Plenty of people try to escape, and then they come shuffling back with their tail between their legs. Is that how it is with you? Are you one of them?"

Are you one of them? The question was almost touching in its barely disguised eagerness to find out who he was. Errki closed his eyelids again. The city was beginning to vanish behind them. Evil intentions, or none at all? He discovered that he couldn't figure out where to place him. Peas, beef, and pork, he thought, blood, sweat, and tears. It was disturbing.

The road began to ascend. Farther ahead, high up on a hill off to the left, was a scenic point. He found himself again, recognized this area. This was one of the roads that he had trudged along for years. They passed through a tunnel, and deep darkness descended over the car. The driver was instantly nervous, as if he feared an attack. He drove with the gun in his right hand, and tore off his sunglasses when he realized how dark it was. Then they were on the other side. Errki blinked his eyes. Now there was only a half mile to the tollbooth. The man would either have to stop and pay, or else crash through the barrier, which was just a wooden bar painted red and white. The thought had evidently occurred to him. He began to slow down.

"Don't try anything!" he snarled.

It hadn't even crossed Errki's mind. The only thing he was trying to do was to remain motionless and invisible, but his body had a life of its own and was refusing to obey.

The driver stopped the car. He had made up his mind. He swung the car to the left and drove up toward the scenic overlook. Errki wasn't sure what he intended to do at the top, but there was no traffic on the road. It was still early and probably deserted up there. The robber gripped the pistol hard and wiped the sweat from his forehead with the back of his hand. Dust and sand spewed out behind the car as it strained up the wooded slope. The road was far below them now, and the cars looked like brightly colored toys. He made one last tight swerve and then steered the car toward the railing. From here they could look down at the toll plaza. They both noticed it at the same time: two police cars were parked on the shoulder to the right of the tollbooth. There was a gasp and then a hiss as the robber exhaled through clenched teeth. He put the car in reverse and backed away from the railing. Stopped again. Began hammering the steering wheel with the gun. Errki could hear the chaos in the man's head. He was about to explode, the sweat was practically gushing from his forehead, and his heart was working hard, close to its limit. A tiny scratch in his carotid artery right now and the blood would spurt out in a red arc, all the way down to the tollbooth.

"OK, my friend. What do you suggest?" the robber said.

Friend? What a pathetic attempt. The poor man was at the end of his tether, it was almost unbearable. Errki wanted to get away. He turned to look out the window, peered at the woods, at what might be a path winding its way through the trees. His glance was quick and almost imperceptible, but the robber saw it. He followed his gaze, his brain starting to function again. He put the car in gear, turned around, and drove across the parking lot. The path was so wide at the beginning that he could drive in fifteen or twenty yards before it narrowed and became a well-trodden track. When he stopped, the car was invisible from the lookout, hidden by the dense foliage. He turned around and grabbed a bag from the backseat.

"We're going to get out and walk."

Errki stayed where he was. The robber opened the door and came around the car, waving his gun.

"You go first. It's a good, dry path. We can wait here until dark. That roadblock isn't going to be there long, they don't have enough manpower for that. Let's go! Get out of here, fast!"

Don't move, don't say anything. In the distance he could hear that the Coat had woken up and was starting to flap as Nestor informed it of the latest details. Their laughter rang inside him, making his whole body vibrate. He put a hand on his chest to ease the pressure.

"What's the matter with you? No use pretending to be sick, you can't fool me that easily. Now get the hell out of that car!"

Errki scrambled out. The robber went behind the car, opened the trunk, and looked inside. For a terrifying moment Errki thought he was going to be locked up in the tiny trunk, unable to move or see out. Instead, the robber rummaged around and pulled out some kind of plastic package. He opened it and took out a tarpaulin, glancing up at the green leaves. The tarpaulin was green. He looked at Errki.

"Put this over the car. You have to fasten it underneath with the hooks. The car will be camouflaged. The longer it takes for them to find it, the better."

The robber tossed the tarp into his arms. Errki stood there holding the green material. It was made of nylon, thin and slippery and hard to handle. It slid out of his slack grip and fell to the ground.

"Pick it up. First you have to open it and then put it over the car."

Errki laid out the green material on the ground and began opening the flaps. There was a little strap with a metal hook in each corner. He lifted the tarp at one end and tried to spread it over the hood of the car. It slid instantly to the ground. He had never held anything so distasteful in his hands as this slippery green fabric. It was disgusting.

"Damn it, man, you're hopeless!"

Errki tried again, feeling the barrel of the gun poking him in the side. Finally he got it spread over the roof of the car, but just as he started to arrange the sides, it fell off again. The robber was sweating and grunting at his incredible clumsiness. He stuck the gun in the waistband of his shorts, yanked the tarp out of Errki's hands, and had it over the car in a matter of seconds. Then he pulled out his gun again.

"We'd better get you back to the asylum—fast. How do you even manage to get dressed on your own? Or do you just keep wearing the same clothes? That's what it looks like. Come on, we're going to take a little hike."

Finally, Errki was allowed to walk. He could walk for hours. He fell into a rhythm that calmed him as he swayed and rolled up the wooded slope. Behind him came the robber with the raised pistol and the bag over his shoulder. The bag with the money. The path grew narrower and the woods closed its canopy above them. Only a small amount of light penetrated the leaves. The robber relaxed. He felt safer far away from everyone. No one could see them here. He should have thought of this a lot earlier. They wouldn't think to search the woods, just check the roads and cars.

And he had kept his promise. He had the money.

Errki strode along with the robber huffing and puffing behind him. It was hot, and the bag wasn't light. Inside he had a travel radio, a bottle of whiskey he would drink to celebrate, a box of ammunition, and the money.

"Slow down, nobody's on our trail."

But Errki kept going. He could hear the other man struggling to keep up with him. He was panting hard after only a few hundred yards. The path was steep, and the trail was getting rougher.

"Hey, you. I'm in command here!"

Three drums performed a sharp roll. Errki heard Nestor cough up a clot of mucus, which was his way of commenting on the robber's statement. Errki kept going without slackening his pace. He had only one speed; he either walked fast or he lay down to rest. But he did slow down as the path continued climbing toward the mountain ridge. From the top they would be able to see the road and find out whether the police were still there. He felt his thin body move from side to side. The other man moved with harsh jerks. He had more muscles than Errki, but not much stamina. But after an hour the robber slipped into a rhythm. His muscles had warmed up. And he had a bag full of money. He felt a surge of joy and decided to share it with the lunatic. He cleared his throat.

"What's your name?" he called.

The voice was almost friendly. The question left a dull slap, as if the drum skin had loosened. Errki didn't reply, just kept on walking. It was harmless enough, but you could never be sure. Nestor was squatting in the dim light, staring up at him. The fire in his eyes gleamed like a low blue flame.

"That much you could tell me!" the man insisted, adding an offended sniff. "If you don't answer me soon, I'm really going to think that you're a mute or something. Or maybe you're a foreigner? You look like a foreigner. A Tartar, for instance. Or a Gypsy. Or maybe they're the same thing. Answer me, damn it!"

Errki veered to the left because a huge aspen lay across the path in front of him. He got tangled up in the thicket and used his thin arms to push aside the undergrowth. The man behind him struggled even harder, with the bag in one hand and the gun in the other. They rejoined the path, and saw light up ahead.

"Since you're playing so hard to get, one of us is going to have to be a little more generous."

He heard the robber stop.

"My name is Morgan."

Errki listened. He said *Morgan* with sharp consonants, as if the name was something he had been wanting for a long time. But it wasn't his real name, that much was clear. Nestor snickered, a sound like someone solemnly pouring an expensive bottle of wine. You could say what you liked about Nestor, but he had style. Errki continued blithely on and heard the other man who wanted so badly to be called Morgan shouting after him.

"We're taking a break. What's the rush?"

Errki kept walking.

"You'd better stop now, or else I'll shoot!"

Keep going. He won't shoot.

Errki turned around. Morgan looked at his face, which made him think of a dry piece of granite. He wasn't smiling, he wasn't shaking now, he had an utterly lifeless expression, and he stared at him, unblinking. A great uneasiness spread through the robber. A mute and stonelike devil of a man, who walked like a machine. Who the hell was he?

"Stop over there by the little hill. We need to rest for a while."

Do as he says. *Sickness, death, and misery.* Nestor whispered through thin lips. Errki obeyed. He headed for a gray mound, twenty to thirty yards away.

Morgan was exhausted. He didn't have the total control that he thought the gun would give him. He couldn't resist spitting out a spiteful remark.

"I'm sorry to tell you this, but I'll be damned if you don't walk just like an old lady!"

Errki stopped short. A thought rose up in his mind.

Don't irritate the alligator until you've crossed the river.

CHAPTER 7

Sejer stared at Gurvin, thunderstruck.

"Say that again?"

"You heard me right the first time."

"You're saying that the hostage is the same person as the escaped patient from the psychiatric hospital, the man who's wanted in connection with the murder of Halldis Horn?"

Gurvin threw out his hands. "I'm positive. That robber is in for an almighty surprise."

Sejer had to look out the window to make sure the view was the same as it always was. What kind of situation did they have on their hands? He turned back to Gurvin.

"But is he dangerous?"

"We don't know."

"When exactly did he escape?"

"The day before yesterday, sometime in the night. Out a window."

Sejer started up the video again, stopping the tape when he had the hostage in focus.

"I thought it was a girl," he muttered.

"I know," Gurvin said. "It's something about the way he holds his head and the way he walks. And his long hair."

"Has he been sick for some time?"

"For as long as I can remember."

"Schizophrenia?"

"I believe so."

Sejer got up and took a few steps, digesting the information. "Well then, the robber is really in for a surprise. So now we've got two wanted men, one of them seriously disturbed and perhaps a murderer, the other a robber with a loaded gun. Quite a pair! Maybe they'll join forces."

"Nobody joins up with Errki."

Sejer gave him a somber look. "The psychiatric hospital? Have you talked to his doctor?"

"Only a nurse, who confirmed that he had escaped. I'll get hold of the doctor later."

"And this child who found the old woman, who saw Errki at the scene—is he trustworthy?"

"At best, once in a while. He lives at Guttebakken, the boys' home. But as far as this situation goes, I believe him. I have to admit that I had my doubts when he came to see me. He seemed a bit manic, in a way. But his story checked out. And as far as Errki is concerned, there's no doubt that the boy knows who he is."

"What was Errki doing at the bank so early in the morning? Cashing his public assistance check?"

"I have no idea. You can bet the robber asked him the same question, and he probably didn't get a sensible answer. I'd really like to know what those two are up to right now. It defies imagination," Gurvin said.

"If they're still together, that is. Maybe the robber let Johrma go out of sheer fright."

"It wouldn't surprise me."

"And Errki isn't going to show up to file a complaint if he's been let go. How on earth are we going to handle this?"

Sejer opened a folder on his desk and read aloud, "A brand-new white Renault Mégane was reported stolen from Frydenlund late last night. The robber had a similar car, so it might be the one. Maybe they've changed cars by now. Maybe he let Johrma go. Let's hope so."

Skarre and Gurvin said nothing. A robber could be many things, but he was seldom truly dangerous, although they couldn't be sure of it in this case.

"Would we even be able to question Johrma?"

Gurvin thought, and said, "I assume we could, with a doctor present. But we might not get answers to our questions. Or at least not answers that we could understand. And even if he did commit the murder, it's not at all likely that he would be convicted."

"I suppose you're right." Sejer rubbed his eyes hard and then opened them again. "Was he committed?"

"Yes."

"That means he posed a threat?"

"I don't know all the details. It could be that he was mostly a danger to himself."

"Suicide attempts?"

"I don't know about that. You'll have to talk to his doctor. He's been at the hospital for several months, so they must know something about him by now. Although I doubt that anyone is capable of truly understanding him. He seems like a chronic case to me. He was different even as a child."

"Are his parents still alive?"

"His father and a sister. They live in the United States."

"Did he have his own place?"

"In the projects. We've been to check. I contacted one of the neighbors, who promised to call if he shows up, but so far no word."

"Is he a Finn?"

"His father is. Errki was born and raised in Valtimo. They came to Norway when Errki was four."

"Ever been involved with drugs?"

"Not as far as I know."

"Physically strong?"

"Not at all. His strength lies elsewhere." Gurvin tapped his finger against his forehead.

Skarre stared at the screen. He tried to make out the eyes under the black hair, but couldn't.

"In a way I can better understand him, now that I look at the tape," he said. "He doesn't behave the way you'd expect someone to in that situation. He doesn't resist. Or even say a word. What do you think was going on in his mind?" Skarre looked over at Gurvin and pointed at the screen.

"He's listening to something."

"Inner voices?"

"It looks like it. I've often noticed the way he walks along, nodding, as if he were listening intently to some sort of internal dialogue."

"Does he ever speak?"

"Once in a while. He has an oddly formal way of talking. Often you can't understand what he's saying. And that desperado with the mask probably hasn't understood much either, if they've even exchanged a single word."

"Is Errki well known in the area?"

"Very well known. He's always wandering along the roads. Once in a while he hitchhikes, but not many people dare stop for him. He likes to take the bus or the train, going here and there. Prefers to be on the move. Sleeps wherever he feels like it—on a bench in the park, in the woods, at a bus stop."

"No friends at all?"

"He doesn't want any."

"Have you ever asked him?" Sejer said curtly.

"You don't ask Errki about anything. You keep your distance," Gurvin said.

Sejer sat lost in thought. The sun shimmered on his closely cropped gray hair. He reminded Gurvin of a Greek ascetic; the only thing missing was the laurel wreath around his head. The chief inspector thought for a long time, absentmindedly scratching one elbow.

"I thought there were only old people in the Beacon," he said at last.

"In the past," said Gurvin. "Now it's a psychiatric unit for young people, with forty patients divided up into four sections, one of them restricted. Or locked up, as we say. In fact, it's known as the Lockup by those who live there. I've been there once with a boy from Guttebakken."

"I have to find out who Errki's doctor is and have a talk with him. Why is it so hard to say whether or not he's dangerous?"

"There are so many rumors." Gurvin looked at him. "He's the kind that gets blamed for everything. I for one don't know of a single situation he was mixed up in that could be called criminal, except for sneaking onto a train or shoplifting. But now I'm not so sure."

"What does he shoplift?"

"Chocolate."

"And he doesn't have any contact with his family?"

"Errki refuses to see them, and they can't help him anyway. The father has given up on his son. But you shouldn't blame him. Simply put, there is no hope for Errki."

"Maybe it's a good thing that his doctor can't hear you," said Sejer quietly.

"Perhaps. But he's been sick his whole life, or at least ever since his mother died sixteen years ago. That says a lot."

Sejer stood up and pushed his chair under the desk. "Let's have a cup of coffee. I want you to tell me everything you know."

———

Kannick was enthroned on his bed like a Buddha. It surprised his listeners, who were sitting in a semicircle on the floor, that he could sit cross-legged in spite of his bulk. At first nobody believed him. How could it be possible that Kannick had found a body up in the woods? And one that had been chopped up, at that. At least that's what he told them. *Chopped up.* It was especially difficult for the oldest boy, Karsten, who generally had a monopoly on the truth. His expression, when Margunn confirmed the story, was still fresh in Kannick's memory. It was one of his greatest victories. Now they all wanted to hear about it from Kannick himself, every little detail. But they had been at Guttebakken long enough to know that nothing was free in the world, and the presents lay in front of Kannick on the bedspread. A Firkløver chocolate bar, a pink pack of Hubba Bubba bubble gum, a bag of chips, and a box of Mocca beans. And still to come: ten cigarettes and a disposable lighter. Everyone was waiting, eyes shining, and it was clear to Kannick that they weren't going to be satisfied with a dry, factual account. They were out for blood, and nothing less would do. Besides, they knew Halldis. It wasn't just a matter of an obituary notice in the paper—this was a live human being. Or at least she used to be.

Kannick had been forbidden to say too much about the murder. Margunn didn't want to get the other boys excited. They were unruly enough as it was. The staff had meager resources, and only just managed to keep the motley group under control.

Kannick squinted his blue eyes. He decided to start with Simon and finish with Karsten. Simon was only eight and reminded him of a slightly melted chocolate mousse. Sweet and dark and soft.

"I went out with my bow and arrows," Kannick began, fixing his gaze on Simon's brown eyes. "Had just shot a fat crow with my second arrow. I have two arrowheads that I ordered from Denmark hidden in a secret compartment of my suitcase. Don't tell anyone. They're illegal here in Norway," he added importantly.

Karsten's face wore a long-suffering expression.

"The bird dropped like a sack of sugar and landed at my feet. There was nobody to be seen in the woods, but I had a bad feeling that someone was nearby. You know me, always going off to the woods. I can sense when something's about to happen. Maybe it's because I spend so much time in the animal world."

He took a breath, pleased with his dramatic opening. Simon was hanging on his every word. No one dared so much as to sigh, for fear of interrupting the account.

"I left the crow on the ground and headed for Halldis's farm."

He turned to look at Sivert now, a freckled eleven-year-old with a braid down his back.

"It was strangely quiet down there. Halldis always gets up early, so I went looking for her. Thought I could bum a glass of juice or something like that. Not a soul in sight. But her curtains were open, so I thought she might be having coffee and reading the paper, the way she usually does."

Jan Farstad, known as Jaffa, looked into Kannick's eyes and waited tensely. "If so," Kannick continued, "I thought I could get a slice of homemade bread with goat cheese. Once Halldis let me have eight slices of bread, but those were the last I ever got."

He blinked his eyes at the memory.

"Get to the point!" Karsten shouted, casting a glance at the Mocca beans lying on the bedspread, his payment for the story.

"I caught sight of her as soon as I came around the well. And let me tell you," he swallowed hard, "the sight is going to haunt me for the rest of my life."

"Yes, but what did you *see*?"

Karsten's voice rose to a falsetto. He was the only one of the boys to have a hint of a mustache and the first trace of acne at the corners of his nose.

"I saw the body of Halldis Horn!" Kannick said, exhaling loudly because he had forgotten to breathe. "Lying on her back on the front steps. With a hoe in one eye. And gray matter pouring out of the socket. It looked like oatmeal." His gaze grew suddenly remote.

"What's gray matter?" Simon asked in a low voice.

"Her brains," said Karsten, sounding bored.

"Brains can't pour out, can they?"

"Jesus, yes. They pour out like crazy. I suppose you didn't know that the stuff between your ears is as thin as soup."

Simon picked at a thread in his shirt and didn't stop until he had pulled it out. "I once saw a brain in a jar. It wasn't runny at all." His voice had a sullen tone, but was also slightly anxious because he was daring to disagree with this experienced group. There was no getting around the fact that he was the youngest.

"What an amateur! It wasn't runny because it was preserved. And then it has the consistency of a mushroom and they can cut it into thin slices. I saw that on TV."

"What does *preserved* mean?" Simon asked.

"Hardened," said Karsten. "They put it in something that makes it harden. But they won't have to do that with Kannick's brain—his was hardened long ago."

"Cut that out! Let Kannick finish."

This time it was Philip who interrupted. If those two started arguing they'd never stop. And Margunn could show up at any minute. Not that she really believed her ban on talking about the murder would be upheld; she knew better than that. The question was how much time they had now. And how many details they could glean.

Kannick waited with the patience of a preacher, frowning at the bounty lying before him. He decided to start with the Mocca beans.

"Her body had already begun to rot," he went on, putting extra emphasis on the word *rot*.

"What did you say?" Karsten snorted. "Give me a break! It happens to take several days for a body to start rotting. If Errki hadn't even managed to leave the scene, you can't tell me that—"

"Do you know how hot it was up in the woods?" Kannick leaned forward and his voice quivered with indignation. "It rots in a matter of minutes in that heat."

"You haven't got a clue. I'm going to ask the police about that if they ever come here. But I guess you're not very important, Kannick, or they would have been here long ago."

"Officer Gurvin promised they would come."

"We'll see about that, but cut out the stuff about rotting, because we don't believe you. I paid for the truth."

"Fine! I can skip over the worst parts. We've got children here, after all. Back to the hoe—"

"What kind of hoe was it?" Philip again.

"The kind you use to work the soil. To dig up potatoes and weeds. It looked like an ax with a longer shaft. Actually it might as well have been an ax because her head was almost split in two. And her eye had come loose and was hanging down her cheek from a thin thread, and—"

Karsten rolled his eyes. "You've been watching too many movies. Tell us about Errki," he said.

"Who's Errki?" Simon asked. He was from a different town and hadn't been there long.

"The terror of the woods," Karsten sneered, picking at one of his pimples. "He's bound to get off. He always gets off. Besides, he's a real nutcase, and crazy people are never convicted. They sit in the asylum swallowing pills, and then they get out and go right on killing. If they put him in a straitjacket he'd go on killing with his bare teeth."

"Is he going to get out?" Simon asked anxiously.

"He is out, you dope. They haven't found him yet."

"Where is he?"

"Up there in the woods."

Simon cast a frightened glance out the window, up toward the trees.

"Errki may be insane, but insane is not the same as stupid," Kannick said thoughtfully. "He noticed that I saw him. Maybe he's going to come after me. I really should have police protection."

He scowled at them with a worried look on his face, to see whether this piece of information had sunk in properly, whether they grasped what it meant to have such a threat hanging over him. A dangerous madman on his heels. It couldn't get any worse.

"Ha. He's probably long gone. Like you said, he's not stupid. What did he look like?" Karsten wanted to know. "Did he have any blood on him?"

"He was standing behind a tree," Kannick said in a low voice. "He was standing in a funny way, with his arms hanging at his sides, staring straight ahead. He has such peculiar eyes. My uncle has Greenland dogs, and Errki has the same kind of eyes as those dogs. Sort of whitish, like a dead fish."

He thought back to that fateful moment, when he stood in Halldis's yard with his heart pounding and stared in terror up at the woods, at the black trees, and suddenly caught sight of that strange figure among the trunks. Motionless at first, but then it moved, and something dark slowly leaned forward, and only then did he realize that it was a face. A face in shadow with staring eyes. The devil himself couldn't have scared Kannick more. He ran like a hare down the road, knowing he should let go of his suitcase containing the bow and arrows, but he couldn't. He kept on running and didn't look back.

"Has he killed anyone before?" Jaffa wanted to know.

Kannick released his body from its lotus position and stretched his stiff legs. "First his own mother. And then the old man up by the church," he said confidently. "And they still let him walk around freely. It's rotten to put a place like this," his eyes took in the room and the courtyard, "a building full of minors, in an area where a mass murderer lives."

"You idiot," Karsten said. "This home was here first, long before Errki went nuts."

"But why isn't he kept locked up?" Simon asked.

"He was. But he escaped. I expect he knocked out the night nurse and stole the keys."

Simon had been given far more to think about than he wanted. Very slowly he moved over to Karsten and leaned against him.

"Relax, Simon. There's a lock on the door," the older boy assured him. "Besides, Errki's the type that can never sit still. He wanders around. Hardly ever sleeps. Right now he's probably on his way to town to kill somebody else."

"Who?" Simon whimpered.

"Somebody chosen at random. He doesn't need to hate the person in order to kill them."

"But then why does he kill?"

"He has to. It's an inner urge."

Simon wanted to ask about this "inner urge," but lost his courage. Kannick picked up the box of Mocca beans and opened the lid, plucked out the little piece of cardboard on top, and then generously passed the box around. His new status overwhelmed him. No one had ever sat still this long listening to him. Everyone took a handful, and for a short time no one spoke as they all munched on the beans.

Karsten was furious. He couldn't get over the fact that he wasn't the one who had found the body. That it had to be this idiot Kannick, that he had actually seen a dead person although he was two years younger and fat. None of the others had seen a corpse.

"Were her eyes open?" he asked.

Kannick chewed as he paused to think. "Wide open. Or at least the one that was still there."

Philip broke in. "I once heard about a girl who had a doll that came alive at night. Its fingernails started to grow. In the morning, when the girl woke up, she was blind. The doll had scratched out her eyes."

"We're not talking about a movie!" Kannick shouted. "This is all real. The trouble with you is that you can't tell the difference between fantasy and reality. That's why you're here, but I'm sure you know that already." He closed his eyes to remember better. "Her eye had a terrified look, as if she'd seen the devil himself."

"That's not so far from the truth," Karsten said dryly. "I wonder if he said anything to her before he did it. Or whether he just charged toward her and cracked her in the head. Was she lying on the front doorstep?"

"Yes."

"With her head out on the steps or in the doorway?"

"Out on the steps."

"That means he must have been inside the house," said Karsten. "He was probably looking for some chocolate."

"If he asked her for some, she would have given it to him."

"Errki doesn't ask for anything, he just takes it. Everybody knows that."

Suddenly they all gave a start. The door opened, and there stood Margunn.

"Don't you look snug!"

She stared at the little group of boys sitting in attentive silence, chewing on the chocolate. No one was going to tell her that they didn't know how to create a cozy atmosphere, even in this soulless place. She knew what they were up to, but she was still proud of them.

"Who's telling stories?" She blinked her eyes innocently.

The boys stared at the floor. Even Karsten fluttered his eyelashes.

"I'm going to treat all of you to a Coke," she said, and left.

Kannick was thinking about that "inner urge" as his blood sugar slowly rose to an acceptable level, and he felt the warm drowsiness come over him that only sweets could produce. He felt comfortably tired and slightly lethargic, as if he were intoxicated. In the intoxication he found peace. He didn't know from what, but he could never get enough of it.

"We'll probably just get a Diet Coke," he sighed as he tore open the pack of Hubba Bubba. There was just enough gum for each of them. His generosity knew no bounds. The murder of Halldis had brought them together like never before. Usually they were a divisive group, everybody fighting one another, each boy struggling for his own pathetic position in this tiny society of outsiders. They had given up their dreams of the future, except for Simon, who was said to have a rich uncle who had hinted that Simon could come to live at his farm where he had thirty racehorses. But first he had to serve a four-month sentence for accounting irregularities, and he couldn't come and get the boy as long as he stood in the atonement line, as he put it. But soon they would make a new start together.

Margunn reappeared carrying, as predicted, some sugar-free Cokes and a tray of glasses.

"Don't spill it on the floor, boys."

She gave Kannick a warning glance. Margunn wasn't one to scold. They were her boys, and she was fond of them. Any attempt to reprimand fell flat, and they all loved her because she was the only person in their lives who cared about them. There were others on the staff, such as Thorleif, Inga, and Richard. And they were all right and did their jobs, but they were young and wanted to move on to something better. For them the boys were just a stretch of rugged terrain they had to traverse as fast as possible. Margunn, on the other hand, was old. She was almost sixty and had no ambition to move on. She had ended up here, in this ugly building covered with sheets of gray asbestos, with the smell of something green and close in all the rooms.

And she liked it, the way people like the moldy places in the back of the cellar because they never give up hope that one day they'll find something of value hidden among the junk. It was easy for the boys to sense that. Only Simon didn't draw his own conclusions. He asked the others and accepted the answers they gave him.

Karsten poured the Coke and sent the glasses around. Everyone was chomping at the bit. Kannick frowned down at the bedspread as he considered whether to share more of his loot or save the rest for bad days to come. This was a golden moment, and it might be a long time until the next one.

"Where is Halldis now?" Pålte asked after Margunn had left. His real name was Pål Theodor, and he was there by mistake, but no one had realized it yet. Somewhere in his future adult life a formidable compensation payment of several million kroner for wrongful incarceration was waiting. That was what kept him going.

"In the morgue," Kannick said, taking a gulp of his Coke. "In a freezer."

"Refrigerator," Karsten corrected him. "There will have to be an autopsy, of course, and if she's frozen, they won't be able to cut her open."

"Cut?" Simon's eyes grew dark with fear.

Karsten put his arm around the boy's shoulders. "When somebody dies, they're cut open. To find the cause of death."

"The cause of death was a hoe in her head," Philip remarked, with a belch.

"They have to find out precisely what it struck. They can't just guess."

"It hit her right in the eye."

"Yes, but they have to write up a death certificate. No one can be buried without a death certificate. I wonder why he used a hoe?" Karsten said. "He could have easily killed her with his bare hands."

"I guess he didn't feel like it at the time," Kannick replied, pursing his lips. Then he blew a big bubble that hid half his face before it finally popped and covered his nose and mouth. He scraped the gum off with his dirty fingers and put it back in his mouth.

"But the police are looking for him now, aren't they?" Simon was pulling on his earlobe, as if to calm himself down.

"Of course they are. They're on a manhunt with their guns loaded, I would imagine. And with bulletproof vests. I'm sure they'll get him."

Karsten tossed his head in annoyance. "The stupid thing is that they have to take him alive and unharmed."

He looked at them. This was something he knew all about. "It's better in the U.S. The police just shoot them dead, and show a lot more consideration for the community. I'm all for the death penalty!" he proclaimed solemnly.

And with this last comment, the meeting was over.

CHAPTER 8

The man who called himself Morgan was sitting on a little grassy mound. His gun lay at his side in the grass. Errki kept stealing glances at his Bermuda shorts covered with palm trees and fruit.

Morgan was trying to assess the situation. Things could be worse. He was out of the bank, out of the city, out of the car. And he had the money, just as he had promised. The car was hidden, and if this path wasn't used much, it could be days before it was discovered. They wouldn't find his fingerprints in the car, because he had never taken off his gloves. He wondered whether they had identified his hostage. Maybe the quality of the video surveillance in the bank would turn out to be poor.

"Listen here," he said in a low voice. The drumroll was more muted, Errki thought, he must have created a greater sense of order in his head. "You can at least answer this question."

He looked up at Errki, who was sitting on a tree stump with his knees pulled up. "Just tell me if you've escaped from somewhere. A home or something like that. Or whether you're on your own and have an apartment, or if you live with your mother. I'm curious. That's not too much to ask, is it?"

While he waited, he took a pouch of tobacco out of his bag. Errki didn't reply. Nestor was about to take up his position, the one where he squatted down with his chin pressed to his knees and his hands linked around his legs. That was the position. When he sat like that, Errki was allowed to speak.

"I mean, have you run away from a hospital or something? Is anyone looking for you? Is there a search going on?"

The question made Errki wag his head back and forth.

"Let's make a deal," Morgan said. "I'll ask you a question. If you answer, you have the right to ask me one, which I have to answer if I want to ask you something else. How about that?"

Morgan felt quite proud of this suggestion as he looked at his hostage. In spite of the black leather jacket and dark trousers, he didn't look sweaty. That was odd. He, on the other hand, was drenched with sweat, and his sleeveless shirt had big dark patches.

"I'd just like to find out who you are," he added. "It's not that easy."

"A person can't see much when the devil is holding the candle," Errki said quietly. He spoke in a weary voice, as if it cost him far too much energy to waste words on a poor man like Morgan.

Morgan started at the sound of Errki's voice. It was bright and pleasant sounding, and he spoke with great solemnity. Errki tilted his head and listened intently to Nestor's whispering. The robber's suggestion sounded familiar. A game they used to play at the asylum. In group therapy.

"I'll start," he said.

Morgan smiled, relieved to hear such a normal remark. "But the same applies to you, right? If I answer honestly, then I have the right to ask you a question and get a truthful reply."

Errki assented by meeting his glance. "What are you going to do now?" he asked, and at the same moment he heard Nestor laughing shrilly down in the depths of the cellar.

Morgan frowned. He scowled at the black-clad figure and licked his lips.

What are you going to do now? That was an unexpected

question. Well, he could just make something up, since this lunatic was barely capable of understanding the answer he gave him. But they weren't supposed to lie. And besides, it seemed impossible to lie to those gleaming eyes. He realized that he felt terribly alone. He began to sweat even more. *What are you going to do now?* Damned if he knew. He was sitting here with a bag full of money and an imbecile he couldn't understand. He hesitated, then shrugged his shoulders.

"I'm waiting for dark."

Waiting for dark. Nestor curled his lips into what looked like a smile. *Tell him, Errki! Make the man open his eyes.*

"It's not going to get dark," said Errki. "It's midsummer."

"I'm not stupid," Morgan snapped back.

Oh yes, he is, Nestor chuckled, rocking back and forth like a devil-may-care old woman.

"Between midnight and two in the morning it will be twilight. Then we'll see what happens," Morgan said.

The voice sounded threatening again, and the drums were once more off tempo.

"Now it's my turn. What's wrong with you?"

Errki spread his fingers. This was what disgusted Morgan. If it hadn't been for the way he splayed his fingers and the nasty way he rocked his head, he would have been bearable.

An honest answer, Errki thought. What's wrong with me? A shudder rushed through and stirred up the gray cellar dust. Nestor snarled gruffly. What's wrong with me? He looked down. A bloodred spot appeared in the grass, right at his feet. It started rising, slowly getting bigger. If he moved his foot an inch, the blood would touch his sneakers.

"Well? Are you going to answer?" Morgan gave him a sullen look. "We had an agreement. What's wrong with you? An honest answer. Come on."

Errki sat frozen solid, staring down at his feet.

"OK, I'm going to be nice, unlike you, since you're a little strange. I'll ask you another question. But if you don't give me a proper answer this time, I'm going to get angry." He stared hard at Errki to emphasize how serious he was. "You moved so damned fast up this hill. I've never seen anything like it. Do you know this area?"

"Yes," Errki said, raising his head. He was careful not to move his feet.

Morgan was excited. "Do you know it well? Then maybe you know a place where we could sit and wait for dark? Or maybe we should build ourselves a shelter out of branches, what do you think?"

Now Errki had more questions. He struggled over them, annoyed at the man's lack of clarity. Know it well? A shelter out of branches?

"Yes," he said as he checked the spot of blood. Several insects had been attracted to it and were crawling around, feasting.

"Yes, you know it well, and yes, we'll build ourselves a shelter out of branches," Morgan said enthusiastically. "OK. You build the shelter. I'll hold the gun. Besides, I can't stand all the prickly branches."

Lazily he brushed aside the lowest branch of a spruce tree. Errki stared at the gun, which lay in the grass a few feet from his feet.

"Tell me," Morgan said, "how good are you at observing details? If you had to identify me to the police, for example. Not that it will come to that, but humor me. How would you describe me?"

Errki whispered, "It's my turn now."

"Sorry, you're right. Fire away."

He licked the paper and stuck the cigarette between his lips, fumbling for a lighter.

"What's wrong with you?" said Errki.

Morgan stared at him in astonishment, his eyes narrowing with displeasure. Nestor snickered. The Coat fluttered its arms a bit over in the corner. He was always so loose. Powerless, in a way. Every now and then it occurred to Errki that he was all bluff. Nothing more than a damned bluffer.

"There's nothing wrong with me, goddamn it," Morgan said harshly. "And so far I haven't given you so much as a scratch. Whether things will stay that way depends on your willingness to cooperate."

He felt uneasy. It was difficult to figure out crazies—they were so unpredictable. But there was a certain logic to them, as far as he knew. It was a matter of finding it.

"Let me tell you one thing," he said, "I'm not completely ignorant of your problem. I did my civilian service in a psychiatric hospital. You wouldn't have guessed that, would you? I refused to do military service. I'm a pacifist."

He looked down at the gun in the grass and laughed. "I remember one odd character there who went around sniffing his underpants. He wouldn't hurt a fly otherwise. How about you? Do you wander around sniffing your underpants?"

It was a dreary discovery for Errki to realize just how childish this man was. He checked the spot of blood. It was still there.

"Before I forget," Morgan said, "back to my question. What kind of description will you give the police if you have to tell them about me? Come on, let's hear it."

A fool of a man, Errki thought. A rumpled clown in silly shorts. Scared most of the time. If he loses the gun, he's helpless. At the asylum they would undoubtedly say that he had been neglected as a child.

Errki proceeded to study him with such blazing eyes that Morgan was unsettled.

Height: about five foot five, definitely no taller.

Morgan kept silent, waiting.

Weight: about forty pounds heavier than me. Age: maybe twenty-two. Thick, sandy hair. Straight, dark eyebrows. Eyes, grayish blue. Small mouth with full lips.

Morgan took a drag on his cigarette and sighed impatiently.

Small ears with full lobes. Short, sausagelike fingers, plump thighs and calves. Puffy looking. Attire: idiotic. Intelligence: average, but in the lower percentile.

It was totally silent. Even the birds were still. Only Errki could hear the sniggering laughter down in the cellar. Morgan stood up abruptly and retrieved the pistol.

"OK, go ahead and be as secretive as you like. Get up. We're going!"

He had a sickening feeling that he was being ridiculed without knowing why.

"It's only a picture," Errki said suddenly.

"Shut up, I said!"

"The kind that nobody bothers to turn over and read what it says on the back."

"Get moving!"

"Have you thought about that?" Errki said. "No one knows who you are. Isn't that shitty, Morgan?"

Morgan looked at him in surprise. Errki got to his feet with deliberate slowness, took a big step to avoid treading in the slippery blood, and started walking back downhill, toward the overlook where they had left the car. From there he would be able to glimpse the sea, cold and blue. And the road with all the traffic.

"No, damn it! We're going to keep heading uphill! Are you a complete idiot?"

"What will you do if I go where I want to go instead?" Errki said in a low voice.

"Put a damned bullet right between your eyes and find a hole to dump you in. Now move it!"

Errki started walking uphill. Faster than ever. He was rested now, and he always felt better when he was on the move.

"OK, that's fast enough. If you really do know the area, then find us an abandoned cabin or something so we can have a roof over our heads."

An old cabin. There were plenty of them, though most were on the other side of the ridge, more than a mile away. It was rough going the entire time, and the heat was fierce. Errki was thirsty. He didn't say so, but he guessed that Morgan was too. He heard the panting behind him, and a little while later Morgan's voice, calmer now.

"If you see a stream or anything, just say so. I've got a hell of a thirst."

Errki kept going. His long black hair swung from side to side, and his jacket and baggy trousers did, too. Morgan stared at him in bewilderment. This guy was altogether different from everyone else. How can I get rid of him? he wondered. Why am I dragging along this black-haired loser? I could have left him in the car. Was it out of fear that he would give the police a description? Or was it something else? He might not even talk if he did fall into the hands of the police. He checked his watch. In half an hour it would be time for the radio news report. He would stop to hear what they had discovered so far. He moved along as fast as he could while thirst ravaged his mouth and throat. He had sense enough not to drink his whiskey yet. Crazy people could be dangerous. This man wasn't in particularly good physical condition, but insanity and a lack of inhibitions might give him tremendous strength. Maybe it would be safer to keep his distance and not provoke him too much. They weren't enemies, after all. He had taken Errki with him on sheer impulse. Rushing out of the bank with him was like holding a thick shield in front of him. Relax, he told himself. He just has a rather bizarre way of talking. Remember the year you worked in the asylum, how scared they all were?

Errki stopped and started patting his jacket pockets, first

one and then the other. He stuck his hand in his trouser pockets, turned around, and stared down at the grass.

"What's wrong?" Morgan looked at him. "Did you lose something? Besides your mind, I mean?"

Errki patted all of his pockets again, one after the other.

"You can bum a cigarette from me if that's what you're looking for."

"The bottle," Errki mumbled, looking around.

"What bottle?"

"The pills."

"You take pills? Where did you lose them?"

Errki didn't reply. In his mind he raced back down through the woods, while he rocked his head back and forth several times.

"Do you take those antipsychotic drugs? Well, OK, you've lost them. Now you'll have to make do without them. You're not going to go berserk because of this, are you?"

Berserk. Nestor was making that humming sound again, like electricity passing through a cable. He doesn't understand the meaning of the word. Errki started walking.

"Chemicals like that are nothing but shit anyway," Morgan muttered as he pondered the problem and what the consequences might be. "They just keep you down. I'll give you a shot of whiskey instead," he decided.

Errki stopped again. Fixed his eyes on Morgan.

"My name is Errki."

"Errki?"

"I'm just here on a visit. If you can't chop off the hand, then you'd better kiss it."

He started walking. Morgan was still standing in the heather, staring after him. It occurred to him that he, who was supposed to be the guard, was trotting after his prisoner like a dog. Errki was strong, and much faster and lighter on his feet than he was. The roles were reversed. Here he was trailing be-hind like an old woman. Nobody knew where they were, no-body was going to come to his rescue if anything happened. He clutched the gun tighter. A shot in the thigh would be suf-ficient. As soon as it was dark, he would continue on alone. Maybe he would tie Errki up to give himself a head start. The guy was repulsive, and yet there was something about him that was also fascinating. His eyes. His peculiar remarks. The air of solemnity that surrounded him, as if he came from another world. Maybe Errki was brilliant, a genius even. He had heard once that it was the people with the sharpest minds who went off the deep end.

Suddenly Morgan realized that the distance between them had grown considerably. He raced to catch up, feeling uneasy. Where, exactly, were they going? How was this going to end?

"We've got to stop now. It's time for the news!"

His voice was unnecessarily loud, as if he were emphasizing his own position, as if he had begun to have his doubts about it, and that scared him. Errki kept going. Rolling and striding along, completely ignoring him.

"Hey, Errki!"

The drum slammed and rattled several times. Errki stopped and turned around. The man behind him was shaking with anger. There's nothing as pathetic as a man who loses his grip, he thought.

"You don't have to act up every damned time I give you an order. I'm the one in charge here."

Wrong. He's the one with the gun. Errki pressed his lips together.

"Sit down. It's time for the news. I want to find out how much they know."

They were almost at the top of a wide ridge. Beyond it was another ridge that was a muted green and infinitely far away in the haze. Morgan fumbled around in the bag for the radio, and spent a moment fiddling with the antenna. Errki lay down on his back in the heather and closed his eyes.

"You look like a ghost lying there."

Morgan tried to pull himself together. He studied Errki with genuine astonishment. "How do you manage to stay so pale when the sun is this bright?" He chuckled. "I guess you live in a different world, and it's damned dark in there, isn't it?"

He found a local station, and drummed his fingers impatiently while the last strains of a military band died out.

"And now for the news." A piece of paper rustled. "A man in his early twenties made off with almost a hundred thousand kroner after he robbed the Fokus Bank this morning. The robbery took place shortly after the bank opened, and the robber took a customer hostage as he left the scene. A shot was fired, but no one was hurt. So far there is no trace of the robber or the hostage, although the police have a remarkably good description of the offender."

Morgan frowned. "A remarkably good description?"

"They left the city in a small white car, but police roadblocks have failed to apprehend them."

"What are they talking about? I didn't take off my mask until we were out of sight!"

He put the radio down in the grass. "They're bluffing!"

Annoyed, he took his tobacco pouch out of his pocket and rolled a cigarette. Errki was listening to a fly buzzing persistently in front of him.

"The police still do not have any leads in the death of seventy-six-year-old Halldis Horn, who was found murdered yesterday morning. The woman was discovered at her home, brutally killed with a sharp object. Her wallet had been taken. The mutilated body was found by a boy playing in the area."

Morgan's eyes took on a remote look.

"Now there's an example of what I mean by a real crime. Do you see the difference? Nobody's going to miss the money I took. The bank has insurance. No one got hurt, and the car doesn't have a scratch on it. Then you have people who murder for the sake of a lousy wallet."

Errki was still listening to the fly. He was convinced that it was trying to get at him; all that buzzing must have a purpose. It was annoying how much that clown Morgan talked. He didn't understand the meaning of a word, of holding on to it, saving it for an important moment.

"An old woman! I don't understand things like that. It must have been a real maniac." He glanced over at Errki. "Are you good at making a shelter out of branches, by the way? Used to be a Boy Scout, maybe?"

Errki opened one eye and stared at him. Morgan was reminded of a lamp behind a thin curtain, giving off a dim light.

"We need to find water, at any rate. You don't know of a little stream, do you? Or a small lake?"

Nestor was rocking back and forth, squatting, as usual, with his chin resting on his knees. Errki was always impressed by this position; he could sit that way for hours without getting tired. The Coat, which couldn't stand up straight or even sit down because it had nothing inside except for foolish remarks, waved the flap of its pocket slightly. Just to show that it was still there and intended to stay until someone hauled it away.

"Do you like whiskey? Long John Silver, room temperature."

Morgan took another drag on his cigarette and stared straight ahead, scratching his calf because there was a twig or insect annoying him. Slapping at insects made him sweat, and for a moment he cast a suspicious glance at the man lying motionless in the grass.

"How can you lie still like that?" he grumbled. "You've got a whole battalion of flies just above your nose."

He ground out his cigarette butt in the grass, stood up abruptly, and went over to Errki. Bent down, grabbed hold of his shoulder hard, and gave him a shake.

Errki flinched. "Don't touch me!"

"So you don't like it when I grab you, huh? Afraid of being infected or something? People like you are always scared of bacteria and germs, isn't that right? But there's nothing wrong with me. I took a shower yesterday, which is more than I can say for you."

A sudden gust of wind made the Coat flutter and roll across the ground. Errki gave a start and raised his hands.

"What's the matter?" Morgan looked at him. "Are you sick? I can't get you those pills, but honestly, I would if I could. I'm not stingy. And as for the robbery," he swallowed hard. "You may not realize it, but the robbery was actually an act of friendship."

The words were spoken with the utmost sincerity. Errki was confused. One minute the man was puffing himself up like a balloon, and the next he was as friendly as a hospital chaplain. He stood up and started walking again. He moved very fast and was far away before Morgan even realized that he had started off.

"Take it easy, I'm coming."

But Errki strode on ahead and disappeared behind a thicket. Morgan could hear branches breaking, dry little snaps.

"Wait right there. This bag isn't exactly light, dammit!"

Errki walked on and on. The two in the cellar watched him go. Nestor turned his head slightly. He seemed to be sending a small signal to the Coat, who waved one sleeve in response. It looked as if they were planning something, or making an important decision. He walked faster. That's what they wanted— to see what would happen. Behind him he could hear the man's footsteps and his ragged breathing. He thought about the gun, about what it could do, about all the power between heaven and earth.

"Errki, goddamn it! I'll shoot!"

Morgan was running. It occurred to him that the woods were so dense that Errki could easily vanish in an instant, simply crouch down behind a bush or sit perfectly still as he ran past. And he didn't know where he was. Would he be able to find his way back to the path where the car was parked?

"I'll shoot, Errki. I've got plenty of bullets. Do you know what a bullet will do if it hits your leg? It'll turn your calf inside out!"

His calf? Errki had to concentrate to remember which part of the body was called the calf. He never saw it because it was always behind him. He kept on going until he heard a sharp crack and something whistled past his ear. The bullet gave off a tiny puff as it flew past. The next instant it slammed into a tree trunk just in front of him. White splinters leaped from the trunk like spikes of hair. He stopped.

"OK! You finally get it. I thought you would."

Morgan was panting like a dog. "Next time I'll aim for your calf. Now slow down. We're going to have to stop soon. I don't feel like trudging around anymore. It's getting late."

Errki bit his lip hard. Something was approaching fast. He could sense that he was getting close, he was almost there, but he wasn't ready. He looked around and knew exactly where they were. The other man didn't. He started walking more calmly. Had to remember not to irritate Morgan. He pictured the wound in the tree, and the same wound in his back, a whole explosion right into the marrow, the skin completely shredded, the blood gushing out as if from an open tap, and the great leap into eternity.

He longed for it. But he pushed it away for when he was ready, until the right day, the right time. It would be soon, he could feel it. So much had happened. The man behind him might have been sent to him as a helper. This is how he saw it: he would plummet into the endless universe, onto a path that was his alone, others passing by on the right and the left, beyond his reach, like faint vibrations in the atmosphere, small gusts streaming past. Maybe his mother was hovering around like that, with her arms spread wide like wings and the light from the stars like crystals in her black hair. Following her would be the dark sound of a flute. The alternative was to continue as he was, with someone always on his heels. I'm tired, he thought. Who forced us to start this run? Who is waiting at the finish line? And how damned far are we supposed to go? Blood, sweat, and tears. Pain, sorrow, and despair!

They had come to a grove where the trees thinned out into a small clearing. Morgan finally caught up with Errki. The bag fell to the ground with a thump. The robber's eyes lit up.

"Hey, look at that! A little cottage, all to ourselves. We can play house here." He looked genuinely pleased. "Jesus, I'm going to be glad to get indoors."

He trotted past Errki, heading for the door. Errki looked at the dark patch on the top step where his guts had spilled out and lay steaming only twenty-four hours earlier. Morgan didn't notice it. He tugged at the rotting door, and it opened slowly with a creak. He peered inside.

"Dark and cool," he reported. "Come on."

Errki was still standing outside in the grass. There was something he was trying to remember, but it slipped away like a rubber band. This had been bothering him for years, the elasticity of his thoughts.

"It's nice inside. Come on in."

Morgan pushed Errki into what had been the living room when shepherds lived in the hut, and went over to the window.

"A little pond. Perfect. I'm sure we can have a swim down there."

He stuck his head out through the broken window and nodded. Errki felt exhausted. He took a few tentative steps toward the bedroom.

"Where do you think you're going?" Morgan looked at him.

Errki opened the door and stared for a moment at the striped mattress, then tore off his jacket and T-shirt, and toppled onto the bed.

"Jesus. A bed!" Morgan smiled. "This is fine with me. Go ahead and take a nap. At least I'll know where you are."

Errki didn't reply. He thought it would be best if he went to sleep, because death and misery were the only things accompanying him, and a person can't commit any sins when asleep. He took deep, steady breaths.

"You've been a first-rate guide. I'll talk to you later."

To be safe, he checked the window in the bedroom to see whether Errki would be able to escape that way. The glass was broken, but the frame was still intact, and the window was jammed shut. If Errki tried to open it, he would hear him.

Morgan left the room. When his footsteps could no longer be heard, Errki opened his eyes. He was lying on something sharp and hard, so he moved over a bit. It was the gun.

CHAPTER 9

The hospital loomed into view between the trees, its presence so forceful that for a moment it took Sejer's breath away. He pulled over to the shoulder of the road, stopped the car, and got out. He stood there for a while, looking up at the building, letting it sink in, feeling as if it were screaming at him: THIS IS SERIOUS!

It stood on the highest point in the area. This was what a psychiatric hospital should look like, as if to show everyone that the path back to sanity was not an easy one. If they didn't know this before, those who came here in the deepest despair would know it when they were led into this monstrosity of an institution.

The road was poorly maintained, narrow, and full of holes. Years had passed since he was last there, and he had thought it would have been improved and widened, but that hadn't happened. He remembered when, as a rookie officer, he had brought a girl here. They had found her locked in the ladies' room at the bus station, naked. They broke down the door. Her face was contorted with fear. In her hand she held a roll of toilet paper, and she started eating the paper, as if it held something of crucial importance, secret information that she had to protect. His hand had hung in midair between them, and she stared at it as if it were a claw. He was holding a blanket that he wanted to put around her shoulders. He talked to her in a soothing voice, and although she listened, it was as if she heard him through a terrible noise and was straining hard to catch his words. Her face told its own story. He had come to mete out a vicious punishment. His words, his assurances, his gentle voice, all these things simply fell away. And so he had to do what he least wanted to do: use force to remove her. He still remembered her screams, and her thin, sharp shoulders.

The Beacon was an impressive building, but up close some of its authority was diminished by the state of disrepair. The red bricks had faded and were gradually taking on a grayish shade, like the asphalt below. It was sinking slowly into eternity. And yet it was imposing, if only because of the magnificent sunlight. It wasn't hard for him to imagine that in different weather, in the winter when the trees spread out their bare branches and the wind and rain battered the windows, the place would look like Dracula's castle. The roof was topped by a copper tower covered with verdigris. The facade was ornate, but the windows were narrow and high, not matching the style of the rest of the building. The front entrance was an attractive arch with its own staircase. Next to it was a classic hospital entrance with big glass doors that would allow an ambulance to drive up and a stretcher to be rolled in.

Sejer went inside. Without noticing, he walked right past the front desk.

"Excuse me? Where are you going?" a young woman called after him.

"I'm sorry. Police. I need to talk to Dr. Struel." Sejer showed her his badge.

"You have to go up to the third floor and ask there."

He thanked her and went upstairs. On the second floor he asked again and was shown into a waiting room with a window facing the garden and woods. The ban on watering grass didn't seem to apply to this area because the lawns were as dark and green as velvet. Maybe they should be using that money on other things. He couldn't imagine that the lawns made much difference to those who lived here. As he thought this he turned around abruptly because he had an uneasy sensation that someone was watching him.

A woman was standing in the open door.

"I'm Dr. Struel," she said.

They shook hands.

"Let's go to my office."

He followed her down the corridor and into a spacious room, where she offered him a seat on the sofa. He sat down in a flood of sunlight and immediately began to sweat profusely. The doctor went over to the window and stood there for a moment with her back to him, staring out at the lawn, fiddling a bit with a drooping potted plant that clearly wasn't thriving.

"So," she said as she turned around, "you're the man who's looking for my Errki?"

My Errki. There was something very touching about the way she said it. Without a trace of irony.

"Is that how you see him?"

"No one else wants him," she said simply. "Yes, he's mine. My responsibility, my job. Whether he killed the old woman or not, he will still be mine."

"Who have you talked to about this?"

"Officer Gurvin called. But I really have a hard time believing it," she said. "I'm telling you this now so you'll know where I stand. Let him stay out there for a while, and he'll come back on his own."

"I don't think he's coming back on his own."

His solemn tone made her realize something was wrong.

"What do you mean? Has anything happened to him?"

"How much did Officer Gurvin tell you?"

"He told me about the murder at Finnemarka, that Errki was seen in the vicinity of the house at what he called a crucial time."

"Not just in the vicinity. He was at her farm. So you can see why we have to find him. It's a very isolated place."

"It's typical for Errki to head for the woods. He tries to avoid people. And with good reason."

She was being awfully curt. Sejer felt something rise up inside him. Irritation.

"Forgive my arrogance," he said slowly, "but I actually do have to take the possibility that he is guilty into consideration. It was a vicious crime and a meaningless one, since it seems as though the only thing missing from her house is a wallet containing a few kroner. Whoever did this is walking around free. People living in the area are frightened."

"Errki is always blamed," she said quietly.

"But he was seen at her house, after all, and she lived in a remote area. It isn't exactly crawling with people. And since he is mentally ill, we can't ignore the fact that he might have something to do with her murder."

"Do you mean that he's under greater suspicion because he's ill?"

"Well, I—"

"You're mistaken. The most he does is shoplift. Chocolate and things like that."

"There are lots of stories about him."

"Just that. Stories."

"And there's no basis for them? Is that what you think?"

She didn't reply.

"But this is only half the story," he went on. "This morning there was a robbery. An armed robbery at Fokus Bank."

She burst out laughing. "Honestly, Errki doesn't have enough discipline to carry out anything that requires a lot of effort. You've just lost your credibility."

"I'm not finished," he snapped. He didn't like that last remark.

"The bank was robbed by a young man who might be a little younger than Errki. He was wearing dark clothes and a ski mask, which means, of course, that we haven't yet identified him. But the biggest problem is that he took a hostage. Someone who was inside the bank. Using a gun, he forced the hostage into his car and disappeared. This hostage has been identified as Errki Johrma."

Now Dr. Struel was speechless. He could almost feel her embarrassment.

"Errki?" she stammered. "Taken hostage? And you don't know where they are?"

"Unfortunately, no. We've set up roadblocks, and we think the car they escaped in is a white Mégane, stolen last night. Most likely they've abandoned it somewhere long ago, but we haven't found it. We don't know anything about what sort of man this robber is, or whether he's dangerous. But he fired a shot inside the bank, probably to scare the staff, and he seemed quite unstable."

She sat down, picked up something from the table, and held on to it tightly.

"How can I help?" she asked in a low voice.

"I need to know what kind of person Errki is."

"That would take all night."

"I don't have time for that. Tell me why you don't believe that he could have killed the old woman. How long has he been your patient?"

"He's been here for four months, but he has spent large periods of his life in one institution or another. The reports and case records on Errki are extensive."

"Has he ever shown violent tendencies?"

"You know," she said, "the truth is that he's incredibly self-protective. Only if he were really backed into a corner would he even think of biting. And I can't understand how an old woman could have made him so angry or provoked him so much that he would harm her."

"We don't know what happened up there, or what the old woman might have done. We know that she is dead and that her wallet is missing."

"Then it's definitely not Errki. He only takes chocolate and things like that. Never money."

Sejer sighed. "It's nice that you have such faith in him. He surely needs it more than most people. And no one else is on his side, are they?"

"Now look here." She stared at him. "I'm not absolutely certain—I can't stand that kind of overconfidence. But I see it as my duty to believe that he's innocent. Sooner or later I'm going to have to tell him what I think. When he's sitting on my sofa where you're sitting right now and asks me: do you think I did it?"

Dr. Struel was in her mid-forties, fair and angular, her hair cut short with long bangs. Her face was surprisingly feminine for such a strong personality, and she had full cheeks dusted with a light down. He could see it in the sunlight that was blazing in through the window. She was wearing jeans and a white blouse, and there were patches of sweat under her arms. Now she ran a hand over her hair to brush it out of her eyes, but the long bangs fell forward again, like a blond wave.

Sejer sat up straight on the sofa. "I'd like to see his room."

"It's on the second floor. I'll show it to you. But tell me, how was the old woman killed?"

"She was killed with a hoe."

The doctor grimaced. "That doesn't sound like something Errki would do. He's such a reserved person."

"That's what anyone would say who believes in him or feels responsible for him." He stood up and wiped the sweat from his brow. "Excuse me, but I'm sitting right in the sun. Would you mind if I move?"

She nodded and he went over to an armchair near her desk. As he did so, he caught sight of a toad. It was dozing behind a stack of papers. It was big and fat, grayish brown on top and lighter underneath. It didn't move, of course, because it wasn't real, but he wouldn't have been surprised if it had started to hop, it looked so alive. Feeling curious, he picked it up. She watched him and smiled as he placed it in his hand. The toad was strangely cold, in spite of the heat in the room. He squeezed it carefully. Inside was a jellylike substance that made it possible for him to squeeze it into different shapes, which he proceeded to do, quite cautiously. He squeezed the contents of the body into the thin legs. It immediately became deformed and looked like a monster. He kept on squeezing, feeling it slowly grow warmer in his hand.

The toad's eyes stared at him. They were pale green, with a black streak. Its back was rippled and uneven, but underneath it was smooth. He began squeezing its bottom, pressing all of the contents into the upper part of the body. Now it looked athletic, with big shoulders and a swelling chest.

Next, he tried another variation, with the contents pushed down into the stomach so the head hung to the side, as slack as a patch of skin. He put the toad down on the desk. The jelly didn't slide back into place on its own as he had expected it to. He picked it up again and began pressing it back into shape as best he could. When he thought it looked like a toad again, he put it back down.

"Clever," he said.

"Useful," responded Dr. Struel, running her finger along the toad's back.

"What's it for?"

"For picking up, just as you did. The way you handled it tells me something about who you are."

He shook his head. "I don't believe that."

She gave him an almost maternal smile. "Oh yes, absolutely.

It tells me something about the way in which every single person approaches things. You, too."

He listened dubiously, but at the same time he was intrigued.

"You picked it up very cautiously and paused for a moment before squeezing it. When you saw that it could change shape, you had to try all of the possibilities, one by one. Many people think it's disgusting, but you didn't. The way you tilted your head to one side as you looked into its eyes tells me that you confront life's surprises with an open and empathetic mind. You squeezed it carefully, almost tenderly, as if you were afraid it might split open. But it won't—or at least it has a warranty from the manufacturer, provided you don't have fiendishly sharp fingernails. You put it down relatively quickly, as if you thought it might develop into a dangerous game. And last but not least, you squeezed it meticulously back into its original shape before you set it down."

She paused for a moment and gave him a long look. "It tells me that you're a cautious man but not lacking in curiosity. You're also a little old-fashioned and afraid of new, unfamiliar shapes. You like things to look the way they're supposed to look, to stay the way they are, to be something that you recognize and know about."

He laughed uncertainly. Her voice was making him soften in a strange way. He felt slightly jellylike.

"With the help of the toad, along with thousands of other little things, other games and tasks, and above all over time, I can end up almost knowing more about you than you do yourself."

You're certainly not lacking in self-confidence, he thought.

"Has Errki seen it?" he asked her.

"Of course. It's always here."

"What did he do with it?"

"He said, 'Get rid of that disgusting, repulsive animal before I bite its head off and spray the contents all over the desk.'"

"Did you believe he would?"

"He has never lied."

"But you say that he's not violent?"

Suddenly she grabbed the toad and began yanking on all of its legs as hard as she could. They stretched out like rubber bands, and the sight made Sejer feel almost sorry for the toad. Next she tied them in knots, first the front legs, then the back ones. Finally she put the toad on its back on the desk. Its utter helplessness was painful to look at. When she saw his expression, she laughed out loud.

"Let me show you his room."

"Aren't you going to untie the knots?" he asked uneasily.

"No," she said, giving him a teasing smile.

A huge wave surged inside him. He registered it in amazement.

They looked at Errki's room. It was sparsely furnished with a bed, a dresser, a sink, and a mirror with a piece of newspaper hanging over it. Perhaps he wanted to avoid looking at himself. The window, high and narrow, stood open. Otherwise the room was bare. Nothing on the floor or the walls.

"It looks similar to what we have to offer," Sejer said thoughtfully. "A cell."

"We don't lock the doors."

He went in and stood leaning against the wall. "What made you go into psychiatry?"

He studied her name tag. Dr. S. Struel. He wondered what the *S* stood for. Maybe Solveig. Or Sylvia.

"Because," she began, as she closed her eyes, "because ordinary people..." She enunciated the word "ordinary" as if it were derogatory. "I mean, those who are successful, the well-equipped, goal-oriented people who follow all the rules, who achieve their objectives without difficulty, who have perfect social skills, who navigate with the greatest ease, who get where they want to go, who acquire what they want to have—is there anything the least bit interesting about them?"

The question was formulated in such a droll way that Sejer couldn't help but smile.

"All the interesting people in the world are losers," she said. "Or rather, those we call losers. Every type of deviation contains an element of rebellion. And I've never been able to understand a lack of rebelliousness."

"What about you?" he said suddenly. "Aren't you one of those successful and goal-oriented people? Are you rebelling?"

"No," she admitted. "And I can't understand it, because deep down I'm full of despair."

"Full of despair? You?"

"Aren't you?" She gave him a long look. "You can't be an enlightened, intelligent, involved human being on this earth without being at the same time full of despair. It's just not possible."

Am I full of despair? Sejer wondered.

"Besides, it's the sterling personalities that do best in this society," she said. "Whole, absolutely confident and consistent people. You know—people with strength of character!"

He couldn't hold back his laughter any longer.

"Here we have room for rebellion, and we're not afraid of trouble. We're not afraid of failure either." She brushed her bangs back from her face. "And I probably couldn't have existed in any community other than this one."

He was fascinated by the way she expressed her thoughts so openly, even though he was a stranger. At the same time, he didn't feel like a stranger.

"What's it like where you work?" she asked.

"Where I work?" He thought for a moment. "Where I work we have order and structure and plenty of disgusting, sterling personalities."

He tried to change his tone, which was becoming a bit too lively. "Not much room for improvisation or imagination. A large part of the job involves searching for tiny little physical things, such as hair, prints, or traces of blood. Tracks from shoes or car tires. But later comes the psychological part, and even though it never gets much space in our reports, it's still there. And of course that's the only thing about the job that's truly exciting. If there wasn't any room for that, I would have done something else."

"And what about the people you haul in and lock up in cages?"

He looked at her in dismay. "That's not exactly how we would describe it."

Now she's trying to provoke me, he thought. Maybe she's so preoccupied with rebellion that she feels she doesn't have to comply with the normal rules of courtesy.

"I would like to send them somewhere else," he said calmly.

He was so fascinated by this woman, by her wide, fair face and her dark eyes with light rings around the pupils, that he was almost nervous about what he might say.

"If there was any other place for them," he continued. "But in spite of everything we've never got any further than... cages."

"Do you care about them?" she asked. He had to look up to see what her expression was. She was teasing him again.

"Yes, I do, although I don't have much time for them. Besides, I'm not a prison guard. But I know that the guards do care about them."

"Ah, yes," she conceded. "I suppose we do have some of the most humane penitentiaries in the world."

"Humane?" He couldn't keep the sharpness out of his voice. "The prisoners dope themselves up. They escape by jumping out of windows, and break their legs or even their necks. They go crazy, rape each other, kill each other, and take their own lives. That's how humane it is!"

He took a deep breath.

"You really do care about them!" She smiled.

"I said I did."

"I had to be sure."

They both fell silent, and once again he was astonished by this strange conversation. It was as if she lacked the usual respect for the authority he represented, which made people speak with deference or not at all.

"Errki," he said at last. "Tell me about Errki."

"Only if you're truly interested."

"Of course I'm interested!"

She went out into the corridor. "Let's go to the cafeteria and have a Coke. I'm thirsty."

He found himself trotting after her, struggling to suppress the commotion in his head, or his chest, or his stomach, or wherever it was right now. He was no longer sure of anything.

CHAPTER 10

"Which way do you think Errki went?"

"Through the woods."

Dr. Struel pointed slightly to the left of the Beacon. "There's a small lake that we call the Well, but we've already looked there. If he went past it and continued on, he would come out on the main road where it passes under the highway. And if he was seen in Finnemarka, that direction would make sense."

A little while later they were sitting in the cafeteria, drinking Cokes. "Would it be possible for you to explain to an ordinary person what psychosis actually is?" Sejer asked her.

"Are you an ordinary person?"

There was something mocking about her tone of voice, and he wasn't quite sure whether the question was meant as a compliment or something else. In his confusion he started fiddling with the cell phone attached to his belt.

"In some ways it's impossible because it's so abstract," she said in a low voice. "But I think of it as a kind of hiding place. It's a matter of having all the normal defense mechanisms totally break down. Your soul is thrown wide open, so that anyone and everyone can step right in. Even the most innocent advance is experienced as a hostile attack. Errki has found himself a hiding place. He's trying to survive by creating a survival strategy, a sort of corrective force that gradually takes over entirely and restricts his freedom and the possibility of making his own choices. Does this make any sense?"

She took a sip of her soda and wiped her mouth with the back of her hand.

He nodded. "Does he want to escape it?"

"Most likely he doesn't, and that's the problem. All forms of illness have their benefits, of course. You know, like having someone to pamper us when we're in bed with a fever. It can be so nice."

That's easy for you to say, he thought.

"But how sick is Errki?"

"He's got plenty of problems, but at least he's not in bed. He eats his food, and he takes his medicine. In other words, he's being cooperative."

"And ... schizophrenia? What is that?"

"We call it that, in all our helplessness, because it's practical to have categories for things. It's when a psychosis has been going on for a while. Let's say several months."

"Has Errki been sick for a long time?"

"He's one of those people everyone has given up on. He wanders from place to place like damaged goods." She sighed heavily. "If he killed that old woman, I'm afraid there's no hope for him. He won't get any more help. Not the kind of help that I want to give him."

"But...," he looked at her as he raised his glass, "what do you know about the cause of Errki's illness?"

"Not much. I have my theories."

"Can you tell me about them?"

"I've often wondered whether it has something to do with his mother's death."

"According to the rumors, he killed her," Sejer said quickly. A bit too quickly.

"Oh yes, I've heard that. He spread the rumor himself."

"Why?"

"Because he believes it's true."

"And you don't?"

"I choose to keep an open mind. We all deserve a chance," she said firmly.

Yes, he thought. I deserve a chance, too. But I probably wouldn't take it even if it fell into my lap. She's not wearing a ring, but that doesn't mean anything. In the past it was a definite sign, it was possible to separate out the ones who were available. The way he had with Elise. Long, smooth fingers and no ring—What on earth am I sitting here thinking about? Sejer wondered suddenly.

"How did she die?" he asked.

"She fell down the stairs."

"He didn't push her?"

"He was eight years old."

"Eight-year-olds push and shove all the time. By accident, or when they're playing. Errki was home, wasn't he?"

"He saw it happen."

"Did anyone else?"

"No."

"What exactly do you know about it?"

"Almost nothing. He was sitting on the steps when help arrived, and he may well have been sitting there for a long time, unable to move." She pulled a pack of Prince Lights out of her blouse pocket. "It happened so long ago."

"One other thing. Officer Gurvin said something about him living in America for a while."

"He lived in New York with his father and sister, for seven years. They came home to Norway at regular intervals, for Christmas, and so on."

"And...is it true that he was in contact with a rather unusual person?"

She smiled suddenly. "I haven't been able to check on that. I talked to his father, but he admits that he didn't keep very good tabs on what Errki did with his free time. He was closer to his daughter. In contrast to Errki, she was good at everything, and socially well adjusted. But you're thinking of the magician, aren't you?"

"Maybe he put some strange ideas in his head."

"I think he had plenty of those already. But it probably didn't help matters. The worst thing is..."

She fell silent and stared down into her Coke. Sejer could see that she was deciding whether to continue, or whether she might be overstepping a boundary.

"The worst thing is," she repeated, "that sometimes I've wondered whether he might really have that ability. Whether he can see more than the rest of us, and even make things happen through deep concentration. I can't explain it in any other way than that he sets things in motion by sheer force of will."

All right. Now she had said it.

Sejer frowned. He had just started to like her, only to find out that she was a little flaky, wasn't the levelheaded and intelligent woman he'd first thought. A close call!

"Go on," he said.

She fixed her gaze on a statue outside, a naked girl on her knees who was staring out at the hospital grounds.

"I'm going to tell you about the first session we ever had, Errki and I. All of our patients are assigned both to a therapist and to a group, where they're given group therapy. It was time for his first session. I was sitting in my office, waiting to see whether he would be on time, after I had shown him where we would meet. And he arrived on the dot. I nodded at the sofa near the window, and he sat down, sprawled out, and remained silent. I couldn't see his eyes. The room was quiet. There's something magical about that moment. The first session, the first words."

She was speaking quietly and very slowly. Sejer could feel himself being drawn into her thoughts, almost as if he were right in the room with them.

" 'We have exactly one hour,' I began. 'And today you will decide how we spend it.' He didn't answer. I didn't try to break the silence; I'm not afraid of silence. It's common for them to say little or even nothing at all during the first hour. Or the second. He seemed comfortable and relaxed, as if he were resting. Not nervous or anxious. After a while I decided to talk about myself."

"What did you say? Are you even allowed to talk about yourself?"

"Of course, within certain limits."

Her voice changed, as if she were reciting a litany. "I must be personable without being personal, involved without being invasive. Firm, without being sharp or authoritarian. Sympathetic, without being sentimental. Et cetera. I told Errki that what we were going to do, he and I, was find a language that was uniquely ours, that only he and I would understand. No others would be able to decipher it. By 'others' I meant the voices inside him that fling him around and make his life miserable. I said that we could find a way to communicate and that it would be our secret. A code. So if there was anything he wanted to tell me, he could put it into code. And I would be able to work it out provided I had a little time, and that cracking the code would be my problem."

She paused to take a breath. "He didn't move. The minutes passed, and I waited for a sign from him. I suppose I slipped into a sort of daze. His presence was somehow soothing. He sat there as if he owned the whole room. When he finally stood up, I jumped. He went to the door without looking at me. That's against the rules, so I stopped him. But he just turned around and pointed at his left wrist, although he wasn't wearing a watch. The hour was over. There was no clock on the wall, and yet he was right. Exactly sixty minutes had passed."

"What did you do?" Sejer asked.

She laughed softly. "I tried a little trick. I told him there were five minutes left, but I said it with a smile. And then the first word passed his lips. The first word he ever said to me. 'Liar.'"

Sejer looked out the cafeteria window at the green lawns. It occurred to him that it was late, that he needed to get back to Headquarters soon. He hadn't taken a phone call in all the time he'd been here. Maybe Errki and the robber had been found, as he sat here getting lost in psychiatry and all of its secrets. Or in her. In everything that might have been, a different future than the one he had imagined for himself.

"Afterward," she said, "I made a note in my journal. One–nil for Errki."

"How do you think Errki would react if he felt threatened?"

She looked at him, and her expression turned anxious at the thought of what he might be going through right now. "He would withdraw as much as possible. He would be on the defensive."

"But what if he couldn't withdraw any further? What if he were sufficiently threatened or provoked? What would he do?"

"I tried to tell you earlier, but you didn't take me seriously. He would bite, to protect himself."

"Bite? Where?"

"Wherever he could."

———

Errki was asleep. Morgan stood in the doorway, looking at him. A jagged red scar stretched from Errki's throat to his navel. It had healed badly. Morgan pondered this for a moment, but couldn't come up with a reasonable explanation for what could have given him such an ugly scar. He stayed where he was and stared, although he had come in to wake Errki up. He had been sitting alone for a long time on the old sofa in the living room, staring vacantly into space, listening to the radio. There were no new details on the news. A hundred thousand kroner, they said. He had counted the money, and they were right.

Morgan stood motionless. There was something intimate about staring at a sleeping man. Staring at a sleeping girl would be quite different. Or so he imagined. Errki was breathing easily, his eyelids quivering slightly, as if he were dreaming. His black jacket and T-shirt lay in a heap on the floor. Why should I wake him? Morgan thought. Why am I standing here like a lonely puppy, feeling like I need company? He can damn well stay where he is. He doesn't speak, and he's much too preoccupied with his own twisted insides to hear what I'm saying. But when he's asleep he looks like everybody else.

He wondered whether the craziness stayed with him when he slept, whether his dreams were crazy, too. Or whether he had a hollow somewhere deep inside where everything was normal. A place he refused to accept.

Suddenly he flinched. Without warning, Errki opened his eyes. In a split second he was wide awake. He didn't stir beforehand, as people usually do as they wake up, twisting a little, grunting and groaning. He just opened his eyes. They were surprisingly big until they focused on Morgan, and then they narrowed.

"What did you do to your chest?" The words slipped out of Morgan's mouth. "It looks like a botched hara-kiri."

Errki didn't answer, because the two down in the cellar were scrambling to get into position. Sometimes they were impossibly sluggish.

"I need company," Morgan declared. He thought he might as well be honest. "It's getting late. Let's have a whiskey."

Errki got up slowly from the bed. Nothing happened. He glanced at Morgan's gun, pulled his T-shirt over his head, and followed him out to the living room. Morgan had rigged up the radio on the windowsill, with the antenna sticking out of the broken window. The temperature inside the old cabin was comfortable, but there was a haze over the woods, and the water far below was shimmering in the warm evening.

"I'm hungry," Morgan said. "So I'm going to have a whiskey."

He fished the bottle out of the bag and unscrewed the top. Errki waited and watched, looking up from downcast eyes, as if he were ruminating on something.

"Whiskey is good for everything," Morgan said as he continued to marvel at Errki's intense gaze. It was as if he knew something special, something crucial about life and death that no one else could see. "It's good for hunger and for thirst. For love troubles and for boredom. For despair and anxiety."

He took a big gulp. His face rippled like rubber at the strong liquor. "There's nothing as nice as a moderate drinking problem," he said. "Do you know what I mean by the word *moderate*?"

Errki did. Morgan wiped his mouth.

"I drink regularly and steadily. But never in the morning and never too much, and never when I'm going to be driving. I'm the one in control."

He took another gulp. "And if you think I'm going to drink myself silly so that you can escape, you're sorely mistaken."

He held out the bottle. Errki looked at it with surprise. He didn't really care for alcohol, but he was feeling dull and empty inside, and if this was all they had, he didn't have to make a choice. It was the only thing available, this bottle of whiskey. And he hadn't asked for it. It was being thrust upon him. He studied the label and turned the bottle around. Then he sniffed at the top.

"Come on, it's not poison."

Errki put the bottle to his lips and took a swallow. The whiskey ran down his throat, without making his eyes water. An unfamiliar warmth spread through his midriff. It started as a stinging sensation in his mouth, then sank down and filled his whole torso. Gradually he noticed the sweet taste, almost like caramel.

"Good, huh?" Morgan smiled. "Where do you live? Do you have an apartment?"

Out by the lake, Errki thought. By the public park, in a beautiful setting and paid for by the county. One room plus a kitchen and bathroom. Upstairs lives the old man who paces back and forth at night; sometimes he weeps. I can hear him, but I don't pay any attention. If I gave him my hand and listened to him, I would give him hope, but there is no hope. Not for anyone.

"Why does it have to be such a secret?" Morgan said, reaching for the bottle.

"It smells bad there," Errki said in a low voice.

Morgan jumped at the sound of his voice. "What smells bad? Your place? I believe it. You smell, too. Maybe it's time you went out in the fresh air."

"Raw meat smells bad. Especially in this heat."

"What are you babbling about?"

"It's on the counter. I eat it for breakfast every morning."

His face was deadly serious as he spoke. Morgan stared at him suspiciously.

"Are you kidding me, or are you having hallucinations? You're just kidding, aren't you? I don't doubt that you're crazy, but I refuse to believe that you eat raw meat for breakfast."

He felt a chill spread slowly along his spine, in spite of the heat. What kind of person was this man, sitting right here in front of him?

"Have some more whiskey. Maybe you're having trouble because you didn't take your pills. If you ask me, whiskey is better for you."

He sat down on the floor and put the gun down next to him.

"So tell me, when did you realize that you were starting to slip?"

Errki gave him a long, sideways glance.

"Was it like it says in books, that you got up one morning feeling terrible, went over to the mirror, and saw to your horror that red worms were crawling out of your eyes?"

He chuckled as he screwed the top back on the bottle.

Errki shut his eyes. A faint drone was coming from the cellar, like a warning. "It wasn't worms," he said in his quiet, clear voice. "It was beetles. With shiny shells. They gleamed in the light from the window, black as oil."

Morgan blinked in confusion. "You're kidding, right? It doesn't really happen that way. I assume," he said thoughtfully, "it's important to figure out why a person gets sick. That's the only reason I asked you. Maybe it's inherited? Was your mother crazy?"

Errki was silent, listening. Listening to the words that were spilling out of his mouth like rubbish. Like wet paper, potato peels, coffee grounds, and apple cores.

"How about you?" Errki said quietly. "When did you realize it?"

"Realize what?" Morgan blinked his eyes and peered out the window. "It's not easy to talk to you. Is there anything that's OK to talk about? You choose the topic." He sighed heavily. "It's a long time until nightfall."

Another pause. Errki sat on the sofa with his legs tucked under him.

"Large parts of the world are at war," he said finally.

"Is that so? I suppose you're right. Why don't you tell me something about the asylum?" said Morgan. He was practically pleading now.

He could do that, of course. If he felt like it. Talk about Ragne, for example, who could never reconcile herself to the fact that she was born a girl and who was always being found mutilated, either in bed or in the shower, in a pool of blood because she had tried to cut off her genitals. And that's not easy to do when you're a girl. Soda pop, tea, and coffee, Errki thought. Beer, wine, and booze. Tell all of that to this curly-haired idiot? Never.

"OK, never mind," Morgan said, resigned. He looked at Errki. "Are you a genius? A sparkling, brilliant mind? I'm not pulling your leg, I can tell that you're sharp, even though you may not seem it."

Errki didn't reply. The man was a real simpleton, completely pathetic.

Morgan sighed. He felt worn out. Errki didn't want to talk, and he was tired of listening to his own voice. Besides, what he said was nothing but babble. He couldn't sleep. Couldn't drink any more whiskey either. He wasn't used to this, sitting in a room with another man and getting no answers. It made him nervous.

"What are you going to use the money for?" Errki asked with perfect friendliness.

"The money?"

"The money from the robbery. Are you going to buy a Nintendo? All the boys want a Nintendo."

Morgan stood up abruptly and went over to the window. He stood there, staring down at the water. It was as shiny as glass, with a deep reddish brown color, like bronze. He looked at the bare island and the dry firs hanging over the water. The news would be on again shortly. He thought about the car and wondered when it would be discovered. When it was, the police would realize that they had gone up into the woods.

"I have to take a leak," he said, and walked across the room. He took the gun with him. "Stay here. I'll be on the steps."

He went outside and inhaled the hot air. It was the hottest time of the day. He longed for a darkness that wouldn't come. Not until autumn. What a mess, he thought dejectedly.

Errki got up from the sofa and sat down on the floor instead, leaning against the wall. He heard the stream of urine strike the dry grass and the faint sound of Morgan zipping up his trousers. The whiskey felt warm in his body. He wanted more.

Morgan came back inside. He could ask for more, but it went against a principle that was impossible to override: it was unthinkable to ask for something. Here came Morgan, with his stubborn stride. He dragged the bag away, and stood with his back turned, fiddling with the radio, twisting the antenna a bit. Errki stared at his sleeveless shirt and down at his muscular calves. Imagine being a man and having all the equipment a man should have, but at the same time looking so discordant, as if he'd been put together using random parts that didn't fit. The room was silent. Errki was about to say a prayer. He couldn't remember when he had last prayed, not in years. He could feel the words balling up into a lump that refused to come out.

Instead he stared at the bag. He concentrated all his strength in one eye and felt his gaze become a ray penetrating the room. It struck the black canvas bag, and the next instant a thin stream of smoke rose up from the black material. He noticed the faint smell of burning. Morgan turned around. A rumbling sound was coming from the cellar, as if great blocks of stone had come loose somewhere and were crashing down. The rumbling grew louder, it was like thunder. Nestor blazed up. A moment later Errki saw something growing out of the filthy floorboards. A river of blood. He stared. It was about an inch from his feet. The bag stood on the other side.

"What's the matter with you?" Morgan asked uneasily. "Are you sick?"

Errki was staring intently at the bag.

"I think you should have some more whiskey. Maybe that would help."

He sounded alarmed. Errki stayed where he was. He was staring at the blood.

"I said, have some more."

But Errki didn't move. He couldn't reach the bag with his hand, he would have to take a step forward to get it. His feet would slip in the thick, hot blood.

"Why do you make everything so damn difficult?! Do I have to put a nipple on the bottle and hold you in my arms?"

Morgan grabbed the bag, took out the bottle, and held it out to him. Errki tore it out of his hands and took a drink. The bag stopped burning.

You were lucky. Don't count on being so lucky next time.

"I'm not stingy," Morgan said. "Say what you like about Morgan, but I'm not a stingy person." He scowled at Errki, who was drinking greedily.

Morgan went out to the kitchen. It was true, Morgan was a strange man, but not stingy. He was rummaging through the drawers out there, then Errki heard him open the door to the pantry. While he was out of sight, Errki took several big gulps. He could hear Morgan cursing softly and things being tossed around. Then a rustling sound that meant that he was fiddling with a candle wrapped in plastic. Next he went into the bedroom. Errki drank some more, listening to him pounding on the walls. Suddenly his voice echoed through the cabin. "What the hell? Take a look at this!"

Errki stood up and tottered forward. "You called, Master?" He was holding the bottle in his hand.

Morgan had put the gun on the windowsill. "Look what I found!"

He held out something to Errki. Dry brown paper, folded over several times. "On the floor under the bed. A map of Finnemarka. Let's work out where we are."

He read aloud, "Map of Finnemarka, National Map Company, 1965. Give me a hand, Errki."

Morgan picked up the gun and went back to the living room. Errki followed.

"Do you know how to read a map? You're going to have to help me. Can you find the location of this cabin?"

He spread out the map, and it almost disintegrated under his fingers. Errki looked at it. Then he put the tip of his finger on a tiny, pale blue spot. "We're here," he said quietly.

"Is it that easy?" Morgan stared. "How can you be so sure?"

"Look at the water outside," Errki said. "See how it's shaped? Then compare it to the map. It's called Himmerik Lake."

"Jesus. You do have your lucid moments."

Morgan went over to the window and looked out. The water had the very same shape as the lake marked on the map. "You're really familiar with this place, aren't you? We haven't gone very far, have we?" he added. "Tonight I can head over the ridge and come out here," he pointed at the map again. "And just for fun I'm going to trade clothes with you."

He grabbed the whiskey bottle. At last he was feeling better. He knew where they were. Everything had a name: the mountains, the lake, and around everything the highway network, clearly numbered.

"You'll go back the same way we came while I continue on—I guess it's northwest. You can borrow my shorts. You'll look great in these Hawaiian shorts. I'll let you go then. Around midnight."

He looked pleased. He had a goal.

"The news," he said suddenly. He stumbled over to the radio and turned up the volume. A female broadcaster this time. Errki sat down on the floor again and closed his eyes. His lips felt numb and pleasantly relaxed from the liquor.

Now to the murder in Finnemarka. The savage murder of seventy-six-year-old Halldis Horn is a top priority of the police force, in addition to the robbery at Fokus Bank. The police are following a clue that may lead them to the killer, but haven't yet revealed what the clue is. In the meantime, the police say that they firmly believe the murder will be solved quickly.

Morgan looked at Errki. "Where do you think she lived? Did you know her?" He scratched his head. "I wonder if they're going to search near here? Can you imagine what he must have been thinking to do something so terrible?"

Errki tossed his head involuntarily, making his hair flutter. But he didn't say a word.

CHAPTER 11

"Why was he involuntarily committed?" Sejer asked. "Did he threaten someone?"

Dr. Struel shook her head. "He stopped eating. When he came to us he was severely malnourished."

"Why wasn't he eating?"

"He couldn't decide what he wanted to have. He would sit at the lunch table, wavering between two different kinds of meat."

"What did you do?"

"When he gave up and went back to his room, I made him a sandwich and took it to him. No milk or coffee, just the sandwich. I put it on his bedside table. The first time, he wouldn't touch it."

"Why not?"

"I made a mistake. I cut the sandwich in half, and he couldn't decide which part to eat first."

"Are you saying that it's possible to starve to death because it's too hard to make a decision?"

"Yes."

He shook his head as he tried to comprehend how inexpressibly difficult it could be to handle daily life. "And you really believe that the man has supernatural powers?"

She threw out her hands. "I'm just telling you what I saw. Other people will tell you other stories."

"Have you ever asked him how he does it?"

"I asked him, 'Who taught you that?' He smiled and said, 'The magician. The magician in New York.'"

"But surely it's a coincidence."

"I don't think so. Once in a while things happen that we simply can't explain."

"Not for me," he said with a smile.

"No?" she teased him, laughing. "You're one of those people who understands everything?"

He felt ridiculous. "That's not what I meant. What else could he do?"

"One time a group of us were playing cards in the smoking lounge. Errki was there too, but he wasn't playing. He can't stand games. It was late at night and dark outside, and the lights were on. Suddenly Errki said, in his peculiar, quiet way, 'We should have candles on the table.' Yes, I thought, that would be cozy. I asked him to get some from the kitchen, but he refused. No one else wanted to go either. They said candles would get in the way of the cards. I felt sorry for Errki. It was the first time he had made a suggestion, and no one listened. The next instant the power went out. The lounge was plunged into darkness, and so was the rest of the building. There was a lot of commotion as we stumbled around looking for a candle. 'I tried to tell you,' was Errki's only comment.

"But he wasn't always successful. Once he wanted to learn to fly, and jumped out a third-floor window. It's a miracle he wasn't killed. But he landed on a bicycle rack, which left him with an ugly scar down his chest. It happened while they were living in New York."

"Were they taking LSD or anything like that?"

"I don't know. And his father didn't know either. He didn't pay much attention."

"Is he as physically repulsive as they say?"

"Repulsive?" She gave him a confused look. "He's certainly not repulsive. Maybe a little unkempt."

"Is he unhappy?"

As soon as he said it, the question sounded foolish, but she didn't laugh.

"Of course. But he doesn't know it. He doesn't allow those kinds of feelings in."

"What kinds of feelings does he allow in?"

"Contempt. Forbearance. Arrogance."

"He doesn't sound as terrible as I thought."

She sighed heavily. "He's actually just a talented boy who wants to do his best. He wants to do everything perfectly, and he's so afraid of making a mistake that he has ended up unable to do anything at all. In school he did very poorly on verbal exercises; he would sit and mutter at the window so that no one could hear what he was saying. Yet in writing he was at the top of his class."

"And eventually you got him to talk?"

"He talks now, if he feels like it. Sometimes he can be devastatingly articulate, even funny. He has a scathing sense of humor."

"Has he ever tried to take his own life?"

"I don't think so, apart from the flight out of the window in New York, which I have never understood entirely."

"So you wouldn't consider him suicidal?"

"No. But in this profession nothing is certain."

"Would you understand it if he did do something like that?"

"I would. It's a human right to take one's own life."

"A human right? Is that how you think of it?"

She stared down at her hands. "I don't agree with therapists telling their patients that death is not a solution. Of course it's a solution for the person concerned. To choose death is a logical consequence of the fact that we're able to make choices. And it's a solution that human beings have always been able to consider."

"But you do what you can to prevent it, don't you?"

"I tell them, 'It's your choice.' And I'm not always happy when I force them to accept a long life, or rob them of a psychosis that, in spite of everything, they regard as their only refuge."

I'm not going to be able to sleep tonight, he thought. Her face is going to hover in front of me in the dark and hold on to me. Her words are going to ring in my ears. He caught himself twisting his wedding ring on his finger. Suddenly it occurred to him that if, against all odds, she might have been interested in him, she would have dismissed the idea at once. Maybe he ought to stop wearing the ring, but then he had decided long ago that he would always wear it, that it would go to his grave with him. Yet it did send out a signal that there was a woman in his life. Now she had noticed it too. The thought disturbed him.

"Errki likes to wander around in the woods and along the country roads. But he doesn't usually go near people, does he?"

"No, he doesn't," she agreed.

"The fact that he did so this time, that he actually went all the way to town and even inside a bank—don't you think it might mean that something is bothering him? That he felt he needed help? Because something had happened?"

She looked genuinely worried. Another big wave surged inside of him. When it retreated he looked inside his own heart, which had long been a deserted shore. For the first time in years a woman was standing there.

———

"Did something happen?" Skarre was looking at him.

"What do you mean?"

"You were gone such a long time."

Sejer didn't answer. He was standing at the sink in his office with his back turned. Skarre grew uneasy. He knew that the chief inspector could sometimes be quite taciturn, and the rigid posture of his back signaled something was up.

"It was very useful," he said without turning around. He filled the sink with cold water and splashed it on his flushed face. Only after he had dried his face and run his fingers over his close-cropped hair did he ask, "Have we got the photos of the footprints from the crime scene?"

"No, but they're coming. According to the lab they're beautiful black-and-white pictures. The prints are probably from sneakers. They have that typical zigzag pattern. And they are long, about a size 10. That's all I know so far."

"Dr. Struel finds it difficult to imagine that Errki would be capable of killing anyone. She says he bites if he's provoked."

"She? Bites?" Skarre gave him a long look. "The doctor is a woman? Did she tell you how she thought Errki would react in a hostage situation?"

"She thinks he would withdraw. Says he's very defensive. But we don't know much about this robber either, what kind of person he is."

"Maybe they're having a nice time together."

"It's happened before. But I've been thinking about something. What would happen if the robber found out that the hostage he took is wanted by the police in connection with a murder?"

Skarre smiled faintly. "Maybe he'd be frightened and let him go."

"Maybe. And it's quite possible that he's listening to the radio."

"But the press doesn't know that the hostage is the same man who was seen at Halldis's farm."

"It's only a matter of time, isn't it?"

He stared at the door leading to the long hall along which the offices were lined up, one after the other. "This is a big place. It won't be long before the news leaks out."

"And then things might get dangerous, right?"

Sejer looked at him. "What would you do? Try to use the part of your brain that thinks like a criminal."

"Oh, but it's such a tiny part!" Skarre protested. "Well, I'd want to let him go. Especially since he's mentally disturbed, and it's probably not easy to deal with him. But if they've established some sort of rapport," he continued, "then it's possible that they're giving each other support. And why would one of them give the other up to the police? They're both on the wrong side of the law. On the other hand, if it comes to any kind of conflict—"

"One of them is crazy, and the other has a gun. We've got to find them," said Sejer, "before they kill each other. I suggest that we leak the information to the press."

"You think he'll let Errki go?"

"Maybe. And I want you to go up to Briggen's Grocery and talk to Halldis's grocer. He's the only one who saw her on a regular basis, once a week for years. They must have known each other well. You also need to find out who Kristoffer is—the person who sent her the letter. Have you had anything to eat?"

"Yes. What are you going to do?"

"I'm going out to Guttebakken to talk to the boy who found the body. And then I'll go over to the Municipal Hospital."

"Why?"

"To see if there are any reports on Errki's mother's death."

"But it was sixteen years ago!"

"I'm sure I'll discover something. But before you leave, find a broom."

"A what?"

"A broom. In the caretaker's closet."

"Nobody uses brooms anymore," Skarre said patiently. "They use mops."

"Then find a mop. Anything with a long handle."

Skarre left the room and came back with a mop. The handle was made of fiberglass, just like Halldis's hoe.

Sejer took up a position. "I'm Halldis Horn," he said, "and you're the killer."

"No problem," said Skarre, standing in front of him.

"I'm standing on the steps, holding the hoe. Of course, I'm taller than she was, and the handle is longer. But I'd probably hold it like this, with my hands together at the middle of the handle."

Skarre nodded.

"You come toward me, from inside the house. Grab the hoe. Do it, Jacob."

Skarre stared at the handle for a moment, then grabbed it with both hands. He automatically placed one hand above Sejer's grip, the other below.

"Stay like that for a minute."

Sejer stared at the four hands. "Halldis's fingerprints were approximately here, in the middle of the hoe. At the very bottom of the handle we found another print, quite small. And another one like it at the top. Which means that he grabbed the hoe out of her hands like this, in a single movement. Then he pulled it away, lifted it up, and struck. But can you tell me, Jacob, where are the other prints from his fingers?"

Skarre thought for a moment. "What if he wiped them off, but he was in a hurry and only got some of them?"

"Leaving her prints untouched on the middle of the handle? It seems unlikely."

"What if his fingers leave poor prints?"

"Why would that be?"

"I have no idea. What if his fingers were once badly burned? The prints would have been destroyed."

"Now I think you're getting carried away."

"Agreed." Skarre scratched his head. "I don't understand it either."

"Do the prints match the ones found in the house?"

"They're still working on that at the lab."

"There's something very odd about this," Sejer said.

"I don't believe in the very odd," Skarre said. "I believe there has to be a logical explanation; there usually is. Maybe Errki is the kind of person who chews on his fingers. He's an odd bird, after all. Did his doctor mention anything like that?"

"About chewing on his fingers?"

"Look at this," said Skarre, holding out his hand. "Look at my index finger, at the tip. What do you see?"

"Not much. It's ... sort of shiny."

"That's right. This finger doesn't leave a print. Do you know why?"

"Because you burned it?"

"No. I got some superglue on it a long time ago."

"But that's only one of ten fingers."

"I'm just saying that there has to be a logical explanation, OK? So the doctor doesn't think that her patient is capable of murder?" he asked.

"No."

"Do you believe her?"

"There's no denying that she has a certain understanding of who he is, along with a solid background as a psychiatrist."

"But generally you don't take that kind of thing into consideration. I happen to think it's quite simple. I think he did it."

"You've been talking to Gurvin too much."

"I'm just trying to think rationally. Errki grew up here. He knew who she was. Nobody ever came by her house except for the grocer. Errki was seen at her farm on the morning the murder occurred. And he's very sick."

"Are you willing to bet on it?" Sejer asked with a smile.

"Sure, why not."

"Then I'll bet he didn't do it."

"If you lose, you have to come with me to the King's Arms and get really drunk."

Sejer shuddered at the prospect.

"And if you lose, you have to take a parachute jump, OK?"

"Um, all right."

"Can I get that in writing?"

"Don't you trust the word of a Christian?"

"Of course."

Sejer shook his head and leaned the mop against the wall. "Better get going now. But there's one thing you should know. Not everything can be explained with the rational mind."

He opened a drawer to signal that the conversation was over. "Buy yourself a pair of tall boots," he said.

"What for?"

"For the parachute jump. So you won't break your ankles."

Skarre looked a little pale as he left the room.

Sejer quickly wrote down some notes from his meeting with Dr. Struel. When he had finished, he opened the phone book to the names starting with S, keeping one eye on the door, as if he were afraid of being caught. He found what he was looking for at once. It came after the name Strougal and before the name Stryken.

Struel, Sara. Doctor.

Sara, he thought. Romantic. Exotic.

And just above it: Struel, Gerhard. Doctor. With the same phone number. He sighed and closed the book. Sara and Gerhard. It sounded so nice. Feeling as disappointed as a child, he shoved the phone book aside.

CHAPTER 12

Briggen's Grocery was so plastered with ads and signs that it looked like an amusement park. Gaudy orange, pink, and yellow placards were everywhere. Tender steaks from our own kitchen. Beef liver, frozen.

Otherwise the building was rather attractive—a red-painted, two-story structure. Skarre assumed that Briggen had an apartment above the shop. He parked his car and went in. The shop had two checkout counters. At one of them a teenage girl sat reading a magazine. A tight perm seemed to be holding her head in an iron grip. She looked up and saw his uniform, and the magazine plopped down into her lap.

Skarre was a handsome man. Handsome in every respect, with a friendly face and a cloud of fair curls. He also had that rare talent of being able to give everyone the same amount of attention, even those who didn't interest him, such as this girl. She wore black-framed glasses, and her plump body was more than twenty pounds overweight. He gave her a dazzling smile.

"Your boss, is he around?"

"Oddemann Briggen? He's in the storeroom, unpacking a delivery from Findus. Go past the dairy section—over there—and through the door next to the vegetables."

He thanked her and began heading through the shop. At

that moment Briggen appeared with a crate of frozen fish in his arms. "The police? Let's go to my office. Follow me."

He shuffled off.

The cashier went back to her magazine, but she was no longer reading. She turned her head to the left, so she could just see her reflection in the Plexiglas that was fastened like a shield around the neighboring checkout counter. Her hair and face were more mellow and slightly blurry, and if she took off her glasses she looked almost like an older version of Shirley Temple. In her mind she went over what she knew of Halldis Horn, because it was just possible he might want to interview her. For two or three minutes he would stand next to the counter, and if she memorized several answers, then she could use the time to study his face and record every detail.

Too bad she didn't know something terribly important that would make him remember her. Oh yes, that plump little cashier at Oddemann Briggen's store? She gave me that tiny but absolutely crucial detail that helped us solve the whole case. Now what was her name?

What a shame that she had such a hopeless name. She looked down at her magazine, at the picture of Claudia Schiffer. From the office she could hear their voices, a secretive murmur.

"How many years have you been delivering groceries to Halldis Horn?" asked Skarre, pulling a notebook from his pocket.

Briggen opened his red and green nylon coat before he answered. "Must be close to eight years now. Before that her husband, Thorvald, used to come in to buy what they needed. I knew him, too. They've lived here forever."

The grocer was somewhere between fifty and sixty, big and stout with a healthy, tanned complexion and red cheeks. Thick hair, cut short. His eyes were dark and his mouth pulled down on one side. He had short arms and legs and small hands with pudgy fingers that he kept clasping and unclasping. His nails were bitten to the quick, with only a stub remaining close to the cuticles.

"What did she buy?" Skarre asked.

"Just the essentials. Milk and sugar and coffee. Paper goods and eggs. She didn't indulge herself much. Not that she couldn't afford it. She had money in the bank. According to her, it wasn't such a paltry sum, either. I suppose her sister will inherit it now—her sister in Hammerfest, Helga Mai."

"She told you that she had a large amount of money in the bank?"

"Yes, she did. She was proud of it."

"Did anyone else know about it?"

"I assume so."

When a rumor like that starts flying, it moves as fast as lizards through hot sand, Skarre thought. The fact that the money is in the bank is forgotten in the rush to latch onto the fortune. And soon the rumor takes on unreal dimensions. Halldis has money, tons of it! Maybe she keeps it under her bed, or somewhere like that. Isn't that where old people usually hide it? She had thought it perfectly safe to tell the grocer, whom she knew so well. But all it took was a little secretive smile, a small hint, and then the news was out. Maybe to one of his other regular customers. Oh, you know Halldis? Well, she's not exactly penniless. Maybe that's what was said when her husband died and someone expressed concern for her. Plenty of people could have heard about it.

"They didn't have any children, you know," Briggen said. "That's why they had saved up a lot of money, and they didn't care much for luxuries. Thorvald fussed over his tractor like a child, greasing and oiling it, polishing it. God only knows what they were planning to use the money for. If they really had as much as she implied, that is."

Skarre wrote himself a note. Check Halldis Horn's bank account.

"What about her sister in the North?"

"She's well-off. Has a husband and children and grand-children."

"So if Halldis had any money, they would be the ones to benefit?"

"I would imagine so. Thorvald didn't have any family, only a brother who died long ago. Some of the money was inherited from him."

"And you went up to her farm once a week? The same day every time?"

"No, she would call me, and the day varied. But I often went there on Thursdays."

"When were you there last?"

"On Wednesday."

"How many employees do you have in the shop?"

"Just Johnna, the girl at the checkout counter."

"No one else?"

"Not right now."

"But you *did* have someone?"

"A long time ago. A young man. He didn't stay long."

"Did he know Halldis?"

Briggen laced and unlaced his fingers. "Hmm...I suppose he did. He came along a few times when I delivered her groceries, but he didn't seem particularly interested in her."

There was something embarrassed and reluctant in his tone of voice.

"I'd better record his name."

It seemed as if Briggen would have preferred not to tell him. He squirmed in his chair and began buttoning up his coat again, even though it was hot.

"Tommy. Tommy Rein."

"A young man?"

"In his twenties. But he didn't show interest in any of us, or in the area either."

"Do you know where he is now?"

"No."

"You stated previously that Halldis kept her wallet in the bread box?"

"That's right. But she never had much money in it. Well, I didn't open it myself, but I watched her open it and take out the money to pay me. She usually had a few hundred-kroner bills."

Skarre made note of this. "And Errki Johrma—do you know him?"

"Of course. He often comes to the shop."

"What does he buy?"

"Nothing. He takes whatever he wants and leaves. If I shout after him, he turns around in the doorway, as if surprised that I'm making such a fuss. Then he holds up what he's taken, as if to show me that it's only a chocolate bar. And since he's the way he is, I've never gone after him. He's not the kind of fellow that you'd want to tap on the shoulder. And of course his pilfering doesn't amount to much, just petty sums. Once in a while I get really angry about it, though. He has no regard for laws or rules whatsoever."

"I see," Skarre said. "Who else, besides yourself, might have known that Halldis kept her wallet in the bread box?"

"No one, as far as I know."

"But Tommy Rein might know, isn't that true?"

"Um ... I'm not sure about that."

"What about door-to-door salesmen, lottery-ticket sellers, or preachers? They must come around here, don't they? Did anyone like that ever go out to her place? Did she ever mention it?"

"They never go up to Halldis's farm. It's not worth it. It's too far, and the road is bad. No, you can forget about anything like that. Focus on Errki. He was seen at her farm, after all."

"So you know about that?"

"Everybody does."

"The wallet," Skarre asked. "Was it red?"

"Bright red, with a brass clasp. She kept a picture of Thorvald in it, an old one, taken before he went bald. You know what?" Briggen said. "I was relieved when they put Errki in the hospital. And now I hope you find him, and I hope that he's guilty."

"Why is that?"

Briggen crossed his arms. They barely reached around his stomach.

"Then we'll have him locked up for good, as the dangerous man that he is. And if he finally gets the blame for something— with physical evidence, I mean—then maybe he won't get out again, and we'll have some peace around here. I mean, who else could have done it?"

"Did Halldis ever have visitors?"

"Hardly ever."

"Who would be the exception?"

"Her sister, Helga, has a grandson who rents a room in Oslo. I know that he's been up there, but not often."

"Do you know his name?"

"His last name is Mai, at any rate. Kristian, or Kristoffer."

Kristoffer, Skarre thought. The one who sent the letter.

"I seem to remember that he worked in the kitchen of a restaurant. And not to be nasty or anything, but I doubt it's a three-star place."

"Why is that?"

"I saw him once. He didn't look like the type."

Skarre found himself wondering what the kitchen hands in a three-star restaurant looked like, as opposed to the kitchen hands in other places in Oslo.

"So there was Mai. And Tommy Rein. Has anyone been here from the newspapers?"

"From the papers and the local radio station. And people have been calling."

"Did you talk to them?"

"No one told me not to."

No, unfortunately, Skarre thought. "We need you to come down to Headquarters. Sometime today."

"Need me? For what?"

"We have to identify the fingerprints that were found in her house."

Briggen looked as if he was having difficulty breathing. "Are you going to take my fingerprints?"

"That's what we had in mind," Skarre said with a smile.

"And why would they be found in her house?"

"Because you've been up there once a week for eight years," said Skarre calmly.

"I only went there to deliver groceries!"

His face took on a panic-stricken expression.

"We realize that."

"So why do you need them?"

"To isolate them."

"What did you say?"

Skarre tried to remain calm. "We have to find an owner for each set of fingerprints. Some belong to Halldis. Some may belong to this Kristoffer, and some may be yours. And some may belong to the killer. We need yours so we can exclude them and end up with fingerprints that don't have a known owner. That owner may be the murderer. Do you see?"

Briggen's face returned to its normal color. "I hope you don't let this get out. People might think that I had something to do with it."

"Not anyone who has even the slightest understanding of police work," said Skarre reassuringly.

He thanked the grocer and left the office. Johnna was making plans to pluck her eyebrows when suddenly he was standing next to her cash register. It was one thing to have beautiful eyes, she thought. But that mouth—and it was the mouth that she always looked at first whenever she met a man—she was overcome by how sensitive it was. Skarre's mouth was absolutely perfect, wide with full lips, not too much of a bow, because that would have made it look feminine. His mouth was symmetrical and even, and his teeth were flawless. The slight bow in his upper lip was mirrored in his brows.

"Jacob Skarre," he said, smiling.

Must be a name from the Bible, she thought.

"May I ask you a quick question? Have you ever been up to Halldis's farm?"

"Once, with Odd." She nodded her head vigorously, but not a curl moved. "One Saturday afternoon when my car had broken down. He offered to drive me home if I didn't mind taking a detour up to Halldis's place. She was out of coffee. It was a long time ago."

She had taken off her glasses and put them in her lap.

"Do you know anyone else who has been up there?"

She thought for a moment. "We had a man working here for a short time. They called from CPC and asked whether we had anything for him."

"CPC?" he said in surprise.

"Criminal Parole Care," she said. "They contacted Oddemann to find out whether he could work here, on a trial basis. It's actually a program for former inmates, and—"

"I know," Skarre interrupted her. "Tommy Rein?"

"Yes, that's his name."

"Did he ever go to her farm?"

"Once or twice. He took off after a while, said it was too boring here. Not even a lousy pub. I don't know where he is now, and I haven't seen him since."

"Did you like him?"

She thought back, trying to remember his face, but she remembered only the blue-black tattoos on his arms. And the uneasiness she felt whenever he was around, even though he never so much as glanced at her, at least not the sort of glance she so seldom received. She was actually a little offended by this, now that she thought about it. Not even an ordinary criminal would look twice at Johnna.

"Like him? Not at all," she said spitefully.

"Briggen didn't mention that he was on parole," Skarre said carefully. At the same time he gave her a confidential look that she couldn't resist.

"Of course not. He's Oddemann's nephew, and I'm sure he's ashamed of the family connection. Tommy is the son of his sister."

"Is that so?!"

He didn't make a note, not wanting her to feel that she was telling tales.

"Do you know what he was in prison for?"

"Simple theft."

"Is Briggen married?"

"He's a widower."

"I see."

"He's been alone for eleven years."

"Is that right? Eleven years." He smiled patiently.

"She took her own life," the girl whispered, using the same tone of voice people adopt when talking about adultery.

Now Skarre gave a knowing nod. That kind of thing explains just about everything, about people and life, and why things are the way they are, he thought. He gave her a look that said he appreciated the information.

"How long have you worked here?" he asked amiably.

"Eight years. Since before Halldis's husband died."

She was making an effort to give clear answers and not add unnecessary details, because he was surely a busy man who couldn't tolerate witnesses droning on and on. But as long as she kept talking, he had to stand where he was, and there wasn't a customer in sight.

"Do you know Errki Johrma?"

"I don't exactly know him. But I know who he is."

"Are you afraid of him?"

"Not really. If I met him alone on a dark road, I would definitely be scared, but I'd be scared of anyone." Except for you, she thought. You look like an angel.

"So, how is the shop doing?" Skarre asked. "Thirteen kroner 75 øre for a loaf of bread? That's a bit steep, isn't it?" He nodded toward the sign next to the bread shelf.

She sighed, resigned. "I'm afraid he's pricing himself right out of the market. There aren't a lot of people around here. We don't make much money, and now they're building a new shopping center half an hour away. That'll be the end of us."

She suddenly looked worried.

"A shopping center?" He smiled encouragingly. "But I'm sure you'll find opportunities there if Briggen has to close."

The idea rushed through her mind, because that was precisely what she had dreamed of, though she never dared tell anyone.

"Let me ask you," he said in a low voice, leaning closer, "just to double check. Was Briggen here in the shop all day yesterday?"

"Not yesterday. I was here alone. He went to the Grocers' Institute to take a course."

"And you can run the shop by yourself when the boss is away?"

"I have to."

He straightened up. "If you hear or see anything, or happen to remember something you think might be important, give us a call. For example, if Errki shows up again to swipe some chocolate."

He winked and pulled out a card from his pocket. She accepted it with trembling fingers. It would never happen. There would never be any reason in the world for her to contact this man.

Then he left, and it was over. She put her glasses back on and no longer felt like looking at her reflection in the Plexiglas. Briggen called her, wanting help with the fish. He gave her a suspicious look.

CHAPTER 13

Morgan stared with longing out the broken window. Below lay the water, glistening and fresh. His body felt heavy from the heat and fatigue, and he had a fierce desire to cool off.

"An ice-cold dip," he muttered. "That would be something, wouldn't it, Errki?"

Errki didn't reply. The thought made him shiver. The whiskey had dulled his senses, and he was half asleep. Besides, he never swam, never even had a bath. His body acted strangely in water, and he didn't like it.

"I'm going to take a dip, and you're coming with me," Morgan cheerfully declared.

He looked at Errki with a determined expression. It was disturbing, and Errki could feel himself growing tense. He didn't want to think about it. Anything could happen down there in the black water.

"You can go in," he said in a low voice. "I'll hold the gun for you."

"Don't be ridiculous. We're both going in, you first."

"I never go swimming."

"You'll go in the water if I say so."

"You don't understand! I never go swimming!" Errki was horrified at the thought of something he hated. He had to raise his voice.

"But God help me, you need it! Come on, I'm not joking."

Errki still didn't move. Nothing in the world would make him go into the water. Not even a gun. He would rather die. He was still not ready, and he would like to depart with a certain grace. But if he couldn't, then he couldn't.

"OK, let's get moving!"

Morgan had made up his mind. He was using almost his whole body to speak. He went over to the sofa, grabbed Errki's T-shirt, and yanked him up. Errki struggled to keep his balance.

"A quick dip and then back out again. It will only take a few minutes. Clear our heads. Except for yours, of course."

He jabbed at Errki with the gun, herding him out to the yard.

"Head down to the left and we'll come out near that little island over there."

Errki looked down at the bare rock and shuddered. He was never, ever going into that black water! There wasn't a peep from the cellar. No one was going to help him now. It was as if they were sitting and listening, wondering what he would do. His body began to itch, a bothersome itch. He didn't know how to swim. He couldn't take off his clothes and show his naked body, couldn't stand that sort of humiliation. Reluctantly he headed down the slope, wading through dry heather and grass. There had been a path once, but it was now almost completely overgrown. He stared at the water, thinking that if there wasn't a shallow part, he would sink straight to the bottom. Behind him Morgan was getting excited.

"I'll bet the water is cold. That suits me fine."

He jabbed at Errki when they reached the crag. "Take off your things. Or go ahead and swim with them on. I don't care. Just get in the water."

Errki stood as if carved from stone, staring at the lake. Here on the shore it no longer looked reddish, merely black and deep. He couldn't see the bottom, only some long weeds floating down there that would twist around his legs like hideous fingers. Maybe there were fish, too, or even worse—eels.

"Are you going to jump in or do I have to push you?" Morgan was impatient.

"I can't swim," Errki muttered. He was still standing with his back turned. The corner of his mouth was twitching.

"Doesn't matter. You can hold on to the edge. Come on. I'm sweating like a pig."

Errki didn't move.

"What's it going to be? I'm cocking the gun."

Errki heard a sharp click through the sound of the drum roll. Morgan had got an idea in his head, and he was going to see it through, no matter what happened. Errki took a few steps closer to the water and felt a rushing at his temples. For him water was just as unthinkable as a sea of flames. His normally pale cheeks were blazing. Carefully he turned around. Couldn't see the gun; maybe Morgan had hidden it in the heather. Now he was coming toward Errki with a menacing expression, his fists raised.

"I want to see what you look like when you're scared," he said.

Errki lunged wildly to the side and doubled over, ready for the attack. Morgan hesitated and gave him a wary look but kept coming toward him. Errki darted up and forward, like a beast of prey, and furiously sank his teeth into Morgan's nose. His jaws slammed together like a pair of scissors, he felt his sharp teeth burrowing through skin and cartilage, all the way to the bone. Morgan teetered, trying to keep his balance, flailing his arms violently, but Errki refused to let go. He held on for a long time and then let go.

At first Morgan didn't utter a sound. He stared at Errki in astonishment, and several seconds passed before he realized what had happened. The tip of his nose was loose, practically dangling from a thread. And then the blood came, pumping out in little spurts. Morgan screamed. He raised his hands to his nose, felt the blood running out and tasted it in his mouth.

"Oh, God!" he howled as he sank to his knees. "Errki! Help me! I'm bleeding!"

He was truly a pitiful sight as he knelt there in the heather with his hands on his face. The blood was gushing out. Errki stood and stared at him. Rocking back and forth, terrified by all the blood but at the same time calmer because he had fought back. From now on everything would be different. He could hear the commotion down in the cellar. They were cheering his effort, hailing him as a hero, the applause was thunderous.

"You shouldn't have pressured me like that. I can't stand being pressured!" Now you're screaming again. How disgusting.

"It's going to get infected!" Morgan whimpered and sobbed. "Do you realize what you've done? You fucking lunatic! You can just fuck off and go back to the asylum. This is going to be the death of me!"

"I tried to tell you," Errki said quietly, "but you didn't want to listen."

"Christ, what am I going to do?"

"You could put a piece of moss on it," Errki suggested.

It was certainly quite a sight: Morgan in those gaudy shorts with his nose falling off.

"I don't have a fucking thing to clean the wound with! Don't you know how dangerous it is to be bitten by a human being? It's never going to heal. You fucking asylum devil!"

"You're different when you're scared."

"Shut the fuck up!"

"You've had a tetanus shot like everybody else, haven't you?"

For once Morgan didn't answer.

"Years ago," he gasped finally. "I don't think it's still good. Besides, it only takes a matter of hours to turn into blood poisoning. You have no idea what you've done! You fucking lunatic!"

"Rinse it with whiskey," Errki suggested. "You can borrow my underpants for a bandage."

"Shut up, I said! Shit, I can't take this anymore!"

He started fumbling around in the heather for the gun, keeping one hand on his nose. Errki caught sight of the weapon, glinting brightly in all the green. Both of them bent forward, but Errki was faster. He picked it up and weighed it in his hand. Morgan began to shake. He uttered a few gurgling sounds of fear and awkwardly tried to scramble backward. His jaw dropped open, and Errki peered inside at several black fillings. A terrified person is not a pretty sight, he thought. Then he raised the gun and threw it with all his might in a great arc right into the lake. It made a modest little splash.

"You fucking bastard!" Morgan collapsed again, in a mixture of relief and despair. "I should have killed you, I should have done it right at the start." His lips were quivering. "I should have shot you in the back and turned your ass inside out! It only takes an hour for a wound like this to go to hell, I should have driven right to the doctor! Who the hell do you think you are?"

"I'm Errki Peter Johrma, and I'm just visiting."

Morgan was still sobbing. In his mind he could picture the putrefaction, the decaying flesh, and poisoned blood spreading with the speed of lightning through his veins, through all the arteries, and with one blow striking right at his heart. He felt as if he was going to faint.

"Before you fall, you should spread out hay," Errki said sagely.

He started walking up the path. A bellow came from behind.

"Don't leave me!"

"The fly that refuses to leave the corpse will end up in the grave," Errki said. But he stopped. He had never heard anyone yell at him like that, like they needed him. He was touched by the sight of Morgan with his ruined nose. He was no longer pitiful. Not in a disgusting way.

"Say something! Help me with the wound. I'll never be able to show my face in public again!" Morgan moaned.

"No, you won't. You robbed a bank, and the police have a good description of you."

"Will you go back up to the cabin with me?"

"I'll go back with you."

"Hurry up. I'm bleeding."

"Why the rush? Where's the fire?" Errki said, and started walking. Then he turned around again. Morgan came staggering after him. He was spitting and coughing to get the taste of blood out of his mouth.

"You taste like lard," said Errki thoughtfully. "Sickeningly sweet lard. Like English sausages."

"You fucking cannibal!" Morgan sniffed.

———

Morgan was lying on the sofa, pale but composed. Errki had taken the whiskey bottle and shaken tiny little drops of Long John Silver onto Morgan's nose. He screamed like a pig. Errki thought his skull would split open.

"Enough, enough! Save some for me to drink, too," he whimpered. Errki handed him the bottle.

"Be careful not to touch the wound with your fingers. I can just imagine where they've been. In the most unmentionable places."

It was easy to talk. The words flew from his lips and whirled around like dandelion fuzz.

"I feel sick," Morgan groaned, taking a big gulp. He lay back down on the couch and closed his eyes.

"Wouldn't it be just as easy to tear your nose off?" Errki suggested. "It's so loose."

"Not on your fucking life! Maybe the doctors can sew it back on."

Errki stood staring at him. They were in the same room again. He had nowhere else to go. It was quiet; the only sound was Morgan breathing heavily through his mouth. It felt as if something had fallen over them from the ceiling. The room was darker, too, making it cozier. And Morgan was no longer the boss. Strangely enough, it seemed as if he was relieved to be rid of the role. It was nicer this way, now they were equals. They could relax a bit, maybe even get some sleep. The day had been so full of trouble. Errki could feel that he needed to rest. To put his thoughts in order.

"Turn on the radio."

Morgan spoke with a slight quaver to his voice, the way people do when they're sick and need tending to. Too bad about his nose, thought Errki. It was so small to start with, and now there's almost nothing left.

"It's time for the news. Turn on the radio."

Errki pressed all the buttons, one by one, until it finally came on. He twisted the volume dial to get it right. Then he sat down on the floor and looked over at Morgan. He looked like a baby sucking on a bottle as he lay there with the whiskey. The music stopped and the news began. This time the speaker was a man.

In connection with the murder of seventy-six-year-old Halldis Horn, the police are looking for twenty-four-year-old Errki Johrma, who disappeared from the Beacon psychiatric hospital the day before yesterday. The missing man, who apparently knew the victim, was observed at the scene by a boy playing nearby. The police emphasize that Johrma is primarily being sought as a witness. He is approximately five foot six, has long black hair, and was last seen dressed in black clothing. He is also wearing a belt with a large brass buckle, and he has a distinctive way of swaying when he walks. Anyone who has seen the missing man should notify the police.

Errki switched off the radio, and a deathly silence spread through the room. Morgan sat up slowly on the couch. What was left of his nose was terribly swollen, and his sleeveless shirt was soaked with blood.

"Were you at the scene?" His eyes were filled with terror. "Did you see anything?"

Errki twisted his hands together. He was staring down at the water again. He was glad he had escaped from the lake. He was going to die anyway, but he didn't want to drown. There had to be better ways to reach eternity than stepping into cold water.

"Are you the one who killed her? Did you do it, Errki?"

Errki took a few hesitant steps forward.

"Stop right there! Don't come any closer!"

Morgan pulled up his knees and moved back. "When they catch you, you'll just say that you don't remember anything, right? Or that the voices told you to do it, so you won't go to prison. Sit down! Do you hear me? I want you to sit down!"

His voice rose to a falsetto. He was trying to collect his thoughts. Errki wasn't just a nutcase, it was much worse than that. He was stark raving mad, he had killed a defenseless old woman, and he was right here in this room! Shivers of fear ran down his sweaty back.

"OK, now listen to me. Sit down and relax. Just take it easy. I'll keep quiet about you, and you'll keep quiet about me. We can split the money, there's enough for both of us. We have to get across the border to Sweden!"

Morgan tried to speak calmly, so as not to provoke him. He was taking big gulps of whiskey, his wide eyes fixed on Errki. At any second the man might kill him with his bare teeth.

Errki had nothing to say. Morgan's nose started to pulsate in a disturbing way. He imagined that the infection had already begun to spread. Errki was sitting on the floor again, leaning against the wall under the window that faced the yard. Morgan was glad to have him at a safe distance. He actually looked quite harmless. And besides, they had been together for a long time now, and if Errki had wanted to kill him, he would have done so long ago. He even had the gun down by the water. There was still no sign of dusk, but the light had changed character and seemed more intense. What had happened? How did things get out of hand?

Morgan set the bottle on the floor. He was alone with an insane murderer, and it was important to stay alert, although he didn't feel very clearheaded right now. His mind was fuzzy. He was asking himself again why he'd brought this damn hostage along in the first place. He could have got away without him.

"So a witness saw you," he said slowly, staring at Errki, who looked as if he were asleep.

"A fat little boy," Errki muttered. "A blimp of a teenager with tits as big as my mother's." He turned to look at Morgan with an inscrutable expression on his face. "Her brains were running down the steps."

"Shut up! I don't want to hear about it!" His voice had an undercurrent of panic, like a raw drone.

"You're scared," said Errki.

"I'm not going to listen to you! There's nothing but insane babble coming out of your mouth! Why don't you talk to your voices instead. I'm sure they understand you better."

A long silence followed. The erratic buzzing of a fly on the windowsill was the only sound. Morgan wondered whether he should go to his sister's place in Oslo and hide there. She'd give him a good piece of her mind, but she wouldn't turn him in. She was a hopelessly silly woman who couldn't stop talking, but Morgan was her little brother. He had robbed a bank, but he hadn't killed anyone, least of all an old woman.

"No!" Errki shrieked and stood up. He leaned toward the window and stared outside.

"What are you screaming about? Are they hassling you? Cut out the bullshit, it's making me tired. There's nobody in there!"

Errki put his hands over his ears.

"Good Lord, the way you carry on, man!"

Morgan touched his nose again. It was throbbing harder now. He felt like laughing. This guy was stark raving mad. Maybe he couldn't even remember that he'd killed someone.

"Hey," he said in a hoarse voice, "maybe it'd be better if you went back to the asylum. What do you think?" His voice sounded tiny and thin.

Errki pressed his forehead against one of the dark mullions of the window frame and felt the fragrant heat from outside fill his nostrils. There was a vulnerability about the room that he liked and disliked. It reminded him of something. There was a faint grumbling down in the cellar.

"This is totally ridiculous, it's insane," Morgan said gloomily. "Here I sit with a mutilated nose and a bag full of money, while you stand there babbling to yourself with a murder on your conscience. And we're both wanted by the police. It's unbeliev-able!" He shut his eyes and made a few strained attempts at laughter. "I don't give a damn," he continued. "I really don't give a damn what happens. We're all going to die anyway. We might as well die right here, in this dusty shack."

He lay back down on the couch, feeling as if he were slowly dissolving, with something swarming inside him that took off and flew away. He was so oddly lethargic. Maybe his mind was slowly seeping out, too.

"I'm going to sleep for a while."

Errki was still standing at the window. He tried to remember her dress but discovered that he was having trouble recalling whether it was red with green checks or green with red checks. He couldn't picture it. But he did remember her braid. And her resigned expression as she hacked at the dandelions in the grass. It was so simple. The weeds were ruining her lawn and had to be removed. And then she had called to him with her voice full of fear.

"Shut up!" he screamed, trembling.

"Excuse me?" said Morgan wearily. "I just wanted to tell you that I really don't give a damn what happens."

"I'll do whatever I want. You can't tell me what to do!" Errki shouted, shaking his fist out the window.

"That's exactly what I'm saying," Morgan mumbled. He rolled over onto his side, keeping one hand like a protective shield over his nose. "When I wake up I'm going to be very sick. Maybe you should go down to the village to get help. I wouldn't mind if you did. I just don't care anymore. I promised to get the money, and I did."

"My name is Errki Peter Johrma. I'm going to lie down."

"Do whatever you want," Morgan muttered. His voice was barely a whisper in the silence. Errki went into the bedroom. He leaned down and rummaged under the mattress until he found the gun, then stuck it into the waistband of his trousers. He was ready. He curled up with his jacket under his head and fell into a deep sleep.

CHAPTER 14

"What Kannick needs right now is to win a trophy," Margunn said firmly. "One he can keep shiny and polished and show to his mother. He could do it, he's certainly good enough. In fact, archery is the only thing he's good at." She nodded twice to emphasize her remark.

They were sitting in her office. Sejer smiled, indicating that he, too, wished Kannick could win that trophy.

"Is he having trouble dealing with what he witnessed?" he asked, staring at her face with fascination. Beautiful she was not. She looked like a man, with a high forehead, wrinkled skin, the hint of a mustache, and a deep voice. But she was filled with an unshakable faith in the goodness of human beings, and especially the individuals in her charge. Benevolence spread like an attractive, blushing eagerness over her rough face.

"He's handling it fine. At least, he seems to be able to focus on the archery competition, and in that way hold everything else at bay. You should also bear in mind that the boys here have already been through a little of everything. It takes a lot to unsettle them."

"I understand," said Sejer. "Tell me about Kannick."

Her chair scraped as she shifted position and smiled.

"Kannick is what we call a good old-fashioned accident. The result of his mother's impulsiveness and lack of character, which, from what I know of her family, she never had a chance to develop. Just like Kannick, she was always in the way. Nothing but a bother. Every summer Polish migrants come here to work on the farms. She was working at the gas station where the men would turn up every week to buy cheap cigarettes and maybe a porn magazine if they were feeling extravagant. No doubt they were the highlight of her week. Different, exotic. And as she told me, much more gallant toward women than the men she was used to. She said, 'They treated me like a lady, Margunn!' It's clear that things like that made an impression on a girl who had long ago lost all trace of innocence and had given up regretting it. One day he turned up at the shop: Kannick's father. He'd been away from Poland for four months and was probably homesick, she said. It's not hard to imagine."

Margunn gave Sejer a conciliatory smile. "Kannick was conceived in the stockroom, after the station had closed for the evening, among crates of chips and chamois cloths. And it never occurred to her to regret it, at least not until she realized that the boy was on the way. He cried a lot as a baby, but she discovered that as long as he was full, he didn't fuss. What this approach to parenting has led to, you'll soon see. The mother was busy trying to find someone who would love her, and she still is. She doesn't want Kannick. She doesn't dislike him, but she just can't believe that he's her responsibility. She feels that he was inflicted on her, like an illness."

"What kind of problems caused him to end up here?"

"At first, he acted up and was much too impulsive to function in a regular school. But now he's starting to close himself off. He spends a lot of time daydreaming, can't manage to show enthusiasm for anything, and doesn't make friends. He craves attention, and when he's in the spotlight, he blossoms. If he doesn't get everyone's attention, then he doesn't want any at all. An instructor comes to give him archery lessons every week, and in that situation he's more lively, because it's all about Kannick and what he can or can't do. But in a classroom he's just one of many students, and then he shows no interest in participating."

"So it's all or nothing?"

"Yes, something like that."

"Where is his room?"

"On the third floor, right at the back. There's a sticker for Freia Marabou chocolate on the door."

Sejer had brought along a bag of candy. He knew he wasn't visiting a sick patient, but the poor boy had been through a terrible experience, and he could do with some extra kindness. But when Sejer saw the fat boy lying on his bed, he regretted bringing the candy.

"Hello, Kannick. My name is Konrad."

He was standing in the doorway of the room that Kannick shared with Philip. Kannick was lying on his back, reading a comic book, and chewing on something crunchy. He glanced up, first at Sejer, then at the bag he held in his hand.

"I'm from the police."

Kannick tossed his comic book aside. "I told the other boys I was sure you would come, but they didn't believe me. They said I wasn't important enough."

Sejer smiled. "Of course you're important. I've been talking to Margunn in her office. Mind if I sit down on the edge of the bed?"

The boy tucked up his legs. Carrying around that much weight must be like carrying a friend on his back, Sejer thought, as he handed the boy the candy.

"Do you promise to share these with the others?"

"OK." He put the bag on the bedside table.

"So you were the one who notified Officer Gurvin?"

The boy brushed back the shock of hair from his forehead. He was wearing cutoff jeans and a T-shirt, with black moccasins on his feet.

"He kept asking me about the time, but I wasn't wearing my watch. I had taken it to be fixed."

"I'm sorry to hear that," Sejer said. "Verifying the time is something that's very important for the police. Knowing the exact time something happened can often help explain everything, or expose people who are trying to trick us."

Kannick gave him a scared look, as if Sejer might be insinuating something.

"Well, I can't trick you," he said, "since I had no way of telling what time it was anyway. But I know that it was seven o'clock when I left here, because of this." He pointed at the alarm clock on the bedside table.

"So you're something of an early bird then. It's the summer vacation right now, isn't it?"

"It was so hot. I couldn't sleep. And Philip wheezes so loudly because of his asthma."

Sejer looked around the room. There was a hollow in the bed where Philip might have been lying before he came in. On the bedside table were bottles of medicine and an inhaler. Through the window he could see the heads of three boys who were examining his police car. Every once in a while they looked up at the window.

"It's still possible for us to arrive at an approximate time, if we help each other. Try to go over the day in your mind, from the moment you left here. You say that it was seven o'clock. And from here you walked up to the woods?"

"Yes."

"And you had your bow with you?"

"Um, yes." He looked down.

"I'm not going to arrest you. It's Margunn's job to discipline you for that. Did you walk fast?"

"Not really."

"Did you stop along the way?"

"Sometimes I stopped to listen for a while. For crows, and things like that. Maybe a couple of times."

"There's a place up there where you like to go, isn't that right?"

The boy tugged on the hem of his T-shirt to cover up his stomach. "There's a flat area up above Halldis's farm, with several paths that cross it, so I can choose whatever way I want to go. I know the place like the back of my hand."

His voice rose and fell. He was sitting on the edge of the bed with his thighs wide apart. It was impossible for him to sit with his legs together.

"So you went up to that spot, up to the ridge, and you stopped twice along the way?"

"Yes."

"Can you estimate how long it took? Maybe if you compare it to something else that you do?"

"About the same time as an episode of *The X-Files*."

"*The X-Files*? Do they allow you to watch that here?"

"Jesus, yes."

"It takes about forty-five minutes, right?"

"Uh-huh."

"So." Sejer crossed his legs and smiled encouragingly. "So, you're up on the ridge and it's about 7:45 A.M.?"

"I suppose that's about right, yes."

Kannick glanced over at the bag of candy. It was a large bag. He made a swift calculation. He knew that the large size held fifty-two pieces, which meant five for each of them, and two for Margunn. If he decided to share, like the policeman had said he should.

"And then you decided on one of the paths?"

"There are four of them. One goes over the ridge. One goes down to the scenic overlook. One goes to the old homestead sites. And one goes down to Halldis's farm."

"And that was the one you chose?"

"Yes. I didn't want to miss breakfast."

"And from the spot where you stood, is it far to her farm?"

"No, but I shot a crow along the way. And lost two arrows. I searched for them for a while, but couldn't find them. That took time. They're very expensive," he explained. "Carbon arrows, 120 kroner each."

Sejer nodded and glanced at his watch. "So you searched for a while, but gave up. Then you headed for the farm. Did that take you longer than when you went up?"

"A little shorter, I think."

"Let's say that it was 8:15 A.M. by the time you reached her farm."

"That's probably a good guess."

"Tell me what you saw."

He blinked, looking frightened. "I saw Halldis."

"When did you first catch sight of her?"

"When?"

"Where were you standing when you noticed her body?"

"At the well."

"So you stopped near the well, and that's when you saw her?"

"Yes."

Kannick's voice sounded more subdued now. He didn't want to think about what he was being asked to recall.

"Can you tell me how far it is from the well to the steps? Since you're good at archery, you must be able to judge distance, right?"

"About thirty yards."

"That sounds about right. Did you go over to her?"

"No."

"But you were sure that she was dead?"

"It wasn't hard to see that."

"No," Sejer admitted. "Let's stop there, with you standing near the well, looking at Halldis. You were scared, weren't you?"

"Yes, I was."

"How did you happen to notice Errki?"

"I looked around," he said in a low voice. "I was frightened, so I looked all around. In every direction."

"I would have done the same thing. Was he far away?"

"A little way up in the woods."

"Did you see him clearly?"

"Very clearly. I recognized his hair. He parts his hair in the middle. Long black hair, like a curtain. He was staring at me."

"What did he do when you noticed him?"

"Nothing. He stood there like a statue. I started running."

"And you took the road straight down into town?"

"Yes. I ran as fast as I could, carrying the case."

"So, by then you had packed up your bow and put it in the case?"

"Yes. I ran the whole way, all the way from the farm."

"Do you know Errki well?"

"I don't know him at all. But he trudges along the roads around here, all year long. A while back he was put in the hospital. He always wears the same clothes, no matter whether it's summer or winter. He always wears black. The only thing that wasn't black was his belt buckle. It was big and shiny."

Sejer nodded. "Does Errki know you?"

"He's seen me a few times."

"Did he look scared?"

"He never looks scared."

"And he didn't say anything?"

"No. He just slipped behind the trees. I could hear the branches. There was a rustling in the leaves."

"What were you going to see Halldis about?"

"I wanted something to drink. I was thirsty. I've been there before. She knows us."

"Did you like her?"

"She was very stern."

"Sterner than Margunn?"

"Margunn isn't stern at all."

"But you were sure she would give you something to drink. She must have been nice?"

"Both nice and stern. She always gave us what we asked for, but she would scold us as well."

"Grown-ups are strange, aren't they?" Sejer smiled. "Did all the boys here know her?"

"Everybody except Simon. He hasn't been here long."

"And occasionally you boys would go up there to talk to her?"

"We'd ask her for juice or a slice of bread."

"Did any of you ever go into her kitchen?" Sejer gave the boy a searching look.

"Oh no. We had to wait at the front door. She was always washing the floor. That's what she said. 'I've just washed the floor.'"

"I see. So you ran to Officer Gurvin to tell him what had happened?"

"Yes. He thought I was making it up."

"He did?"

"I had to tell him my address," he said, resigned. "You know how it is."

"Right. I understand," Sejer said. "So I hear that you're good at archery, Kannick."

"Very good," he said proudly.

"Who gave you that bow? It must be expensive, isn't it?"

"The social welfare office paid for it so that I would spend my free time in a meaningful way. It cost 2,000 kroner, but that's not really expensive. When I'm . . . when I can afford it, I'm going to get a Super Meteor with carbon limbs. In sky blue metallic."

Sejer blinked, impressed. "Who's teaching you how to shoot?"

"Christian comes twice a week. I'm going to be in the national championships pretty soon. He says I have talent."

"You know that a bow is a deadly weapon, don't you?"

"Sure I do," the boy replied defiantly.

He knew what was coming. He bowed his head and shut his eyes to receive the rebuke. By closing off his ears he could reduce the words to the sound of a fly buzzing round and round.

"And when you sneak around, other people can't hear you. If you come upon someone picking berries, you could kill them by mistake. Have you ever thought of that, Kannick?"

"There's never anybody up in the woods."

"Except for Errki?"

Kannick blushed. "Yes, except for Errki. But he doesn't exactly go around picking berries."

They both fell silent. Sejer could hear muted voices coming from the courtyard. The boy looked up at him and bit his lip.

"Where is Halldis now?" he asked softly.

"In the basement of the Municipal Hospital."

"Is it true that they put them in a refrigerator?"

Sejer gave him a melancholy smile. "It's actually more like a long drawer. Did you know her husband?" he asked, to change the subject.

"No, but I remember him. He was always driving his tractor. He never talked to us, like Halldis did. He wasn't interested in children. And besides, he had a dog. When Thorvald died, the dog died too. It stopped eating."

This seemed to amuse Kannick.

"How long do you think you're going to stay at Guttebakken?"

"I don't know." He stared at his knees. "I'm not the one who decides."

"You're not?" Sejer looked at him questioningly.

"They do whatever they want, no matter what I want," the boy said sadly.

"But you're doing well here, aren't you? I asked Margunn, and she said you are."

"I don't have anywhere else to go. My mother is unfit to take care of me, and I need help."

Sejer could hear the whine in his voice. "Life isn't easy, is it? What do you think makes it especially difficult?"

Kannick thought for a moment and then repeated the words he had heard so many times. "I act before I think."

"That's called being impulsive," Sejer said, consolingly. "And it's all part of being a child. Most things sort themselves out, over time. Most things. But I wonder," he asked, "could you see if Errki was wearing gloves?"

Kannick blinked in surprise, his eyes widening. "Gloves? In this heat? I didn't really notice his hands. Maybe he had them in his pockets. I'm not sure."

"The reason I ask," Sejer said "is that it's important to identify fingerprints. We found several inside the house. You're sure that you didn't see or hear anyone else up there?"

"I'm sure," said Kannick, nodding vigorously. "I didn't see anyone else up there."

"If there was someone else," Sejer said, "Errki might have seen him, even if you didn't."

"You don't think it was Errki?" he asked in surprise.

"I'm not assuming anything, one way or the other."

"But he's crazy."

"He's not exactly like the rest of us," said Sejer, smiling. "Let's just say that he needs help. But I suspect that a lot of people around here are hoping that Errki is guilty. People like to be right, you know. What do you think Halldis would say," he asked, "if Errki came wandering into her garden? She knew him, didn't she?"

"I suppose she did."

"Do you think she was scared of him?"

"She wasn't scared of much, I'll tell you that. But Errki's the kind who just takes whatever he wants. In the shops. Maybe he went right into her house. That's how he is."

"And then she got furious?"

"She could get really angry if we didn't do what she said. Errki never does what people say."

"I see. So it's probably best if we find him, wouldn't you say?"

"Will they put him in a straitjacket?"

Sejer laughed. "Let's hope he doesn't have to go through that. But maybe you boys should stay close to home while this is going on, and not go running around in the woods for a while. Until we find out what happened."

"That's OK with me," said Kannick, nodding. "Margunn took my bow away."

The boys stood in a group, watching Sejer as he got into his car. He didn't have time to talk to them, to bring a breath of fresh air from the outside into the closed world in which they lived. They looked at him with a mixture of defiance and awe. A few of them had already had trouble with the police; others lived with it hanging over their heads as a constant threat. The little dark-haired boy named Simon waved as Sejer drove off. He thought about them as he headed toward the Municipal Hospital. That small group of sullen boys who hadn't managed to find their place in the world. The kind of group that would interest Sara Struel. A group of rebels.

CHAPTER 15

"Elsi Johrma." Sejer looked at her expectantly. "Born September 4th, 1950. She died in an accident on January 18th, 1980, and was brought here to the Municipal Hospital. I don't know whether she was dead on arrival or whether she died later from her injuries. But somewhere in this building there must be a file on her. Would you please see what you can find?"

Curiosity was apparent in the nurse's eyes, but at the same time she looked reluctant. It was the vacation season, they were understaffed, and it was unbearably hot. Sejer looked around the room, a cramped office with files and books piled up in big heaps. The place was not exactly spacious.

"That was sixteen years ago," she said, as if he hadn't worked that out for himself. "Since then we've acquired computers, but her case probably isn't entered in the database, so I'll have to go down to the archives in the basement to look for it."

"Look under 1980, the letter *J*. I'm sure you know your way around down there, and I have time to wait," he told her.

She was in her mid-twenties, tall and sturdy with her hair in a ponytail. She slid her glasses down her nose and stared at him over the rims of the red frames.

"If I don't find anything right away, you'll have to come back later."

She left, and he sat patiently, looking around for something to read. The only thing he found was the Cancer Association journal, which didn't tempt him. Instead he sat lost in thought. In a place like this he couldn't keep at bay the memories of the time when he restlessly wandered endless hallways, while Elise's body was being tested and analyzed, medicated and irradiated, growing weaker and weaker. It was the smell and the sound of muted voices. He was worlds away when the nurse reappeared in the door.

"This is all I could find."

She handed him a brief, one-page admittance form.

"What about the autopsy report?" he asked.

"It wasn't there."

"But could you look for it? It's very important."

"It'll have to wait until Sunday, if I have some extra time. For now, this was all I could find."

"Thank you," he said humbly. "Can I take it with me?"

She handed him a form, which he signed.

"Do you have two minutes, while I read through it?" he asked. "There's probably some terminology I won't understand."

She let her eyes roam over the page and then read aloud: "Admitted, January 18th at 4:45 P.M. Dead on arrival. Visible fracture of arm and jaw. Significant blood loss."

"Excuse me?" Sejer responded swiftly. "Significant blood loss? Didn't she fall down the stairs?"

"I wasn't there. I was only ten at the time," she said curtly. But then curiosity got the better of her. "She really fell down the stairs?"

"That's what I was told. Her son was there when it happened," he explained. "But he was only eight."

"I suppose it's possible," she said uncertainly. "But I can't help you with this. Not unless I have the autopsy report."

She read through the document again. "Yes," she said at last, "it's strange. There was a great deal of bleeding, and that alone could have taken her life. But the actual cause of death is unclear based on what we have here."

"How badly can you injure yourself by falling down the stairs?"

"Quite badly," she said, "especially if you're elderly."

"But she wasn't elderly." He pointed to the document. "Elsi Johrma, born in 1950. That means she would have been about thirty when she died, isn't that right?"

"Can't you get hold of her son? After all, he was there when the accident happened."

"We're trying to find him."

He stood up and thanked the nurse. When he was outside he stopped and stared at the Institute of Forensic Medicine. Halldis's body was somewhere inside. He headed toward the main entrance without really knowing what he was going to do. It was much too early to be asking questions, it would be at least a week or two before it was Halldis's turn for an autopsy. He showed his badge at the front desk and was immediately allowed in. Snorrason was in one of the autopsy rooms, just as Sejer had expected. He was standing with his back to the door, pulling on a pair of rubber gloves. On the table lay a white form, not very big. In fact, it was no bigger than a dog. The idea that it might be an infant made Sejer frown.

The doctor turned around and raised one eyebrow. "Konrad?"

"Who's that?" Sejer asked, nodding at the white form.

Snorrason looked at him. "It's not Halldis Horn, but I'm sure you can see that. I am, however, wondering what you're doing here at this unlikely hour."

Sejer smiled crookedly. "Of course I know that you haven't got around to her yet. But I was in the neighborhood and thought I might find you here."

"I see."

"Just to have a look at her. Nothing else. To get me thinking."

"Are you hoping that she'll talk to you?"

"Something like that."

Snorrason pulled off his gloves. "She doesn't have much to say."

"No, well, I'll just take a quick look. Maybe I can say a few words myself, if the silence gets too oppressive."

"But you'd rather I stood next to you, thinking out loud. That's what you're hoping, if I know you. Even though you know I hate doing that."

"Just a quick peek."

"Didn't you see her at the crime scene? And didn't you get some good photos?"

"Yes. But that was yesterday."

Finally Snorrason gave in. Sejer followed him out to the left and down into the bowels of the building, to the refrigerated room where Halldis lay. After ferreting out the correct number in the files, he pulled one of the drawers all the way out.

"There you are, sir." He folded back the sheet.

It was not a pretty sight. The eye that was still intact was pitch black. In the place where the other eye should have been, the hoe had made a deep gouge. It had sliced the nose in half, and internal bleeding had stained the forehead and temples a dark reddish violet.

"Three and a third inches wide, five and a half inches deep. The exact width and length of the blade," Snorrason said briskly. "A slight defensive wound on the underside of the right arm, where the blade grazed her. Obvious monocular hematoma in the loose connective tissue of the right eye. Secondary to the broken bones in the skull."

Sejer forced himself to bend closer to the face of the dead woman. "Can you say anything about the angle?"

"It's one of two things." Snorrason was struggling against his principles. "Either she was lying down when the hoe struck her. Or she was standing up and lifted her head in horror when she saw the blade come crashing toward her. As you can see, the blade entered the eye socket right under the brow and was driven down and back into her head."

"It happened quickly and suddenly, didn't it?"

"I have no idea," Snorrason said. "But there are no outward signs of a struggle. Her clothes, for example, were intact, and as you no doubt recall, she was still wearing her clogs. So you're probably right. And that surprises me. Since she was killed with her own hoe, the murderer couldn't have planned to do it. He grabbed what he could find, in a moment of panic. A terrific anger or terrific fear, or a combination of both. Statistically, this is a rare type of murder—a crime of passion. You got a lot of fingerprints, didn't you?"

"Yes," said Sejer. "Inside the house. And two slight prints on the hoe. Fortunately for us, she lived alone. Only a few people had been inside and touched things. Time is on our side."

"Seen enough?"

"Yes, thanks."

Snorrason pulled the sheet up and pushed the drawer back in. "You'll get my report in due course."

Sejer drove to Headquarters, noticing how the thought of Sara Struel had crept into his mind and was pushing aside the ruined face he had just seen. Sara's smooth, downy skin. Her dark eyes with the light-colored rings around the pupils.

All those years of loneliness. Yet I wanted to be alone, he thought. Why do I want something else now?

He thought again about Elsi Johrma. Why had she stumbled on the stairs? There had to be an explanation, something had made her lose her balance. She fell down the stairs in her own house, stairs she must have gone up and down countless times. Maybe she was running, or maybe there was water on the steps. There had to be a reason, just as there was a reason why her injuries had caused her death, when they could just as easily have led to a concussion and a broken wrist. When I get old, he decided, I'm going to take up all the unsolved cases that we have at Headquarters. Work on them without any kind of time pressure, without being pestered by the press, work on my own terms. Make the job my hobby. While Kollberg keeps my feet warm. While I live on my pension. While I drink whiskey and roll my own cigarettes. What joy.

———

It was as in the scriptures, like the parting of the sea. The scurrying, white-clad people moved aside at the sight of Skarre standing in the open door. He peered into the enormous, sweltering kitchen, and looked in the direction the cook pointed. Over there, by the dishwasher. That's Kristoffer Mai.

Skarre could only see his back, broad with a short neck and red hair. He was the only one in the room who had not noticed the stranger walk in. He was busy lifting a rack holding dozens of steaming wine glasses out of the dishwasher. He didn't register the silence descending over the place until he put the rack down. Then he turned around and saw Skarre.

"Kristoffer Mai?"

The youth nodded. He looked as if he were frantically searching through his memory for an explanation for this visit. Then he remembered. Aunt Halldis, of course. He pulled himself together and nodded curtly as he dried his hands and shut off the machine. Beads of sweat covered his forehead.

"Is there somewhere we can go to talk?"

"The break room," Mai said, showing him the way. He kept his eyes lowered because he could feel that everyone was watching him. Since they had always ignored him before, he didn't know how to deal with it.

The room was long and narrow. They sat down in a corner

with their backs to the door. Skarre looked at the young face and was seized with a keen melancholy. How many people am I going to meet in my life, he thought, on account of some gruesome and brutal murder? How will I feel about it ten years from now? What will it do to me as a person, to be constantly asking innocent people: Where were you yesterday? When did you get home? And what's your financial situation at the moment?

He took his notebook from his back pocket.

"It's certainly hot in here," he began in a friendly manner. He looked at the red face.

"It suits me fine." Mai said with a quick smile. "I'm from Hammerfest. We were always freezing up there."

Skarre opened his notebook and began. "When did you find out that your aunt was dead?"

"My mother called me last night."

"And what did she tell you?"

He raised his eyes toward the electric fan on the ceiling and sighed heavily. "That someone had broken into her house and stolen all of her money, killed her with an ax, and then run off."

"A hoe," Skarre corrected him.

"Same difference," he said in a low voice. "People say she had a lot of money."

"What do you know about that?"

"She had half a million," Mai replied. "But the money was in the bank."

"You knew about it?"

"Hell yes. She was proud of it."

"Did you tell anyone else?"

He gave Skarre an intent look. "Who, for example?"

"Friends. Colleagues."

"I keep pretty much to myself," he said simply.

"But there must be a few people you talk to?"

"The man I rent a room from. Nobody else."

He shifted position and gave Skarre a long look. "You're here to interrogate me regarding the case, aren't you? Isn't that what you call it?"

Skarre put down his notebook and looked at Mai. Not for an instant had he imagined that this young man might be the murderer. That he might have killed his own great-aunt for her money. But his visit would be interpreted that way, and now he wondered how that must feel. Was it enough to know deep inside that your conscience was as pure as snow? Or was there a nagging uneasiness in knowing that someone had contemplated the possibility? Kristoffer Mai had green eyes. They looked innocent. It struck Skarre that everyone did, everyone he had interviewed, interrogated, questioned. Maybe it was enough that at one time, in dire straits, each had entertained the thought. Halldis has lots of money, and here I am, slaving away in a kitchen, earning a miserable wage. What if?

"You visited her now and then, is that right?"

"If three times a year is now and then, the answer is yes."

Skarre attempted a smile, to soften the next question. "How long has it been since you were last there?"

Mai looked out the window and shrugged his shoulders. "Three months, maybe. Whether that's a long time ago or not depends on how you look at it."

"You sent her a letter? Postmarked six days ago?"

He shifted uneasily. "That's what I've been thinking about. That in the last days of her life she was waiting for someone who never showed up."

"Why didn't you come as planned?"

"We had a lot of people call in sick, and I had to work extra shifts."

"Did you call her to say that you had been delayed?"

"No, unfortunately. I suppose I'm like most people," he mumbled. "I'm so busy with my own life. At least that's what I've realized now."

Skarre recognized the feeling of guilt that always surfaced when someone died. Even if there was no good reason for it, people felt guilty.

"Do you like working here?" he asked. It seemed ridiculous to be sitting here questioning one of the few relatives the dead woman had, one of the few people who did occasionally visit her. At the same time he couldn't understand his discomfort. This was exactly what he had intended to do. Maybe I'm overworked, he thought, and this is a sign that I need a vacation.

"What's your landlord's name?" he asked. "You live in a rented room?"

"It's actually a small apartment with its own entrance and bathroom. It costs 2,500 a month. But it's OK, and he's a nice man. Sometimes he makes waffles, and knocks on my door. He's rather lonely, and must be in his late sixties. Just so you know that if I had mentioned Halldis's money, he wouldn't have made it up there to the woods to steal it."

Skarre smiled. "I see what you mean. It's unlikely that I'll need to go and see him. Let's just say that the man has been crossed off by virtue of his age."

As he spoke, it occurred to him that he had just made an error. Maybe the man was much younger. Maybe they spent a lot of time together. Had a drink, talked about all kinds of things. This young man from the North was lonely, hadn't managed to make any friends, but he had a great-aunt who lived somewhere up in the woods. And the aunt had money. It slipped out over a double whiskey. Half a million. What if?

"But I'd better have his name," Skarre said.

Mai pulled his wallet out of his back pocket. He looked through it and then took out a receipt that he slid across the table.

"My rent," he said. "There's the name and address. Go ahead, write it down."

Skarre's eyes widened. He almost gasped in astonishment. An address in the East End. And the name Rein. *Thomas Rein.*

"Excuse me," he said in a low voice. "There's just one small detail I need to check. You're renting from a man named Rein? Thomas Rein? Does he use the name Tommy? And could he be a little younger than you have said?"

Mai looked at him in surprise, but he was also on guard. There was a mixture of honesty and fear in his expression.

"No, he's old," he said firmly. "But he has a son named Tommy, and my apartment actually belongs to him. I'm only renting it while he's away."

"And where is he right now?"

"I don't know. All I know is that he's away."

Skarre tried to maintain his composure. Hastily he scribbled some notes, breathing as calmly and evenly as he could, striving to keep a poker face, his expression smooth and unruffled, just the way his boss always looked.

"And when did you start work yesterday?"

"At midday. And there are a number of people who can verify that. But apparently the murder occurred early in the morning, so of course I could have done it."

His tone was insolent. He could tell that the officer was on full alert, and he was trying to defend himself against a danger that he couldn't see.

"Do you have a car?"

"An old banger."

"I see," Skarre said. "Were you close to Halldis?"

"Not really."

"But you visited her?"

"Only because my mother nagged me to. You know, because we're her heirs. But the few times I was there, I did have a good time. I didn't really think about it until afterward, now that she's gone."

"So you've never met this man named Tommy Rein?" Skarre asked.

"No. Why do you ask?"

"It's just the second-to-last question on my list."

"Pure routine?" Mai asked.

"Something like that."

"So what's the last question?"

"Errki Peter Johrma. Have you ever heard of him?"

Kristoffer Mai stood up and shoved his chair under the table. A lock of red hair fell over his forehead as he put the wallet back in his pocket.

"No," he said. "Never heard of him."

CHAPTER 16

Errki was awake. He rolled slowly onto his side and lay there, staring at the wall. He was still hovering on the verge of sleep. Bit by bit he collected his thoughts and remembered where he was. He had slept heavily. He remembered the pistol. He had never fired a gun, but he knew that it required considerable strength. He walked across the room with the gun in his hand, through the kitchen and into the living room.

Morgan was asleep. His curly hair was wet, and sweat glistened on his forehead. Maybe he really was developing an infection. But that wasn't Errki's concern. He merely registered the fact, without any feeling of guilt. Setting his teeth in Morgan's nose had been pure reflex. Besides, he hadn't asked to come along. He had set off for town because he'd had a horrible dream that had shaken him to his soul. He had tried to run away from it. When he felt safe, he slept for a long time in an empty barn, with a sack under his head, so that when he woke up his face and neck itched. Then he went into town. He needed to see that the world still existed, with people and cars. It was even hotter on the asphalt streets, and he went inside the bank because it was cool, with comfortable-looking chairs in the window. For no other reason.

He stopped by the couch where Morgan lay and hid the gun behind his back. For a moment he imagined himself taking aim and pulling the trigger, the blond head on the green sofa splitting open like a melon, its contents spraying in all directions. And Morgan gone. Vanished from one second to the next. Just like the old man at the church.

Morgan turned over and whimpered softly, then opened his eyes.

"You're sick," Errki said.

Morgan muttered that yes, he was very sick indeed. He could feel a weakness spreading through his body, a sensation of sinking. If only he could surrender to someone who would take care of him. Take over responsibility.

"Is there anything you want?" Errki asked in a friendly voice.

Morgan groaned. "Just a bullet in my forehead, that's all."

Errki brought the gun out from behind his back, bent down, and placed the barrel right between Morgan's eyes.

"Checkmate," he said, smiling. "The king is dead."

"What are you looking at?" Skarre asked. He pulled his notebook out of his pocket and dropped into a chair next to Sejer.

"Footprints," Sejer muttered. "I've been sitting here studying them, and I have a strange feeling that something doesn't mesh."

He slid the photos across the table to Skarre, who patiently put off telling his boss about his own discoveries.

"Tell me what you see," Sejer said.

Skarre looked at the pictures. "Seven footprints, three of which—no four—are virtually useless. But three of them are quite clear, with visible patterns. Grooves," he said. "Or waves. Medium-sized shoes. Size 9, wouldn't you say?"

Sejer nodded. "Go on."

"Is there anything else I should notice?"

"I think so."

Skarre studied the photos again and put one aside, leaving two. The same two that Sejer had pulled out and stared at for an eternity.

"Both of them are right shoes," Skarre said quietly. "Most likely a sneaker of some kind."

"I agree."

"One of them is clearer than the other."

"Correct."

"And one of the waves here," he pointed with his finger, "is broken. A gash in the sole, I suspect."

"But it's not on the other print, is it?" Sejer stared at him intently.

"But it's the same shoe, isn't it? They're both right shoes, aren't they?"

"Is it the same?"

"I don't know what you're getting at. Maybe it's a stone. A stone that's stuck in the grooves and leaves a white spot on one of the waves."

"A stone under the shoe that later falls off? Is that what you mean?" Sejer was still staring at him.

"Well, yes, it's possible."

"Or the rubber sole could be damaged," Sejer said. "Another thing: one of the impressions is fainter than the other. As if that sole is more worn."

"What are you getting at?" Skarre asked.

"The possibility that there were two of them."

"Two killers?"

"Yes."

"And both of them had sneakers with grooves in the soles?"

"That's what people wear nowadays. Especially young men."

"Then it's unlikely to be Errki," he said slowly. "Since he's always alone."

"Your parachute jump is getting closer," Sejer said merrily. "I thought we should take it from five thousand feet, so you'd have a good jump."

Skarre felt a wave of anxiety wash over him. He inhaled deeply to clear his head.

"The worst moment is when they open the door," Sejer said. "The roar of the wind and cold air. You'd be surprised how cold it is at five thousand feet."

"I have something to show you," Skarre said, quickly changing the subject.

He opened his notebook and pointed. Sejer read the page with a frown and then nodded slowly. "Did you find him?"

"According to Mai, Tommy is away, but he says he doesn't know where he went. I went to the house, but the father was out, and a neighbor claimed that he was gone for the weekend."

"Then we'll try again Sunday night. Maybe someone will be there. And while we're on the subject, maybe you ought to take out some life insurance. Duo Insurance. I'll find the number for you."

"It worries me that the son is away somewhere, and the minute I go looking for the father, he's gone too."

"Maybe he has a cabin in the mountains. Do you have ski gear, or anything like that? You don't want to buy a skydiving suit for just one jump. But boots are important. And you can buy some knee pads at the pharmacy, just to be safe."

Sejer leaned back in his chair and smiled brightly.

"Did you know that at the King's Arms they have fifty different kinds of beer?" Skarre said with venom. "They're open until 2 A.M., so if we start at 8 P.M., we should be able to try quite a few of them. I'll reserve a table close to the men's room."

"The wind pressure is so great that if you open your mouth during a free fall, you can't close it again. It turns inside out and you look like a monkfish."

"That whiskey you like so much? Famous Grouse? I checked with the bar, and they have it."

"Just keep your mind on the jump. Maybe this isn't what we thought. Someone must have been after the money. If Tommy Rein has gone underground, he probably has his reasons. And maybe he's working with someone."

"They would have struck at night. Not early in the morning. Besides, they would have come by car so they could make a quick getaway." Skarre stood up. "Don't forget to fill the fridge with beer. Nothing is better the day after."

Sejer didn't hear her knock. Suddenly Sara was standing there with a bag in her hand. She had been home and changed. Home to Gerhard, he thought.

She took a few steps forward and stopped in front of his desk, as he tried to hide his surprise and the emotions that overwhelmed him.

Sara Struel stared at him. The chief inspector looked different. Caught off guard. It was obvious that he was struggling hard to collect himself and regain his composure.

"What can I do for you?" he stammered.

"I don't know yet," she said, smiling.

There was a dead silence. Her eyes were dancing. He smiled sheepishly, feeling his face begin to stiffen.

"Aren't you going to ask me why I'm here?" she said, still smiling.

You're taking a trip with Gerhard to Israel, and you need a new passport, and the passport office is on the first floor, so you thought you would kill two birds with one stone.

"Aren't you curious?"

Actually, I'm scared.

"Right at this moment you're as helpless as the toad." She smiled. "I came here because I wanted to see you again."

Soon I won't be able to tell the difference between a dream and reality.

"I'm so thirsty." She looked around his office. "Do you have anything to drink?"

He stood up as if asleep and brought her a glass of water.

Maybe Gerhard beats her. And she's ready to leave him.

"I'm sorry," she said softly. "I've embarrassed you. I just think it's good to speak candidly."

"Yes, of course," he said seriously, as though she were a witness who had revealed something important, and he was determined to deal with the matter.

"I realize that other people might feel differently. But we're grown-ups, after all."

"Nothing wrong with that."

He drained a whole glass of water in one gulp and fixed his eyes on the desk. He was staring at the blotter, at the African continent where wars were raging. Something was raging inside him, too. He felt as flammable as an oil drum. A tiny spark would set him on fire, like if her hand came close to his. It was resting on the desk, soft and slender, inches from his own.

"It wasn't a death threat," she said, smiling gently as she patted his hand.

"A death threat?" he asked.

"I just said that I wanted to see you again. Nothing more."

"We're grateful for all the help we can get," he said awkwardly. Obviously she had thought of something important in relation to the case.

"I'm going to help you out a little," she said, looking deep into his eyes. "Just answer one question."

He nodded, amenable and proper, clutching his glass.

"Are you glad to see me?"

Konrad Sejer, chief inspector, weighing 183 pounds and standing six feet five inches tall, got to his feet. He hadn't thought it possible. He went over to the window and looked down at the river and the boats.

My defense system, he thought, is caving in. I'm open all the way to my soul. I have nowhere to hide.

"I have plenty of time," she said gently. "I'll wait for your answer."

Will I start something if I answer? Pull yourself together, man. It's not about confessing to a murder. All you have to do is say yes.

Slowly he turned around and met her gaze.

———

The sightings were flooding the police station switchboard. Errki had been seen in four places, spread across a geographic area that would have been impossible for him to cover in such a short time. A young woman pushing a stroller had met him on Highway 285; she remembered his T-shirt. At the same time a woman at the Shell station outside Oslo claimed that he had been a customer. He had arrived on foot and disappeared on foot. A truck driver had taken him across the border into Sweden at Ørje.

Unfortunately, it was only the last sighting that reached the ears of Kannick Snellingen. Pålte was the one who mentioned it. "He's on his way to Sweden; that's what they just said on the radio. Just think of that poor driver, Kannick. He has no idea who he has in his cab!"

Scared? Not that boy. Kannick had lost two arrows up in the woods. Two Green Eagle carbon arrows with genuine feathers that cost 120 kroner each. The thought of having to wait any longer to search for them was unbearable. There were animals up there, and they might get trampled on. Or maybe it would rain, and slowly but surely they would sink down and be swallowed by the earth. He knew exactly where he was standing when he shot those two arrows, and in his mind he could follow their flight through the trees, to where they should have landed. He had intended to go looking for them as soon as he'd heard about Errki, but it was getting late, and his excursion hadn't been sanctioned from above. Now he sat in his room and stared out at the courtyard. Gave a long, satisfying burp, and tasted again the leeks and turnips from the stew they had eaten for dinner. There was no swimming today, and Margunn was always so preoccupied with paperwork and things like that. His bow was in her office, inside the big metal cabinet where she kept the few valuables they owned. Karsten had a camera, Philip a jackknife that he was only allowed to use in the presence of an adult. The cabinet was locked, but the key was in her desk drawer in a little plastic box along with other important keys. Everybody knew that.

He gazed with longing in the direction of the woods and caught sight of several big crows sailing overhead. He also saw a couple of gulls. Not more than half a mile away was the dump, where they found plenty to eat, and grew as big and fat as albatrosses. He could also see Karsten. He was by the incinerator, bending over his bicycle, trying to attach a bottle holder to the frame. The clip must have been too big, because he was in the process of wedging in a piece of rubber hose that he'd cut up to make it fit. He kept wiping his forehead, and he had bicycle grease and dirt all over his face. Inga was standing next to him, watching. She was taller than everyone at Guttebakken, even taller than Richard, as thin as a Barbie doll, and as beautiful as a madonna. Karsten was trying to concentrate, but it wasn't easy. And Inga was enjoying herself, that much was clear.

The advantage of living at Guttebakken, Kannick thought, is that it couldn't get any worse. At least not much worse. If he ran away, or broke a few rules, he would just be sent home again. To Guttebakken. Nobody could send him to some hellish place because he was still too young. Places like Ullersmo or Ila prison were still a long way off. They belonged to a future that did not really concern him. But that was what the grown-ups were always talking about. How are things going to be for you in the future, Kannick? Nothing like the here and now, was the answer. This ugly building with all its rules. Sharing a room with Philip and listening to him wheeze night after night. Washing dishes and vacuuming the TV room. And listening to Margunn's nagging.

He made up his mind. He moved away from the window and opened the door to the hall. In the distance he could hear Margunn's voice and the sound of running water. That might mean she was washing clothes and that Simon was with her, chattering away like he always did. If so, she was down in the laundry room, which was on the second floor, next to the showers. Her office, where she had locked up his bow, was at the other end of the building. Kannick was fat, but that didn't mean he was sluggish. He slipped out and sneaked downstairs, taking the outside staircase, which was actually an emergency exit and always stood open, as was required by law. They had already had two fires, because Jaffa was so enamored of the firemen's uniforms. The steps creaked. With the utmost caution, Kannick distributed his considerable weight on the narrow boards of the stairs. He made his way to the door of her office, fearing for a moment that she might have locked it. But it was Margunn's belief that the boys shouldn't find themselves standing in front of locked doors. Kannick slipped inside and stared at the cabinet, pulled out the drawer with a finger and found the box of keys. He tried to work fast without making too much noise. He unfastened the little padlock. There was the case. His own Centra, deep red with black limbs, his pride and joy, was inside. With his heart pounding, he pulled out the case, locked the cabinet, put the key back, and left the office. He made his way through the basement and out the back door. No one could see him from the courtyard. Off in the distance he could hear Inga laughing.

He knew the woods well, and he soon found the path he had taken hundreds of times before. His footsteps, which were heavier now that no one could hear him, made the birds stop singing, as if they sensed the terrible weapon that he carried. Kannick stayed on the path that led west of Halldis's farm. He didn't want to get too close. The thought of the dead woman bothered him too much, and he knew that if he caught sight of the house again and its door and front steps, everything would come rushing back to him with all its horror. And that wasn't where the arrows were, anyway. It was the arrows he wanted to find. After he found them, he'd try to shoot a crow or two before he went home. Maybe he'd even have time to put the bow back so that Margunn would never know it had been missing. He'd done it before. Kannick was amused by people like Margunn, who always thought the best of others. It was like a religion with her, something about which she felt a moral obligation. Like the time he exchanged a 1,000-kroner note in the cashbox with 500 kroner, and she couldn't let herself believe that any of them would do such a thing. So she blamed her own faulty memory, saying that "all the notes look alike these days."

Kannick trudged on. Although he was fat, he was reasonably fit, but even so he was breathing harder, and he was sweating. As he walked he could feel himself gradually drifting into his favorite fantasy. A secret space that no one knew about, where he almost forgot time and place, and the trees around him changed shape and became an exotic forest with a rushing river far in the distance. He was Geronimo in the mountains of Arizona. His mission was to find sixteen horses in order to win the beautiful Alope as his bride. He shut his eyes, opening them only for brief intervals so as not to stumble.

The wind whispers Nimo, Nimo. In his bed he had five hundred white scalps. He caressed the case with his hand and thought, as the great chief had thought, Everything has power. Touch it, and it will touch you.

He heard a dog barking in the distance. Otherwise the woods were silent.

CHAPTER 17

Morgan could feel the sweat on his forehead. The muzzle of a gun was wavering in front of him. Perhaps he wasn't wide awake yet. Maybe the infection that was spreading through his body was giving him these surreal visions. Fevered hallucinations.

He looked at Errki and thought what hell it must be for him to constantly see visions like this, threats of death and destruction and punishment, insane terrors, year after year.

"I'm sick," he moaned. "I think I'm going to throw up."

He had slept for a long time. The light outside had changed, and the shadows had grown longer.

Errki noticed that Morgan's skin had taken on a yellowish tinge. He lowered the pistol.

"Go ahead and throw up," he said. "The floor in here is filthy enough already. It won't make a difference."

"Where the hell did you get that gun? I saw you chuck it in the water!" Morgan struggled to sit up and take a closer look. "You had it all along, didn't you?"

He curled up in a ball to make himself less of a target. "Why didn't you use it on the old woman? They said on the radio that you beat her to death!"

Errki felt anger begin to boil in his cheeks. He raised the gun again.

Morgan screamed, "Go ahead and shoot. I don't give a damn!" It surprised him, but he realized that he meant it, that he just didn't care anymore.

"You've got to go to the doctor," Errki said thoughtfully.

The gun shook. If he fired now, he was bound to hit something, either Morgan's stomach or the couch.

"Since when did you start worrying about my health? Do you think I'm going to believe that? Do you think anyone would bother to listen to what a lunatic has to say? Ha! I don't have the strength to go back down to the road. I'm too sick. I feel faint. Cold sweats, that's a sign of shock, isn't it?"

He lay back down and closed his eyes. The lunatic might very well shoot him. He lay there motionless, waiting for the shot. He'd read somewhere that it didn't hurt much to be shot, it just felt like a big jolt in your body, and then it was over.

Errki stared at Morgan's nose. It had swollen up and taken on a hideous blue color. He ran his tongue over his teeth. He could still remember the taste of skin and fat in his mouth, and then the sickening taste of blood.

Morgan was still waiting. No shot came.

"Goddamn it," he groaned. "You've really made a mess of things. I'm going to die of blood poisoning."

Errki let his arms fall to his sides. "I'll shed a tear for you."

"Go to hell!"

"You're nothing but an egg in the hands of a child."

"Cut out that crazy bullshit!"

Morgan was caught up in some kind of farce, he was sure of it. Not a single thing about this day seemed real.

"Can't you see that it's infected? I'm shaking with cold, man."

"Go ahead and call for your mama," Errki said. "I won't tell anyone."

Morgan snorted miserably. "Call for your own mama."

"She's dead," Errki said somberly.

"I'm not surprised. You probably killed her, too."

Errki wanted to reply. The words were on the tip of his tongue, ready to spill out. He stopped himself.

"Can I borrow your jacket?" Morgan mumbled. "I'm freezing." He glanced at Errki. "What's wrong with you? You look so weird."

"She stumbled on the stairs."

Errki tensed all his muscles and clutched the gun hard. It was so easy, they were just words, but they had betrayed him, had spilled out on their own, without letting him think. Suddenly he dropped to the floor. The gun slid over to the wall, and he heard the little crash as it hit. He bent nearly double, as if convulsing, trying to hold everything in with his hands. It poured out of him. He could sense the smell of his own insides, spoiled meat, waste products, venom, and bile. Little, shiny blisters that burst, the gurgling sound of slimy organs being squeezed together and spraying out, air and gas that made the strangest noises. He squirmed around on the floor, wallowing in his own misery.

"Are you going to get sick now, too?" Morgan said in horror. "You can't. You have to go for help! I'd rather sit in jail for a while than die of tetanus in this shithouse. You know the way, so go and get somebody, damn it, and we can get out of here!"

There was no answer. Errki groaned and thrashed around, his shoes banging against the floor. It sounded as if someone were beating him, as if someone were yanking and tearing at him and tossing him around. After a while he started coughing and gasping, or maybe he was belching and vomiting. Morgan shuddered. Dear God, what a madhouse! Something in this room had poisoned them both. Maybe there was a curse in the cracks of the floorboards that had begun slowly seeping out as soon as they stepped inside. It felt like a lifetime ago that he had stood inside the bank, pointing the gun. They must have sent people out to search, they must have found the car! Why had they put that damn tarpaulin over it?

Errki grew still down on the floor. He was lying there, breathing hard. Morgan glanced at the gun.

"That was quite an attack, wasn't it?" he said softly. "What's going on?"

Errki began gathering up his body, piece by piece. To Morgan it looked as if he were searching for something that he'd lost. His black hair fell in his eyes as he fumbled like a blind man.

"Are you seeing things?" Morgan asked uneasily. "Could you get me the whiskey?"

Errki pulled himself into a sitting position. He was bent over, holding on to his stomach, with his eyes closed. Every muscle in his body was wound as tight as a steel spring. Drool was dribbling down his chin.

"Don't nag me," he gurgled.

"I didn't mean to nag you. It's just that I'm freezing. I thought you might lend me your jacket. Is there any whiskey left? Could you take a look, after you're done with... your attack?"

"I said, don't nag me!"

There was a faint rustling sound from his polyester trousers as Errki finally stood up. He walked across the room, hunched over like an old man, still clutching his stomach. First he picked up the gun, then he went into the bedroom. His jacket was on the bed, rolled up into a pillow. He snatched it, keeping one hand on his stomach, then tottered back to the living room. The bottle stood next to the radio, and it was open. He picked it up and took a big gulp as he stared out at the water. His body needed time to calm down. This time he had split in half without the slightest warning. The life that lay ahead of him didn't seem very appealing. He stared at the dark surface of the water. Not a ripple. The water was dead. Everything was dead. Nobody really wants you. They just want what you can give them. Morgan wants your jacket and the whiskey. Do you have anything else to give, Errki?

He stood holding the jacket, drinking the whiskey. He could put the jacket over Morgan. A friendly gesture. The question was, did it make any difference? Did it make life worth living?

"Don't drink it all!"

Errki shrugged. "You've got a real drinking problem," he said vaguely.

"My nose hurts like hell."

"Plundering together is a joy. Dying together is a party," Errki said, handing him the bottle. Morgan drank until tears filled his eyes, then put the bottle down, gasping for air. He tucked up his knees and lay down on his side, as if making room for Errki to sit at the end of the couch. Either he would sit down, or else he would shoot him. But he no longer felt threatened, and he didn't know why.

Errki hesitated. He looked at the place on the couch and realized that it was meant for him. Cautiously he put the jacket over Morgan's shoulders. A chorus of laughter rose up from the cellar and roared in his ears.

"Shut up!" he shouted, annoyed.

"I didn't say a word," Morgan said. "What on earth do they say to you, anyway? Your voices. Tell me about them, tell me what it's like. Then at least I'll die a wiser man."

The whiskey was burning hot in his stomach; he was already feeling better. "Why do you listen to them? You know they're not really there, don't you? I once heard that crazy people know that they're crazy. That's what I don't understand. I hear voices, they say. Damn it, I do, too, once in a while. Inner voices, like in my imagination. But I know that they're just imaginary, and it would never occur to me to do what they say."

"Except when they tell you to rob a bank, I suppose?"

"Hey, that was my own decision."

"How can you be so sure?"

"I can recognize my own voice when I hear it."

Errki was still staring at the empty place on the couch. Morgan looked at him with genuine curiosity. "Tell me about them. Can you see what they look like? Do they have fangs and green scales? Do they ever say anything nice? You shouldn't let them get to you. Christ, I thought they were going to finish you off. Maybe I should talk to them. Maybe they'd listen to an outsider."

Morgan giggled hollowly. "Mad dogs and children often have to be dealt with by the neighbors."

With great effort he pulled himself into a sitting position nearer to Errki, lifted one hand, and tapped Errki three times on the forehead. "Hey, you in there! Stop terrorizing the boy. He's exhausted. Find some other skull to plunder. Enough is enough!"

Errki blinked uncertainly. Morgan sounded dead serious. Suddenly he began to snicker.

"Is there more than one? A whole gang?"

"Yes. Two."

"Two against one? Damned cowardly. Tell one of them to get lost, and then you should have it out with the one who's boss, man to man."

Errki laughed nervously. "You don't have to worry about the Coat. It just lies in the corner, shivering."

"The Coat?"

Morgan looked at him in surprise. The full extent of Errki's madness was finally becoming clear to him.

"It hung on a hook in the hall."

Time abruptly spun backward. Everything came back to him as it had once been. He saw glimpses of faces and hands, raised eyebrows, turned backs, silk and velvet, reels of thread in many colors. He flew backward along a road full of potholes and lined with green ditches, and approached the house. The open door, the narrow hall, the stairs leading up. He was sitting on a stair, almost at the top. His father had built the stairs out of pine. The wood was full of narrow, squinting eyes that were always watching him.

"It just hung there. Father's coat. It didn't contain anything, just air. Shivering, shifting in the draft from the attic. One time it turned inside out, and at the same instant she tumbled down and set the air in motion."

"Tumbled down?" Morgan gave him a quizzical look.

"My mother. She slipped on the stairs. I pushed her."

"Why did you do that?" Morgan lowered his voice. "Did you hate her?"

"I told everybody that I pushed her."

"But you didn't? Or aren't you sure? Why did you say that you had?"

Errki saw the images in front of him, flickering above the rough timber. He raised his hand and pointed. Involuntarily, Morgan turned to follow his gaze. The only thing he saw was the filthy wall. Errki was silent.

"You know what?" Morgan said, hauling himself up into a better position. "Wouldn't it be great if your voices could talk to the other voices instead of to you? I mean, to the voices of the other patients in the asylum. Then they could fight among themselves and leave all of you in peace. Damn, sometimes I'm a fucking genius. You know how you should get rid of them? Use an ancient tactic. Set them up against each other, and they'll end up obliterating each other. Give me the bottle!"

Errki picked up the bottle from the floor and held it in his hand.

"Give it to me. I want more!"

Morgan stretched out his arm for the bottle. Errki held on to it. "The one who fights the source will die of thirst," he said gravely. Then he let Morgan have it.

He took two gulps. "Why did your mother fall down the stairs? Tell me about it. We can pretend I'm your doctor. I'm good at that, you just have to give me a chance. Come on, tell Uncle Morgan. Talk about it, my friend, and it will be all right."

He gave a low chuckle. He was very drunk.

Errki's hands began fumbling over his thighs. He put one hand on the gun and felt it settle down. The gun fit his hand like a glove. There was a significance to that; it meant something.

"She did sewing for people."

"She was a seamstress?"

"Bridal gowns made of silk. Suits and coats. Or customers brought old clothes that had to be ripped up and resewn. That was what she did most. She ripped up old suits."

"Have a drink," Morgan interrupted him. "It's tough to recall old memories."

Errki took a drink and passed back the bottle. The cellar was silent. The dust had settled, everything was gray. For a wild moment he thought they might even be gone. In the silence his voice became crystal clear. His own voice. The words weren't planned in advance, they emerged gradually, and if he felt doubtful and held them back, new words appeared, wanting to come out. One word led to another, and he was powerless to stop them.

"I was playing on the stairs," he said quietly. "I was eight years old."

You weren't playing. You had set a trap. Let's not disguise the facts, we were there and saw everything. The Coat saw you, it was hanging in the hall.

Errki moaned. His rage was growing stronger and stronger. Or was it despair? How could he sit here with his mouth open, letting this rubbish spill out? Sickness, death, and misery. Snails, worms, and toads. He tossed his head angrily. Morgan was listening. Errki could feel him listening in a thoroughly physical way, like skin against skin, and he couldn't stand to be touched. Not even by Sara with the wave. In his mind he heard the lovely harp that accompanied her voice.

"Why on the stairs?" Morgan took another drink. For the moment he had no other plan than to get stinking drunk. A shortsighted but pleasant goal. "I mean, that's a hell of a place to play."

"The stairs," Errki said heavily. "The attic. The light in the hall was on. I could hear the sound of the sewing machine. Like a clock ticking. I was playing on the stairs because I wanted to be near her."

"So the stage is set," Morgan said, "and the play can begin. The light is on, the sewing machine is going, and little Errki is eight years old."

"I had found an old fishing line in the basement and erected a cable car out of it, going from the top step in the attic all the way down to the first floor."

Morgan gaped at him. "You strung up a goddamned fishing line?"

"I stuck holes in some empty matchboxes and made cars out of them, filled them with almonds and raisins, and then sent them off below. The phone rang. She called, 'Can you get that, Errki?' I didn't want to, I was busy playing, had just filled up a car with almonds. I sat on the stairs and waited. She appeared in the doorway and took two steps. Her foot caught in the line and she stumbled forward. She was always so quiet, but this time she screamed. She toppled over and fell, just like a piece of furniture that had been tossed downstairs."

Morgan was speechless. His eyes were shining, as if he were a child listening to a story that was a bit too frightening.

"I was sitting on the third step, close to the wall. She crashed past and didn't stop until she hit the floor, wrapped around the banister."

"Did she break her neck?" Morgan was whispering. "You're so damned weird. One minute you seem so normal, talking like a regular person. Why are you so normal all of a sudden?"

Errki seemed to wake up. "First you yell at me for being crazy, and now I'm supposed to explain myself for being normal. Of course I'm normal. Are you normal? You rob banks, and your nose is rotting away."

"But why did she die?"

"All the blood ran out of her body."

"What did you say?"

"All of it, out of her mouth. It just gushed out like a waterfall and made a puddle at the foot of the stairs. I could see the light in the ceiling reflected in the blood, and the Coat was like a dark shadow. The phone was ringing, but I couldn't pick it up. I would have had to put my foot in the big pool of blood and drag it with me all through the house, over the carpets and floors. Eventually it stopped ringing. I unfastened the fishing line and put it in my pocket, then sat still and waited. The blood stopped running out of her mouth, her face was gray as a stone. Sooner or later somebody will come, I thought. Father, or a customer. Somebody. But no one came. Not until all the blood had turned dull, and I couldn't see the light reflected any more."

At last Errki fell silent. He didn't feel relief, just emptiness. He touched the gun. A single bullet in the chamber. That must mean something, it must be intended for him.

"Yes, but blood coming out of her mouth? Why did that happen?"

"Give me a little whiskey."

"Did she crack her skull open?"

"She was a seamstress."

"You already told me that."

"She was ripping up an old suit. Stitch by stitch, using a razor blade. She always put the blade between her lips if she had to tug at the material a little, or change the position she was sitting in. Then the phone rang. She walked across the room with the blade between her lips, and stumbled on the fishing line. The razor blade vanished down her throat."

Morgan choked, and clutched his hand to his throat. He could feel his pulse throbbing gently under his clammy skin. The thought of swallowing a razor blade nearly made him throw up.

"You seem totally clearheaded to me," he said cautiously. "Maybe you've just been in the asylum too long. Your mother's death was an accident. It wasn't your fault. And by the way, it was fucking stupid to hold a razor blade between her lips. And fucking stupid of you to take the blame."

"I was the one who strung up the fishing line."

"But you were just playing, right? The incident is hereby filed away as an accident."

The remark was meant to be consoling, but it didn't look as if it had any effect.

"We humans think that we can control our own lives," Errki said slowly. "But we can't. Things just happen."

They were both silent for a long time.

"What are you thinking about?" Morgan asked finally.

"About a farmer back home. Johannes."

"So tell me about Johannes, now that we're making some headway."

Morgan felt as if time had stopped. The future no longer existed, only the present. It was just him and Errki here between four rough wooden walls. Dimly lit and comfortable. The whiskey was burning in his veins, giving him a floating sensation.

Errki thought about Johannes. A gray, wrinkled, dry old man with dead eyes. He seemed to recognize himself in those eyes, as if he and Johannes were related. Eyes without hope. And then one day, there he was, at the top of a ladder.

"He'd started drinking. His wife was dead, and Johannes shrank to almost nothing in just a few months."

"Sounds like my mother after my father died," Morgan remarked.

"He started drinking. He drank all the time, without stopping, for months. People kept coming over to try and help him, but it didn't do any good."

"So he drank himself to death?"

"No. In the end he woke up and put a stop to it, after sharing a bottle of liquor with the minister."

"Sounds like a great minister."

"The minister saw me and started yelling, but I didn't stop. I could have stopped, but I went out the door as fast as I could and hid behind the greenhouses."

"Why was he yelling?"

"Stop nagging me like that."

Errki turned around and grabbed for the bottle. Morgan let him have it.

"Johannes got a job working for the minister as a handyman. He was whitewashing the church, standing at the top of a tall ladder, working hard. Then Errki Johrma came along. Johannes didn't hear anything because he was busy with his work, and besides, he was whistling, happy and sober as he was. That's exactly why I was disappointed. He'd started to look like everyone else.

"But I shouted at him. I shouted, 'Hey, you up there!' And good God, what a fright I gave him! He shoved against the wall out of sheer fright, and the ladder made a big arc, and he fell backward."

"Holy shit!"

"He slammed on to the stone. I stood there staring at his crushed skull. His legs kept twitching for a while, until he lay still. I hid behind a headstone. Then the minister came running, and I heard him shouting and wailing."

"And so they said it was your fault?"

"It was my fault."

"How on earth does a guy get to be so incredibly unlucky?" Morgan said. "Were you born on Friday the thirteenth?"

"Afterward they came and got me from home."

"What did you tell them?"

"Nothing. Nestor told me to keep my mouth shut."

"Nestor?" Morgan rubbed his eyes. "How you've managed to get yourself mixed up in so much misery is more than I can comprehend. I thought I was unlucky. But what about the old woman they found yesterday? Was that an accident too? Just tell me what happened."

Slowly Errki turned to face him. "As I said. Things just happen."

"That's a rather glib response, don't you think? The police are going to interrogate you. You need to work out what you're going to say."

"I'm a wave," Errki said dramatically. "I break only once."

"Then I think that's what you should tell them. And you'll land right back in the asylum." He wiped his brow. "My nose aches," he complained.

Errki shrugged. "You could fix your nose with your own willpower if you'd just make the effort."

"Is that right?"

"You have to scare off the infection using all the powers you possess. You have to heal yourself."

"I'm not a fucking shaman. I don't believe in that kind of stuff."

"That's why you're sick."

"Can't you do it for me?" he said sarcastically. "Besides, I'm in no shape to exert myself. My bones are like jelly."

"You have to do it yourself."

"I thought as much, but thanks anyway," he said. "You know, I once saw a guy on TV who could break glass just by thinking about it. It was really impressive. But it's all just a stunt."

"Breaking glass with your mind isn't very impressive," Errki said. "I can do that too. Glass is under constant tension; it's easy."

"Wow, listen to him! How come you don't travel around giving performances?"

"Don't feel like it."

"And who taught you this?"

"The magician. In Central Park."

"It's good you have a sense of humor. We're going to need it."

"Do you know what he could do?" Errki asked. "He could stretch out the skin on his hands until it burst."

"So give me a demonstration. But don't break the whiskey bottle."

"There isn't any glass here," Errki said thoughtfully. "All the windows are already broken."

"I suppose someone was here before you and did the job."

"But there are still some big pieces left in that window over there," Errki said, pointing at a window that faced the yard.

"OK, then break them," Morgan said, full of anticipation. He was enjoying himself, although at the same time he had a nasty feeling that something could go horribly wrong.

Errki got up unsteadily from the couch. He stared at the window and sank down to the floor, bent his head and shut his eyes. Morgan looked at him with a mixture of glee and sadness. He stared at the piece of glass in the upper right corner of the window frame. The sun shone through, making it light up. Not a sound came from Errki, he sat like a statue. Morgan wondered hazily if he ought to make a decision about what they were going to do next. But the heat and the whiskey had drained his energy, and it was so nice just to sit still and doze. Life hadn't turned out exactly the way he'd expected. It hadn't for Errki either. He looked ridiculous sitting there on the floor, a rock-hard knot of stubborn willpower. Morgan was struck by how thin he was, as fragile as an insect. And now he was going to perform a magic trick for him. It was almost painful to imagine how disappointed he'd be when nothing happened. He wondered what he should say to console him. Maybe put the blame on the whiskey, say that it had sapped him of his strength.

Then the glass broke. It didn't split apart with a little tinkling sound, just for fun. It shattered with a bang, and glass rained down in the room. Morgan jumped, feeling his heart jolt with fear. Errki was still sitting on the floor. Then he raised his head and looked around. He looked sleepy, at first. But then he looked surprised.

"Something's not right," he said, and headed for the door.

"Something's not right? How the hell did you do that?" Morgan looked bewildered. "Where are you going?"

"Outside," Errki replied. "I need to check on something."

CHAPTER 18

Kannick lowered his bow. He was standing approximately thirty yards away, looking at the empty window. What he'd hit was no great feat, but it was still a challenge to aim for the transparent, shimmering glass, and the arrow had made a great sound as it struck. In his mind he had just skewered the eyeball of General Crook. He went closer and stared at the house, which was empty and abandoned and looked dilapidated in the afternoon sun. He knew that he would find the arrow inside, sticking out of a wall. He looked around for another target because he had one arrow left in his quiver. It was getting late, but he wasn't worried about the unpleasantness that awaited him back at Guttebakken. He knew exactly what would happen and had been through it many times before, so it didn't scare him. It was all so pitifully predictable. Grown-ups had so little imagination. Margunn might find somewhere else to hide the key to the cabinet. It probably wouldn't be any worse than that. Besides, she would be glad that he'd found the missing arrows, since she knew he was worried about them. He would discover her new hiding place. And that would be it.

He stared at the old house, at the gray wood, the flat stone steps in front of the door, and the empty windows. He had been inside many times, had been through all the cupboards, had even slept on the old couch in the living room. He stared at the door. There were several black spots in the wood, and he decided to choose one of them.

He was Geronimo. The door was a Mexican soldier, and the dark spot was his heart. The enemy. They were the ones who had raped and killed the tribe's women and children. He hated them from the depths of his warrior soul!

This time he wanted to shoot from a kneeling position, the way the chief used to shoot. It was a big challenge. He went down on one knee and pulled an arrow from the quiver. This one had yellow and red feathers. He put the arrow into the bow and straightened his back. Through the sight he made sure the bow was level. He looked at the dark spots and chose the one in the middle of the door, a little to the left of where the door handle had been. Then he drew, felt the plate slide under his chin and the string of the bow move into place just above the tip of his nose.

Long live the Apaches!

Just the slightest adjustment and he had the spot in his sight. Vaguely he noticed that something was happening. The door opened and a black shape appeared in the entrance. But his brain had already given the command; his grip loosened and he wanted to lower the bow, but he couldn't stop the arrow from releasing. It flew from the string at a speed of over two hundred miles per hour.

There was not a sound as it struck. Errki stood on the steps and gave only a tiny gasp of surprise. Kannick saw the yellow arrow sticking out of his black trousers. Errki looked astonished but didn't say a word. Hesitantly he moved his hand to pull it out. Then he caught sight of Kannick. *The fat boy.*

He recognized the ragged trousers and the bulging body. Now he understood what he had in the case he was clutching as he'd raced down the path with madness in his eyes. A bow. The boy lowered it now, it gleamed red in the sunlight, and the arrow the boy had just shot was sticking out of Errki's right thigh. It didn't hurt. He gripped the arrow close to his trousers and clenched his teeth. It slid out, quite easily. Instantly he felt something give way, a tight clamp that suddenly let go. The boy turned and ran.

Errki did something he hadn't done in years, he ran after him. Hot blood was starting to pour down his thigh. Kannick was gasping for breath, but otherwise not a sound came from his mouth as he tore away. He dropped the bow; he'd never thought he could do such a thing, but it was hindering his flight, and the black shape that was Errki Johrma was after him! As the seriousness of the situation dawned on him, the strength drained from his body, leaving him empty for a moment. He lost his concentration and began to stumble over the branches and undergrowth. He thought, If I fall now, there's no hope. He was running for his life; he wanted to go back home to Guttebakken. Home to Margunn and all the others, to the safe familiar life in that ugly building, to Philip wheezing in bed beside him. Home to Christian, to the dream of defeating all the other contenders for the national championships, home to dinner and freshly baked bread, to the flickering TV set and clean sheets every other week. Life suddenly seemed so precious, something he wanted to fight for, and the feeling overwhelmed him.

Then he stumbled and fell, facedown in the dry grass. But he didn't give up, he was still fighting; he had to find something to defend himself with so that he could kill his pursuer before his pursuer killed him! He looked around for a stick but found only twigs; there wasn't even a rock he could throw. Exhausted, he saw his life vanishing, slipping away before his eyes. He surrendered, rolled up into a ball, and lay still. Kannick had never imagined he would die so young. He used the last of his strength to prepare himself. Errki's footsteps were coming closer. Finally they stopped right beside him. The man was crazy. He wasn't going to behave like anyone else. That was the worst part, not knowing what to expect. All the stories he'd heard about Errki raced through his mind.

"He who fears the wolf shouldn't go into the forest," Errki whispered.

Kannick heard the low voice. He didn't move, he was already as good as dead. Cautiously he turned his head and caught a glimpse of the leg of Errki's baggy black trousers. The wound didn't seem to be bothering him. Yet another sign that the man was inhuman. He probably didn't feel pain, not his own, and definitely not anyone else's. He was without feeling. Being inhuman meant that you have no feelings about anything.

"Get up."

The voice was not menacing. It actually held a trace of surprise. Kannick got to his feet unsteadily, keeping his head bowed. The beating would come soon, and he had to take the brunt of it on his forehead and temples. A hard slap on the cheek was the worst thing Kannick could imagine. That kind of blow was so humiliating. But nothing happened.

"Back to the house," was all Errki said.

There was something unnerving about the fact that he didn't raise his voice. That's the way a sadist talks, someone who enjoys causing pain, Kannick thought. The voice was so clear and quiet; it didn't match the rest of him. He was overwhelmingly sinister up close. Kannick didn't dare look at his eyes. That was something he wanted to avoid for as long as possible, because when he saw them he would be utterly lost.

Back to the house. He was hiding out in the old cabin, had been up there the whole time. He wasn't on his way to Sweden like they'd said on the radio. Going inside that house with Errki was like entering the realm of the dead. Once he was inside no one would hear him scream for help. He started shaking violently, thinking that now he would be punished for everything he had ever done.

If you don't shape up, Kannick, I don't know what's going to become of you in the future.

The future, which had never worried him before, was not just catching up with him, it was about to vanish. Maybe he would die painfully. The only thing Kannick really feared was pain. His body began shaking so badly that his rolls of fat quivered and sloshed. Maybe he still had time to faint and disappear, to sink unseen through the heather, anything to escape this nightmare. But there was nowhere for him to go, and he didn't faint. Errki was waiting. He was patient, because he was sure that he would win, sure that Kannick didn't have a chance of escaping.

Then Kannick saw the gun. In the midst of his despair, a thought occurred to him, a thought from a soul that faced death: if only he could get a bullet in the head instead of being tortured. That was Kannick's last hope. He began walking slowly through the grass. He had no idea how his legs managed to carry him; they moved against his will, back toward the house, in the direction he didn't want to go, to his end. Errki followed behind. He had stuck the gun in his belt with the big eagle on the buckle, and was holding one hand over his wound. His leg was bleeding badly, but he would be able to stanch the blood by tying something around it; it wasn't more serious than that.

"You're scared," Errki said.

Kannick stopped and tried to understand what the crazy man meant. Was this part of the torture? To make him feel safe and then deal him a deathblow? To enjoy his terror as he realized that he was going to die? He pondered this so long, standing still on the path, that Errki had to give him a little push. Kannick cringed and whimpered softly, but no shot was fired. He started walking again until the house was visible through the trees. He thought they had run forever, but in reality it was only a few hundred yards. They stopped in what had once been a garden, and Kannick had his second shock. A man with blond hair and a wounded nose was standing in the doorway in brightly colored shorts.

There were two of them. One to hold him down and one to administer the torture! He tried again to faint, tried to make himself fall forward, but his knees refused to obey. I'm going to die here, he thought, closing his eyes. With bowed head he waited for the shot. Errki gave him a shove in the back.

"That man over there wants to be called Morgan."

Morgan stared at them, wide-eyed. "Hey, Errki! Have you been to the butcher to buy some lard?"

He was leaning against the door frame, looking in disbelief at Kannick's impressive double chin and thighs as wide as Errki's waist.

Kannick scowled at his nose.

"He shot me in the thigh," Errki replied.

"Damn it, Errki, you're bleeding like a stuck pig!"

"I said he shot me." He bent down and picked up the arrow. "With this."

Morgan examined it with curiosity, stroking the yellow and red feathers. "I'll be damned. Were you playing Indians? Is there a cowboy out there too?"

Kannick shook his head vigorously. "I was j-just out here p-practicing."

"Practicing? For what?"

"F-for junior national ch-champion."

He barely managed to gasp out the words. Errki heard quite clearly the sound of a bagpipe, not entirely pure in tone.

"Take him inside." Morgan moved aside to let them pass. Errki shoved Kannick ahead of him, wondering what he could use to tie around his leg to stop the bleeding.

"I have to go home," Kannick squeaked.

"Sit down on the couch," Morgan said harshly. "We need to assess the situation first. Maybe we can use you for something."

The sight of Morgan's nose made Kannick stare. It looked

worse than ever, with the loose part dangling hideously. Its color reminded him of a rotten potato. He noticed the whiskey bottle on the floor, the radio on the windowsill, and his arrow sticking out of the wall next to it. The man with the curly hair was obviously drunk. That didn't make him feel any safer. He sank onto the couch, and sat there feeling dazed, with his hands in his lap. Then came the question he had dreaded.

"Does anyone know where you are?"

No. Nobody knew. They wouldn't even know where to start looking, unless Margunn was sharp enough to check the cabinet, find that the bow was missing, and realize that he had gone to the woods. But the woods were enormous. It would take forever for them to find him, and besides, they would wait a long time before they even started looking, and at first she would only send out Karsten and Philip. And they were hopelessly lazy and didn't know their way around very well.

"Answer me!" Morgan said and hiccuped.

"No," he whispered. "No one knows."

"Not very pleasant, is it?"

Kannick lowered his head. It was worse than unpleasant, it was the beginning of the end.

"You don't have an ice-cold beer, do you?" Morgan licked his lips. As he asked the question, he was suddenly overwhelmed by a terrible thirst.

This was not what Kannick had expected. "I've got some lozenges," he mumbled.

"OK. Let's have them. I haven't got a drop of spit left."

Kannick stuck his hand in his pocket and took out a box of liquorice lozenges. Morgan grabbed the box, struggled for a moment with the sticky clump of lozenges, and put three in his mouth.

"Allow me to introduce ourselves," he said, smacking his lips. "This is Errki. He's possessed by evil spirits that talk to him and harass him. My name's Morgan, and the police are after me for a little show I put on this morning. We've been killing an afternoon together." And then he added, "It's that lunatic over there who wrecked my nose. Just so you know what kind of person you are messing with."

Kannick nodded somberly. He already knew.

"And what about you. Who are you?"

I'm the one who wants to be called Geronimo. The pathfinder. The champion shot.

"Excuse me? What did you say?"

"Kannick."

"Do you really go by that name?"

"I do the best I can," he said, trying to catch his breath.

"Aha! The boy has a sense of humor!"

Errki had sunk down onto the floor. He had found his leather jacket and wrapped it around him, gripping his thigh with both hands. "I've seen him before," he said in a low voice.

Morgan looked at him in surprise.

"Where?"

"At the dead woman's farm."

"What'd you say?"

Morgan turned to Kannick. "He saw you? Are you the boy who was playing nearby? The one they were talking about on the radio? Are you?"

Kannick lowered his eyes.

"Oh no, this is serious. Damn it all, he saw you, Errki. We've got to get rid of him!"

Kannick gave a startled little squeak, as if someone had stepped on a rubber toy. His long eyelashes fluttered with fear.

"And I heard that you've been talking to the police, right?"

Kannick didn't reply.

"Never mind. That doesn't bother Errki. He's a little strange that way. And we're actually very friendly. It's just that we're bored. We're sitting here waiting for night to come. Which reminds me, at night Errki gets really crazy. His teeth start to grow and his ears get pointy. Isn't that right, Errki?"

Errki didn't answer. He was studying Kannick out of the corner of his eye. Fear was making the boy's eyes light up in his pudgy face. He was chewing hard on his lip, and the color had left his cheeks.

"Hey," Morgan said, "you didn't bring along a lunch and a thermos, did you? We're starving to death."

"I've got some chocolate in the case. But it's probably melted by now."

Errki reacted at once. He scrambled to his feet and starting waving his hands. "Go and get that case!"

"Calm down," Morgan said softly. "Get it yourself. Otherwise he'll just run off. And you have to share it with me!"

Errki limped out and began searching for the case. Shambling around in the bushes, he kept one hand clamped tight on his wound. Eventually he found it, and farther away he found the bow. He dragged everything back and flung open the case. Inside lay more arrows and some other things that he didn't recognize, and the chocolate. A Mars bar and a Snickers. His fingers shook as he picked them up and went into the house, holding a bar in each hand. Snickers and Mars, Snickers and Mars. Soft, slightly melted chocolate. One with peanuts and caramel, the other with toffee. The paper rustled. He walked across the floor, weighing them in his hands. Both were good. He liked Snickers bars, but Mars bars had always been his favorite; it was impossible to choose, and he could only have one. Morgan jumped up and grabbed the Snickers. "I'll take that one. You can have the Mars. Fatty can have a whiskey in exchange."

Kannick glanced at the bottle standing on the windowsill. He'd never had anything against beer. He enjoyed getting drunk, as long as it didn't happen too fast, but he'd never cared for liquor. He shook his head. The others were busy eating the chocolate, smacking their lips like two children. In the midst of his despair he felt like laughing, but he only managed a pitiful little gasp.

"We're not going to hurt you," Errki said, giving him an odd smile as he spoke.

"That's not something we've decided yet," Morgan said, swallowing the last of his chocolate.

"He doesn't have anything we want. Except for the chocolate."

"Maybe the little dough boy here could help us," Morgan said. "It's all gone to hell, anyway. With or without Jannick."

"Kannick," said Kannick.

Morgan wiped his mouth on the back of his hand. "I suppose you want to go home to mama, don't you?"

"I'd rather not."

"Is that right? Then where do you want to go?"

"To Guttebakken."

His voice had taken on a defiant tone, as if he had regained hope that they weren't going to kill him after all. The fact that they had eaten the chocolate with such glee made them seem much more human.

"And what's that?"

"The boys' home."

Morgan snickered. "Christ, it looks like we're all cut from the same cloth. And just what have you done in your young life for you to end up there? Aside from eating too much?"

"It's a metabolic disorder," Kannick said.

"That's what my mother always said when she was at her worst. Have a shot of whiskey, that should help your metabolism."

"No, thanks." He thought about Margunn, tried to picture what she was doing. How many times she would have checked the clock. It would take a while before she started to worry. He made a habit of staying out for long stretches. She probably wouldn't begin wondering what had happened to him until evening. But she knew that he'd never miss supper. So she'd start looking out the window around eight o'clock, and another hour would pass before she'd send Karsten and Philip out to look for him. Anything could happen by then! It was a while until evening, a sea of time, alone with two drunk nutcases, and one of them had a gun! Desperation made him cast another glance at the whiskey bottle. Morgan noticed.

"Go ahead. No reason to hold back here."

So Kannick took a gulp. It was his only hope of escape. The first swallow created an internal explosion that started in his throat and worked its way with intense fire down to his stomach. He gasped for air, wiping away a few tears.

"Take three or four more," Morgan said encouragingly. He sat on the floor licking his fingers. "You'll feel great after a while. Tell us why you're living in a boys' home."

"How should I know?" Kannick said, sounding a little annoyed, which he instantly regretted. Maybe he had insulted Morgan.

"You have no idea why the grown-ups put you there? What an idiot you are. Do you think I blame my mother because I became a bank robber? Do you think Errki blames his mother because he's had all the furniture moved around in that brain of his?"

Kannick gave Morgan a lightning-swift glance. Bank robber?

"Just read what it says on his T-shirt. I guess he blames 'the others.'"

"Am I being attacked?" Errki said simply. He was busy picking a pebble out of the sole of his sneaker. Then he started pulling out the laces. He was going to tie them around his thigh, which was still bleeding.

Kannick was squirming on the couch, and every time he moved, the springs creaked.

Morgan suddenly felt dizzy and faint. What were they doing? How long were they going to sit here? For some reason he couldn't stand the thought of being alone. He couldn't stand thinking of them being caught and then each sent off somewhere different, that Errki would be separated from him, that they would never see each other again. He had no one else. This hot, filthy room, the buzz from the whiskey, Errki's pleasant, low voice, and the fat boy with the downcast eyes—suddenly he didn't want any of it to end. The very thought took his breath away. Confused, he grabbed for the bottle. "Root, stem, and leaf," he muttered.

Kannick realized that they were both mad. Maybe they'd escaped from the asylum together. Two ticking time bombs. It was best to stay calm. He breathed as slowly as he could.

Errki had moved away. He was sitting on the floor, leaning against the old, broken wardrobe. It was peaceful now. The drums and the bagpipe had finally stopped. He was resting with his hand on the gun.

CHAPTER 19

A forest-service employee turned his red Massey Ferguson tractor onto the plateau, heading for the small stretch of forest road where he intended to park. Surprised, he stared at the green tarpaulin, then switched off the engine and got out.

He shoved the smooth green fabric off the roof of the car and peered inside. Empty. Except for a little pill bottle with a screw-on lid lying on the floor in the front. He opened the door, picked it up, and read the label. *Trilafon, 25 milligrams, three times a day.* For someone named Errki Johrma, prescribed by Dr. S. Struel. A small, white, abandoned car. Unlocked. He remembered something about a bank robbery that morning; it had been on the news. The car was a Renault Mégane. He went back to his tractor, swung it around again, and set course for home.

Less than an hour later two cars turned onto the plateau. Five men and three dogs spilled out. The three excited Alsatians were immediately growling and whining. A five-year-old male named Sharif was first, followed by Nero, who was slightly smaller and a lighter color. He was just as agitated as Sharif, tugging on his leash. The third dog had a shaggier coat and moved more slowly than the other two. His name was Zeb, and his handler was Ellmann. Every time they went out on patrol together, he wondered if it might be the last time. He looked down at the dog's dark head. It was almost time to retire him, and he didn't know if he had the energy to train a new dog. It seemed to him that after Zeb, any other animal would be a disappointment.

The starting point was not ideal. The dry, crackling forest wouldn't hold scents for long.

Sharif leaped into the white car. He sniffed at the driver's seat and the floor, at the carpet under the rubber mats, then at the passenger's seat, his tail wagging. He came back out and began sniffing at the dry ground, continuing to wag his tail vigorously, then started down the path. The other dogs repeated the procedure. The men stared at the dense woods and locked their cars. The dogs stared at their masters, waiting for the magic words that would release them.

All five men had guns. The hard weight at their belts was both comforting and frightening. The assignment was an exciting one for the three dog handlers. This was what they had pictured when they joined the police force as young recruits, before applying for the dog patrol. All three were mature men. If between thirty and forty could be considered mature, as Sejer had said wryly. They had hunted for many different things during their years of service, and been successful many times. They loved the peace of the woods, the not knowing, the work with the dogs. The sound of panting dogs, of twigs breaking, of rustling leaves, the buzzing of thousands of insects. All their senses were on high alert, their eyes fixed on the ground, taking in the smallest detail: a cigarette butt, a snapped twig, the remains of a fire. Studying the dogs, the way their tails moved, whether they were wagging briskly or were suddenly lowered, stopping altogether. At the same time they were waiting to hear something from Headquarters: word that the two had been found elsewhere, perhaps. Or that the bank robber had struck again, that the hostage had been found in good condition or lying in a ditch with his skull split open. Anything was possible.

It was the not knowing that excited them; no two days were alike. They might find someone hanging from a tree. Or sitting under a tree trunk, exhausted but happy to be discovered. Or dead from an overdose. And afterward, the release. The eased tension. But this time it was different. Two individuals on the run, and most likely desperate.

Track!

The magic word! The dogs were instantly attentive. For a few seconds they meandered around at the start of the path. But very quickly they set off, focused on only one thing: following the scent they had picked up in the car. Ellmann whispered softly, "No doubt about it, the dogs have picked up the trail."

The others nodded. The dogs pulled them up the slope, their muscles straining. All three animals were on it, with Sharif in the lead. The men panted after them, hot in their overalls. The three dogs stayed together. They had been given plenty of water before they set off, and they had the kind of stamina that the men could only envy. The men were in good condition; working with the dogs had seen to that—years of strenuous training. But the cursed heat was sapping their energy. How far could the two fugitives have gone?

The woods looked dead, as if screaming for water. The men had a map, and they knew where the paths led and the location of the old homesteads. One of the men stuck his hand in his pocket, looking for chewing gum. He kept his eyes on Nero. The dog swung his nose from side to side, every so often taking a detour, making a little circle, as if he wanted to turn around. But then he kept on going. Sharif was still in the lead. The fur on his head and back was black, his coat looked thick and shiny in the fading sunlight. His tail was like a big golden banner, and his paws were broad and powerful. None of the men could imagine anything more beautiful than a well-groomed Alsatian. An Alsatian was the perfect dog, the way a dog ought to look.

After fifteen minutes the handlers changed places and let Zeb go first. The competitive instinct was immediately aroused, and the dogs intensified their efforts. Even so, they gradually began to waver, their tails started to sink, they no longer sniffed so eagerly. At first Nero and Sharif pressed on, but then they wanted to turn back. The men took their time, seizing the opportunity to rest a little after the difficult climb. They were up on a ridge. From here they could look down at the main road and the barrier outside the tollbooth.

"Bet they stopped here to rest," Sejer said in a low voice.

The others nodded. They had stood here and looked down at the barrier and the squad car. Then they had pressed on. But in which direction?

"Here's a cigarette butt."

Skarre picked it up. "Roll-your-own. Big Ben paper."

He slipped it inside a plastic bag and put it in his pocket, then kept on searching, but found nothing more.

"Let's keep Zeb in the lead, and let the others reconnoiter," Ellmann suggested.

Nero and Sharif began sweeping the area from side to side, covering a range of about fifty yards. Zeb trotted on, sticking to the path. The scent was unclear. The dogs no longer seemed so confident, pausing now and then, acting distracted. The men looked back. Not down to the farm where the murdered woman lived. Maybe up to the old homestead sites? In this heat it seemed most likely that the fugitives had stopped to rest in one of the old mountain huts. If so, the dogs would find their trail up there, stronger than in this dry terrain.

It was utterly quiet in the woods. In the autumn there was much more activity, with hunters and berry pickers. But right now it was too hot for anyone to be taking a walk in the woods unless they had to. Or were being paid to, and were plagued by an incurable lust for adventure that coursed through their veins like tiny little ants and gave them no peace.

Sejer ran his hand over his forehead and then checked his gun. At the range he was a good shot, but he realized that wouldn't mean much when it came to a real exchange of gunfire. And that made him uneasy. A single error in judgment could have disastrous consequences. Suspension. Disability. Death. Anything could happen. For some reason he was feeling vulnerable, as if life had taken on more meaning. He forced the thoughts out of his mind and strode briskly on, casting a glance at Skarre, who had pulled down the bill of his cap to keep out the sun.

"God only knows what's happened to that poor man from the asylum," Sejer murmured.

"In my mind there's just as much basis for worrying about the other guy," said Skarre, looking at the chief inspector.

"We don't know that he killed her, only that he was there."

Skarre was wearing steel-rimmed glasses with clip-on sunglasses. "Take a look around," he said. "Not very populated up here, is it?"

"I only mention it to keep the facts straight. Let's just say that their positions are equal."

"Except that one of them has a gun," Skarre said.

They kept walking. The dogs led the men through the large wooded area and circled around on either side. Now and then they plodded through dense thickets, and in other places the path led them through clearings. Hot blood pumped through their bodies. The light was beautiful, a luxuriant gold, and the many hues of green in the trees were astonishing. Dark and intense in the shade, golden yellow out in the open. Leaves and boughs softly intertwining, needles that pricked at them, grass that caressed their legs, branches that snapped back and struck them in the face. Insects circled, but the men quickly gave up slapping at these pests because it wasted too much energy. Only once did Skarre wave his hand at an angry wasp that was trying to fly into his curls.

A while later they stopped at a trickling stream to let the dogs drink. The men splashed the cool water on their faces and necks. The dogs were still preoccupied with the scent, perhaps more impatient because it was faint. Tenacious and eager, never willing to give up as people might be if the fugitives turned out to have gone a long way. Maybe they were lying in the shade somewhere, resting, with their legs dangling in one of the small ponds. The idea of a cool dip began to pass from one mind to another. It was idiotic, but once the idea presented itself, they had no peace. Ice-cold, rippling water. The thought of submerging their burning-hot bodies, of rubbing the sweat out of their hair.

"In Vietnam," Ellmann said suddenly, "when the Americans hiked through the bush in the heat of the day, their brains would start to boil under their helmets."

"Boil? Good God." Sejer shook his head.

"They were never the same again."

"They wouldn't have been the same, no matter what. But honestly," he turned to looked at the others, "do you really believe that's possible?"

"Of course not."

"You're not a doctor, either, are you?" Sejer said dryly as he mopped his brow.

The men chuckled quietly. The dogs were not disturbed by the conversation. They kept on going, occasionally sticking their noses into the weeds along the path, but they didn't stop. They were making slow progress, but they stuck to the path, and the men guessed that the fugitives had preferred to stay on it, rather than veer off into the dense woods.

"We'll find them," Sejer said grimly.

"One thing that strikes me," Ellmann said, sighing as he followed Zeb with his eyes, "is the tragic nature of a man's destiny."

"What are you babbling about?" Skarre turned around.

"Testosterone. It's what makes men so aggressive. Testosterone, right?"

"And?"

"Well, that's why we almost never go searching for women on these assignments. Just think how scantily dressed they would be in this heat!"

Sejer made a low clucking sound. Then he thought about Sara. About the light rings around her pupils.

Skarre noticed the sudden shift in his expression. "Worried, Konrad?"

"I'm fine, thanks."

Their mood was still upbeat. A small plane appeared in the blue sky, white and shiny in the sunlight. Sejer stared at it for a long time. Up there it was cool and airy. In his mind he was aboard the plane with a parachute on his back. He opened the door, paused for a moment to look down. Then he threw himself out and plummeted for a while before he began to float comfortably on a column of air.

"Do you see that, Jacob?" Sejer turned around and pointed.

Skarre stared anxiously at the plane. His imagination began working overtime.

———

"Does anyone have a mirror?"

Morgan tried to focus on his nose, looking very cross-eyed.

"He who has friends doesn't need a mirror," Errki mumbled from over by the cupboard.

Morgan looked at Kannick. "The fellow's got a quick tongue, hasn't he? It's hard to believe."

"I think I may have one in my bow case," Kannick said. He was still afraid to look Errki in the eye. Maybe he was sitting there deciding on a horrible way to kill him. He had such a strange look on his face.

"Go and get it, Errki," Morgan told him.

Errki didn't reply. He was still feeling pleasantly drowsy,

tired in a good way. Morgan gave up and went out to the steps where the case stood and dragged it back inside along with the bow. He rummaged through the arrows and other equipment and found the mirror. A little square mirror, about four by four inches. Hesitantly he held it up to his face.

"Oh, fucking hell! That's the worst goddamn thing I've ever seen!"

Kannick hadn't thought about the fact that Morgan hadn't seen his own nose. And it was true. It did look awful.

"It's infected, Errki. I knew it!" He started pacing, holding up the mirror.

"The whole world is infected," Errki muttered. "Sickness, death, and misery."

"How long does it take for tetanus to set in?" Morgan wondered out loud. His hand shook so hard that the mirror swayed.

"Several days," suggested Kannick.

"Are you sure about that? Do you know about these things?"

"Not really."

Morgan sighed like a sullen child and threw down the mirror. The sight of his nose was about to strip him of his courage. It didn't hurt much anymore, and he didn't feel so sick either. Just listless, but that was due to other things, like the lack of food and water. It was important to think about something else. He looked at Kannick and narrowed his eyes.

"So you were a witness to a murder, huh? Tell me about it. What do you think happened?"

Kannick's eyes widened. "No," he said. "I wasn't a witness."

"You weren't? On the radio they said you were."

Kannick ducked his head and whispered. "I just saw him running away."

"And is that man present in the courtroom? Raise your hand and point him out for the jury," said Morgan theatrically.

Kannick clasped his hands on his lap. Not on his life would he point at Errki.

"Did you have to go blabbing to the police?"

"I didn't blab. They asked me if I saw anything. I just answered their questions," he said.

Morgan had to bend forward to hear what the boy was saying. "No use trying to wriggle out of it. It's obvious that you blabbed. Did you know the old woman?"

"Yes."

Errki had his head tilted to one side. He looked as if he were asleep.

"He couldn't help it," Morgan said. "He's all mixed up in the head."

"Mixed up?"

"He doesn't even remember it."

"He doesn't?"

"Maybe he doesn't even remember that I took him hostage when I robbed Fokus Bank this morning."

He gave the boy an amused look. "He was standing there so conveniently in the bank, and I needed him to help me escape. Do you know what?" Morgan chuckled. "Robbing a bank and taking a hostage is like buying an Easter egg with a prize inside. Some people are lucky and get a whole toy. But I just got a bunch of separate pieces to put together."

He had forgotten about his nose. "He doesn't remember anything. And besides, he just does what his inner voices tell him to do. I doubt you can understand that, but I feel sorry for Errki."

Morgan sat back down on the floor and looked at Kannick with a serious expression. "You know what? When I was a child, I went to a nursery school. We had school assembly every morning. We had to sit in a circle on the floor while one of the teachers read or sang. We had a game that was all about trying to catch a thought. The teacher would look deep into our eyes and whisper, 'Think about something!' And we would think really hard. Then she'd scream, 'Catch it, catch it!' And she'd reach her hand out into the air as if she were gathering up one of them. And we would do the same thing."

Morgan paused. "'Hold on to it!' she'd shout, and we'd hold on tight, terrified that it would fly away. And it did. Because when we opened our hands, there was nothing there. Just dirt and sweat. I suppose it was meant to be an exercise in concentration, but it only made us feel terrible. Grown-ups do so many damned strange things to children."

He shook his head in resignation at the thought. "Errki has the same problem. Either he's confused and can't hold on to his thoughts, or else he thinks the same thing over and over again. It's called obsessing. I know about problems like this; I worked with those kinds of people."

They could hear Errki grunting softly over by the wardrobe. "Do you know why he bit me on the nose?"

"I have no idea," Kannick whimpered.

"I wanted him to take a swim down there, and he refused. He can't swim. He doesn't like it when people nag him. You shouldn't nag him. All of a sudden he'll be hanging on to your ear, or worse."

"Can I go now?"

Kannick's voice was as thin as a thread. He spoke as softly as he could so that Errki wouldn't hear him.

Morgan rolled his eyes. "Can you go now? Why the hell do you think you should? Are we going to let you get off more easily than us? Did you do anything to earn that? This is our destiny," he said solemnly. "We're trapped here, waiting for the police to come and lock us up. But we refuse to give ourselves up. We're proud and brave, and we won't give up without a fight."

Morgan's voice was full of drunken pathos. He talks like Geronimo, Kannick thought. Errki wasn't the only one who was crazy. They both were. Maybe he was mad, too. It wasn't easy to tell, when it came right down to it. But he was living in a reform school, after all, not in a nuthouse. Or was it a nuthouse?

He suddenly felt sick and tried to gulp back the sensation that something woollen was growing in his throat. In a certain way he belonged here with these two men. He knew that.

"Is your mother still alive?" Morgan asked abruptly. He had pulled Kannick's arrow out of the wall and was studying it.

"I think so," the boy said glumly.

"Now, hold on a minute," Morgan snapped. "Are you really that bitter? Don't try to tell me that you don't know whether she's alive or dead. My mother's alive. She's on the dole. And I have a sister who runs a beauty parlor."

"So she should be able to fix your nose."

"Cut the sarcasm. She's doing really well. Is your mother alive, Kannick?"

"Yes."

"At the government's expense?"

"Huh?"

"I mean, does she have a job, or is she on the dole?"

"I don't really know."

"Does she send you money?"

"Just packages once in a while."

"Here's a tip, for the next time you have a birthday. Ask for a package of SlimFast."

Kannick had no idea what SlimFast was. He sat there thinking about his mother, whom he seldom saw. She only came if Margunn called and nagged her to. Usually she brought him chocolate. It was hard for him to remember what she looked like; they didn't even talk much. His mother didn't really look at him, she just gave him furtive glances, and then she'd cringe and look away in sheer fright. Suddenly he thought of something that had happened a long time ago. He had come home from school one day, stopped in the doorway of the kitchen, and stared at his mother. She looked different. Her hair had suddenly grown a foot longer, all in one day, in the few hours he'd been sitting at his desk.

"Did you get a wig?" he asked.

She tossed aside the tabloid she was reading and reluctantly turned to look at him. "No, I didn't. This is genuine hair that's been attached."

"Huh?" He was so surprised that he sat right down at the table. It wasn't just her hair, either. Her fingernails were suddenly long, too, dark red and as shiny as the paint on a new car.

"What do you mean 'attached'?" he asked with genuine curiosity. "Is it glued on?"

"Yes. It'll hold for weeks."

She swept her hair back, fanning it out to demonstrate for him. This new mane of hair had given her dignity. Her expression was different, she held her back straighter, carried herself like a queen.

The temptation was too great. Kannick lunged across the table and with a dirty hand grabbed a hunk of hair and pulled. It didn't budge. It was incomprehensible.

"You idiot!" she shrieked, getting up from the table. "Do you realize how much this cost?"

"You said that it was stuck on."

"And you just had to try to ruin it, didn't you?"

"Who did it?"

"My hairdresser."

"How much did it cost?" he asked sullenly.

"You'd like to know, wouldn't you? But that's none of your business. You don't have any money."

"No. Not even pocket money."

"What do you need pocket money for? You never do anything for me!"

"You never ask me to."

"What exactly can you do, Kannick?" Suddenly she leaned across the table and gave him a challenging look. "Is there anything you can do, Kannick?"

He picked at a spot of dried jam on the tablecloth. He couldn't think of anything, not a single thing. He wasn't good at reading, and he was terrible at sports. No one could beat him at darts, but he didn't mention that.

Later, when she was in the shower with her new hair tucked up under a plastic shower cap, he peeked inside her handbag. He knew there wouldn't be any money. She was smarter than Margunn, and she'd taken her money into the shower with her. But he found the receipt from the hairdresser's. It was hard for him to decipher the grown-up handwriting, but for once he made an effort. Hair and nails, 2,300 kroner, paid in full. He felt as though he couldn't breathe. Went roaring into the bathroom and tore the shower curtain aside.

"That was enough for a bicycle!" he shouted. "All the other children have bikes!"

She pulled the curtain back in place.

"Hair grows all by itself," he yelled, "and it's free!"

"Leave my things alone," she shouted back. "You need a father who can discipline you. I'll never get my hands on a proper man if I look like a witch. I have to make myself look good. It's all for your sake."

He could see the outline of her body through the shower curtain. It would be an effort to get her out of there, if he really wanted to. He could go over to the sink and run the cold water. Then the water in the shower would be so hot that she'd scorch herself. But he didn't feel like it. That was an old trick.

Kannick felt completely exhausted. He rested his forehead against his knees and sighed. He was hungry, too. The others had eaten all of his chocolate. But his thoughts were still pulling him back to the past. Once he had arrived home before his mother and found the box of drain cleaner inside the kitchen cupboard. He had a sudden, funny idea. He knew quite well how it worked: tiny, round, bluish white beads that were sprinkled over the drain in the sink when it blocked, which was all the time. Contact with the water turned the beads into a corrosive, foul-smelling gas. He found an empty milk carton, rinsed it out thoroughly, and dried it carefully. Then he sprinkled a generous quantity of beads in the bottom and went into the bathroom. He lifted up the grating from the drain in the shower, put the carton inside, and replaced the grating. He'd never forget his mother's howl when she went to take a shower. She turned on the hot water, and poisonous gas filled the whole bathroom. She came storming out, coughing and sputtering, while she screamed the ugliest curses she could think of, and there were plenty. He had created his own gas chamber!

Morgan interrupted his thoughts. "What else have you got in that case?" he asked. "Do you have anything I could use as a bandage?"

Kannick thought for a moment. He had nine different kinds of arrow. An extra bowstring. A bag of nocks with a tube of glue. String wax. Pliers. And a cotton cloth to clean the sight.

"A cotton cloth," he said.

"Is it big enough for my nose?"

Kannick glanced up at the discolored stump. "Yes."

Morgan stood up at once and walked over to the case. The cloth was yellow and fuzzy, the kind that was used to polish glasses.

Kannick looked at him. "You'll get lint in it."

"I don't give a shit. I want something to cover it. I can feel air in the wound every time I move my head, and I don't like it. I see you've got tape here, so I'll use that too. Give me a hand!" he said, waving the cotton cloth.

Kannick struggled a bit, but he did the best he could with his thick fingers, placing the cloth lightly over Morgan's nose and biting off a piece of tape with his teeth. It was on good and tight.

"How attractive," he remarked.

"So let's party!" Morgan said hoarsely, grabbing the bottle. "With a bottle and a girl, you lose track of time!" He winked at Kannick.

Errki was asleep. Morgan looked funny with the yellow rag on his nose. It's like the one my mother wore on the first sunny days of spring, Kannick thought, to stop her nose from getting burned when she sunbathed behind the house. She had lain there with her legs apart so the sun could reach every inch of skin. Sometimes he would spy on her. He could see a little bit of the dark curly hair up there. That's where the Polish man had been, and that's where he had been created. It wasn't something his mother had told him in so many words, but he knew it was true. He tried to remember the exact moment when this fact became apparent to him, but it was no use.

He thought about Karsten and Philip, and wondered whether they were out looking for him. What if they showed up here at the house? Maybe they would storm straight in! Every once in a while he glanced at the two men, wondering what they had talked about. He couldn't really see that Errki was a hostage, since he was the one with the gun, and it didn't seem as if that bothered Morgan. He reached for the bottle and took a gulp, then handed it back. The whiskey no longer burned his throat. He was almost anesthetized. His body was numb and felt oddly sluggish. He had to get away before he fell asleep.

"Can I go now?" he begged humbly as he glanced at Errki in the corner.

"Errki will decide," Morgan said curtly. "He's the one in charge in this house, and right now he's asleep. You'll just have to keep me company until he wakes up. A meatball like you should be able to keep me going for a long time." He snorted.

They were both beginning to feel very drunk. Morgan could no longer remember what he was doing here or what his plans were. He liked the quiet room, which was surprisingly dark compared with the dazzling light outside, and he liked listening to Errki breathing over by the wardrobe. People shouldn't have plans at all. Or appointments to keep. They should just sit still and let their thoughts drift. The fat boy sitting near him had slumped a little on the floor. There wasn't a sound from outside, no birds, not even a tree rustling. The whiskey was nearly gone. That worried him a bit. In a few hours he would be sober again. Sooner or later he would have to pull his heavy, lethargic body up off the floor and do something. But he had no idea what that would be. He had money, but no energy to leave the house and go back to the road or try to escape. He had no friends, except for the one who was in jail for robbing a post office and would soon be paroled. Morgan had driven the getaway car. They barely managed to escape and had parted company as soon as they reached safety. Two days later his friend was caught, arrested because of the pictures from the robbery that were shown on TV. The idiot had debts, and someone got their revenge. He had hidden the gun, somewhere in the woods he'd said, but they found the money in his apartment. He hadn't told the police about Morgan. It was so amazing, really incredible, that he had withstood the pressure and taken the punishment all alone. No one had ever done anything like that for Morgan before! Only afterward did it come creeping over him, the feeling of being eternally indebted. And later, the little hint in the visitors' room.

"When I get out, I won't have anything. Can you do something about that?"

Robbing Fokus Bank was only the beginning. A hundred thousand kroner, half for each of them, wouldn't last long. He knew his friend, knew his habits and his thirst. As soon as the money was gone, he'd be back. It would have been better if the police had caught him, too, Morgan thought dejectedly. There was a low buzzing in his brain. Maybe he was going mad, just like Errki. This was the first voice: an insect flying in circles inside, trying to get out.

CHAPTER 20

Morgan woke up with a start. Kannick was asleep next to him, his head tilted forward, pressing his double chin down and making it spread out against his chest in an indescribable mass of skin and fat. He stretched out his stiff legs and put his hand to his head. His nose wasn't aching as much; it felt almost completely numb. Maybe it was already dead. Soon it would come loose and fall off like a piece of rotten fruit.

Kannick opened his eyes. He noticed the bluish light outside.

"It's evening," Morgan whispered.

"I have to go home," Kannick pleaded. "They'll be looking for me!"

Morgan glanced over at Errki, trying to catch sight of the gun. It was stuck inside the waistband of his trousers. He stood up slowly, swaying a bit to get his balance, and then he walked over to the wardrobe. He stood there a moment, thinking, and bent down. It was dark in the corner. He put one leg on either side of the sleeping body and hesitantly placed a fumbling hand at Errki's waist. Suddenly he slipped in something wet and sticky and toppled over. In two seconds he was back on his feet, with a puzzled look on his face.

"Fucking hell!"

Kannick gave a start and blinked. "What's going on?"

"There's blood everywhere! He's bleeding like anything!"

Kannick felt a cold terror creep across his shoulders.

"Errki!" Morgan screamed, lurching back. "He's bled to death. He's cold!"

"No!" The scream was shrill and hoarse. Kannick clambered to his feet but immediately had to lean against the wall.

"He's dead!"

As if in a nightmare, Kannick watched Morgan slowly turn around and stare at him. "Do you realize what you've done? You've killed Errki with your bow. Damn it all, Kannick!"

Kannick shook his head. A sound came from his lips, like a shriek that dissolved before it was fully formed.

"I only hit him in the leg."

"You must have hit a vein in his groin. Maybe an artery."

Morgan moved back farther, keeping his eyes fixed on Kannick. "I've had enough of this. I'm getting out of this madhouse!"

He swayed violently. He needed the gun, but to get it he would have to touch the cold body, maybe even get blood on his hands.

"You've got to help me!"

Kannick was clinging to the wooden wall. He started to cry. "I didn't mean to! He opened the door, and I couldn't help it. You have to tell them what happened. Nobody else saw it!"

Morgan paused, moved by the sight of the fat, desperate boy. He swallowed hard, cast another glance at Errki's body, and sank down to the floor. "Things are bad enough for me without this. I robbed a bank and took a hostage. I'll get a stiff sentence."

"We could dump the body in the lake. We can say that he escaped!" Kannick was wringing his hands helplessly. "I didn't mean to do it. It was an accident! Let's dump him in the lake!"

"All you have to do is tell the police the truth. But I've got to get out of here."

Morgan's eyes narrowed. He was trying to pull himself together sufficiently to think of a way out.

Sobs gushed out of Kannick, a sea of tears, an outpouring of despair.

"It won't help to dump the body in the lake," Morgan said urgently. "There's blood all over the place in here. A whole pool of it."

"We can put the wardrobe over it."

"That won't help."

"Please!"

"They're looking for us. They could be here any minute. We don't have time. And we can't carry him down to the water without getting covered in blood. It's no use, Kannick. Besides, you're too young to end up in prison. You'll get off. Just like Errki would for murdering that old woman, because he's nuts. But I," he yelled, pounding his fists on the floor in fury, "I'm not going to get off. I don't have any goddamned excuse!"

He groaned and yanked at his hair, trying to remember how the day had begun. It struck him how unbelievably long it had been. It felt like a lifetime. A terrible feeling of paralysis overwhelmed him. His brain refused to function. It was that fucking whiskey. Kannick was stretched out on the floor, gasping.

"There's a steep slope behind the house," he sobbed. "Maybe the body would roll downhill all by itself."

"Jesus Christ. I can't take any more of this!"

Kannick stood up, walked across the room, and began shaking Morgan vigorously. "You have to. You have to!"

"No, I don't."

"We'll do it together. And then we'll take off. We have to! Nobody is going to miss him."

"You're wrong," Morgan said quietly. Surprised, he realized that this was true as soon as he said it.

He peered out the window, sobbing. The landscape off in the distance looked hazy. He had to get away, or go crazy, like

Errki. He would start rambling right now, if he allowed himself to. He could feel it: how he could sink down and leave the world behind. How he could look in astonishment at people talking, unable to understand what they said. But he wouldn't care. He would just let them carry on. It's not my concern. This society is fucked. There are too many things to think about. Like the blackmailer waiting in prison. Like the fat, wretched boy standing in front of him.

"We have to!" Kannick screamed.

Morgan let his head fall onto his chest. He could hear Kannick gasping, and something else, off in the distance, something that was getting closer. Dogs barking, far away.

"It's too late," he groaned. "They're coming."

———

Sejer studied the map.

"We're getting near the old homestead sites." He squinted and pointed. "I'll bet they're hiding out in one of those old houses over there."

"What are we going to do when we find them?" Skarre asked.

Sejer looked at each man in turn. "I don't think we should do anything dramatic. I suggest we stop a good distance away and shout, making it clear how many men we are and that we're armed."

"But what if he comes out with the hostage in front of him, holding a gun to his temple?"

"Then we let him go. He won't get far. We're five against two."

Skarre wiped the sweat from his face.

"Nobody draws his gun," Sejer said. "I don't want to end up having to carry one of you home in this damned heat. When it's all over, we're going to have to account for every detail. In writing. Truthfully, and with a clear conscience. Nobody even looks at his gun without my say-so. If I change my mind, I'll let you know."

He started walking, and the others huffed and puffed after him. They had complete confidence in him, but sometimes they thought he was a little too cautious. Assignments like this were rare. Not that they really wanted to be here, in this sweltering forest, but the taste of adrenaline was sweet.

"I think Himmerik Lake must be down there," Sejer said, pointing. "It's close, according to the map, although I can't see it from here. I bet you a round of beer the dogs head in that direction."

"I can't see any buildings." Ellmann shaded his eyes with his hand and peered at the dense grove of trees ahead of them.

"Maybe beyond those trees over there. At least they won't be able to see us."

They kept going. The dogs raced ahead, straight toward the grove. Occasionally Skarre glanced up at the sky, hoping that God was keeping an eye on them. There was something menacing about the quiet woods. There was a sense of foreboding about the silence, as if it were gathering force for a violent storm. But there were no clouds, only a faint haze above the trees. Steadily and relentlessly the ground was being sapped of all moisture; it rose up and settled like a milky mist over the landscape. Maybe the two men were waiting for them at an open window, with their guns ready. Or maybe they had gone over the ridge long ago. The grove of trees slowly came closer. No dwelling in sight.

They decided to use Zeb to listen out. Ellmann called him in, and the men stood and watched the big black and tan dog. His head swung gently from side to side, his ears turned like antennae, quivering faintly. Suddenly they pricked up, and Zeb turned his head toward the trees. His ears stood straight up, aimed at a spot they couldn't see. In his mind Ellmann drew a direct line from the dog's ears into the thicket.

"There's someone in there," he whispered.

Sejer went to investigate. Zeb tried to follow, but was held back with a yank on his leash, which made him utter a sharp yap. Sejer's hair shone like silver against the green as he crept forward. The seconds ticked by. Skarre was sweating. The men stroked their dogs. Sejer kept going. Just as he reached the thicket he veered to the left and stepped into the undergrowth at the edge. He tried to make his body relax. He could make out something in the trees now, something darker and denser. He put one hand on his gun. The leather holster felt hot to the touch. Soon the trees began to thin out, giving way to a clearing up ahead, and in the clearing stood a house. Dark and heavy. A log cabin. He stared at the windows, which were all broken. There was no one in sight. He crouched down in the grass, certain that he couldn't be seen from any of the windows. Of course they might still be inside, even though it was as quiet as the grave. Maybe they were sleeping or resting. Maybe they were waiting for him. Grass was growing on the roof of the house, dry and sun scorched. The windows were small, with mullions, and didn't admit much light. It was probably nice and cool inside. He could sense that someone was there, but still didn't hear a sound. Standing up and walking to the door seemed unthinkable. They might jump up and start firing in blind terror. He stayed where he was. A pinecone would make a dull thud if he threw it against the wooden wall, and might be enough to make one of the men come to a window to investigate. He searched under a dry pine tree and found a big cone. Maybe he should aim for the door. If anyone was there, they'd hear it. He could see a dark, brownish red patch on the stone steps. It looked like blood. He frowned. Was someone injured? He raised his arm and threw the pinecone. It made a small tap. Quickly he sank back down to a crouch. Nothing happened. He gave himself a full minute. The seconds ticked by. It was hard to crouch wearing overalls that were already too small for him.

The minute passed. He turned around and crept back to the others.

"I'm going inside the house."

Skarre gave him a worried look. "I don't think they're in there. It seems so quiet."

"Zeb heard something," Ellmann said.

Sejer and Skarre walked back to the cabin while the others stayed with the dogs. Sejer gave the door a shove.

"Hello! Police. Is anyone there?"

No one answered. Everything was quiet. He didn't expect the bank robber to storm out and shoot him. That wasn't how he was going to die. Besides, the house seemed completely deserted. He peeked inside the living room. Caught sight of a green couch, an old wardrobe, and, of all things, a gray case. He took a few steps forward, and whispered over his shoulder to Skarre, "They've been here."

For a moment he stood in the middle of the dusty floor and looked around the room, letting his eyes adjust to the dim light. Then he noticed the figure in the corner. A gaunt man with dark clothes and black hair. He was half-sitting and half-lying, his head leaning against the wardrobe. It looked very uncomfortable. Sejer was no longer thinking about his own safety, about whether someone might come rushing out at him. He walked across the room and knelt down next to the lifeless man. The first thing that struck him was how small he was. Thin and delicate and lacking any sign of strength. His eyes were closed, his face ghostly pale. He looked like a severely malnourished child, with a tangle of black hair reaching to his shoulders.

"Errki," Sejer whispered.

The body was lying in a pool of blood. He felt for a pulse on the thin neck, but found none. It was hard to see where the wound was, but he had clearly been struck somewhere in the abdomen. There was still a little warmth left in the body. Sejer was about to stand up when he heard a sound. He thought at first that it was Skarre, but suddenly something dark slid into his field of vision. He heard an ugly creaking noise. The wardrobe door swung slowly open on its squeaking hinges. The hair on the back of his neck stood up. He took a big breath. The creaking stopped, there was no one there. He couldn't see inside the wardrobe from where he was sitting, but no one could be inside. The bank robber wouldn't shoot his hostage and then hide inside an old wardrobe. He must be long gone. The door had swung open, but only because Sejer had walked across the floor and shaken the floorboards. He moved back and took a few steps, then stared inside the wardrobe. There was a flash of metal.

The gun was shaking violently. Sejer gasped in surprise and went to take out his own gun, but changed his mind. He stared uncomprehendingly at the creature standing there gaping back at him, at the terror in the pale face, at the raised gun. Inside the wardrobe stood Kannick. Sejer didn't understand it. He stared at the gun and the way the boy was holding it.

No mistakes, now. Steady, very steady. The boy is at breaking point and completely unpredictable. Stay calm, keep your voice down. Don't show you're afraid.

"I didn't mean to do it!" Kannick screeched. His voice cut through the silence and made Sejer jump even though he was prepared for it. "He got in the way! You can ask Morgan!"

He was aiming at Sejer's chest and would certainly hit him. If he were able to fire.

Sejer let his hands fall. "It's not cocked, Kannick." And then he added, "Who's Morgan?"

Kannick stared in surprise at the gun. Bewildered, he began fumbling with the safety catch, but his fingers were numb with fright and refused to obey. Finally he managed to do it. But Sejer had pulled out his own gun, and behind him stood a curly-haired man, also holding a drawn gun.

"He's in the bedroom," Kannick sniffled. And with that he dropped his gun on the floor, bent double, and began to throw up violently. He was still standing inside the wardrobe, vomiting over the rotting planks. Stew and wn.skey, everything poured out. He leaned against the wardrobe and let it happen. Sejer waited until he was done. Then he cautiously picked up the gun, handed it to Skarre, and left the boy with his colleague as he went off to find the bedroom.

Morgan had been standing behind the door, waiting. Now he made for the woods, using what little remaining strength he had to race across the yard toward the trees. Ellmann saw the blond hair and colorful shorts through the leaves. The poor man didn't have a chance.

The officer leaned down, grabbed the big dog's head, and whispered in his ear, "Zeb. Attack!"

The animal bounded forward and raced off like a furry bolt of lightning. Morgan was running. He didn't hear the dog come chasing after him, or anyone shouting. In fact, he only heard the sound of himself crashing through the undergrowth. He ran, but all his strength was drained in an instant. Zeb saw the white hands and aimed for the left one. There was nothing aggressive about what the dog was about to do; it was years of training and a clear command, nothing more. Morgan stopped and gasped for breath. His knees were about to buckle under him. He had to check to see if anyone was after him. At that moment he stumbled and landed on his stomach. He rolled over and sat on his behind in the grass. Terrified, he stared at what was coming toward him. A black and tan animal with gleaming jaws, his red tongue, the yellow teeth. The dog crouched down, preparing to jump. The white hands that he had been aiming for were gone. All he saw now was the red face, and in the middle of it, the yellow cloth. A perfect target. With one mighty leap he rushed forward and snapped his jaws. Morgan gave a heartrending shriek. When the men reached him, he was sitting there, sobbing, with his face buried in his hands. Sejer paused for a moment to listen. The whimpering held a clear element of relief.

CHAPTER 21

Sara sat very still, on the edge of her chair. Sejer was telling her the whole story. She wanted to know everything: what position Errki was lying in, whether he had felt any pain. Sejer said he didn't think so. Most likely he was exhausted, and the loss of blood had drained him of all strength. Perhaps he felt as if he were falling asleep. Sejer sat there for a long time, trying to remember all the particulars. There was only one small detail remaining.

"I can't believe Errki is dead," she whispered. "That he's really gone. In fact, I can see him in my mind, quite clearly. Somewhere else."

"Where?"

She smiled with embarrassment. "Floating around in a vast darkness, without a worry in the world, looking down at us. Maybe he's thinking: if only they knew how beautiful it is, all those people down there, struggling away."

The image brought a smile to Sejer's face, a brief, melancholy smile. He searched for something to say, something that might take away the sting of what he was going to have to tell her.

"I untangled the toad," she said suddenly.

"Thanks. That's a relief."

She was wearing a thin jacket, which she pulled tighter. He

hadn't turned on the ceiling lights, only the desk lamp, with its green shade casting a watery glow over the office.

"There's something you should know."

She looked up, and tried to read his expression.

"We found a wallet in Errki's jacket." He cleared his throat. "A red wallet, which belonged to Halldis Horn. It contained approximately 400 kroner."

He fell silent, waiting. The greenish light made her look pale.

"One–nil, in Konrad's favor," she said, smiling sadly.

"I haven't won." He couldn't think of anything else to say.

"What are you thinking about?" Sara asked.

"Is someone coming to pick you up?"

The question slipped out before he had time to think. Maybe he could drive her home. But Gerhard no doubt had a car, and if she called him, he'd be there in a flash. He pictured the man in his mind. He was sitting in a living room somewhere, staring at the clock, glancing at the telephone, ready to come and get the woman who belonged to him and no one else.

"No," she said, shrugging her shoulders. "I came by taxi. The boss is in a wheelchair. Shut up in the house with me. He has multiple sclerosis."

Sejer was surprised. He couldn't imagine Sara with an invalid husband. He had pictured things so differently. A thought that wasn't entirely pure crossed his mind.

"Why don't you let me drive you home?"

"Would you mind?"

"There's nobody waiting for me. I live alone."

It didn't make a difference, one way or the other, that he had finally managed to say it.

I live alone.

Had he ever described himself that way before? Or had he merely given his status as "widower" or "single"?

Neither of them spoke in the car. Out of the corner of his eye he could see her knees; the rest was merely a presence, an inkling, a longing. His hands rested on the wheel, giving him away. Sejer felt as though they were screaming out loud that they needed something to hold. What was she thinking? He didn't dare turn and look at her. Errki was dead. She had worked with him all those months, and she had not been able to save him.

She gave him directions to her street. When he reached her house he realized that he would have preferred to drive with Sara beside him to the ends of the earth and back.

"I know it's irrational," she said suddenly, "but it's so hard for me to comprehend."

"That Errki's dead?"

"That he could have killed Halldis Horn."

He sat with his hands in his lap, twisting and turning them, and said awkwardly, "There was something you said, earlier today. That sometimes, once in a great while, things happen that we simply can't explain."

She shrugged. "I refuse to give up."

"What do you mean?"

"I'm going to have to search for an explanation. Find out how it happened."

"Where will you search?"

"In my papers. In my memory. For what he said, and all the things that he didn't say. I simply have to understand."

"Will you let me know what you find?"

At last she looked up and smiled. "Could you see me in?" she asked.

He was puzzled by her request, but he obediently escorted her to the door, and watched as she put her key in the lock after first giving a brief tap on the doorbell. Maybe it was a signal to Gerhard that she was home. Sejer didn't want to meet her husband. If he saw him, his fantasies about their relationship would become all too real. Her home was a single-story bungalow with extra-wide doors, equipped for a disabled person. They were standing in the door of the living room. Sejer thought of a book he had read as a young man. The main character, who was deeply in love, escorted a woman home. He had lost his heart to her and thought that she lived alone. On the way she told him that Johnny was waiting for her. At that instant, his heart broke, until they stood in the living room and he discovered that Johnny was a hamster.

Gerhard Struel was sitting at a desk, reading, wearing a knitted jacket in spite of the heat. The man was actually older than Sejer. He was bald, and his dark eyes were framed by glasses. On the floor next to him lay an Alsatian. The dog raised his head and stared.

"Papa," Sara said. "This is Chief Inspector Konrad Sejer."

Gerhard Struel was not a hamster. He was a father!

Sejer tried to pull himself together as he clasped the outstretched hand. Why did she want him to see this? The house. The father who needed care. Perhaps she was saying, "Take me away from all of this!"

"I must get home to my dog," he said apologetically.

"Oh, I'm sorry," she said, fumbling with her jacket. "I didn't mean to take up your time."

Gerhard Struel gave Sejer a long look. "So it's over, then?"

Yes, he thought, it's over. Even before it started. I can't make a move now. It's not right. He had landed himself in that awkward situation where he would be forced to pick up the phone and call her if he wanted to see her again. She had made the first move. Now it was his turn.

Sara held out her hand. "We made an excellent team, don't you think?"

She had planted a seed. Maybe it would grow. An excellent team.

He found her name in his name book. Sara. It meant "princess."

Later he lay in bed, staring at the ceiling, carrying on an imaginary conversation with her.

I knew you would turn up. I've been waiting for you.

Tell me something about yourself, she said with a smile.

What do you want to know?

A childhood memory. Something beautiful.

Here's something beautiful: The summer I turned five, my father took me to the cathedral in Roskilde. I had no idea what was inside. I left the warm sunlight outside and stepped into the nave. The church was filled with sarcophagi. Father explained that people lay inside them, all of the ministers who had worked at that church. They lay there in full view, for everyone to see, row after row, on either side of the pews. The coffins were made of marble, and they were unbelievably beautiful. It was cold in the church, and I was freezing. I started tugging at my father's hand to make him take me back outside. Eventually he took pity on me. "They're sleeping the eternal sleep," he said with a smile. "While the two of us have to go home and work in the yard, even though it's so hot! I have to mow the grass, and you have some weeding to do."

I couldn't stop thinking about the sight of all those coffins, until my mother came out to the yard and brought us strawberry pudding. It was chilled from being in the cellar, but the cream was warm. I ate the pudding and thought that it couldn't really be true. There wasn't anything inside those coffins, just cobwebs and dust. And the pudding tasted so wonderful it seemed impossible that life wouldn't last forever. I looked up at the blue sky and suddenly caught sight of a flock of angels with white wings hovering overhead. I thought they had come to get us, but we hadn't even finished our pudding! Father saw them, too. He smiled happily. "Look, Konrad! Look how fine they are!"

It was fifteen parachute jumpers from the national guard, and they landed on the soccer field nearby. I will never forget how beautiful they were, how silently they drifted down.

Sejer lay awake for a long time. He was beyond tired now, but his eyes seemed to be lit from within. They were wide open, staring into the dark. He tossed and turned, and every time he moved, Kollberg's ears pricked up. It was too hot to sleep. He started scratching. Resigned, he climbed out of bed, got dressed, and went into the living room. Kollberg padded after him. Did he really want someone so close? Beside him in bed in the morning, every morning, year after year? What would Kollberg say? And two male dogs, that wasn't going to work.

"Want to go out?" he asked. The dog barked and trotted to the door. It was 2 A.M. The building stood like a lonely pillar in the starless sky.

At first he thought of going into town, to the cemetery, but he changed his mind. He couldn't believe that he felt guilty. He'd read about this happening, and he didn't know how he was going to deal with it. Maybe I should move, he thought. Get a new car. Draw a kind of line: before and after Elise. I can't cope otherwise. Something is holding me back.

He was in his shirtsleeves. The night air against his bare arms soothed the itching. He walked and walked, just as Errki had walked and walked.

If you're going to remain in this world, you have to live life, he decided. He turned around and looked back at his apartment building. There was something about the structure, the heavy pillar of gray cement with its muted lighting, that seemed to evoke human anxiety. I have to get away from here, he thought, I want to be on the ground. Stand in the grass and see trees.

"Shall we move, Kollberg? Out to the country?"

The dog's eyes gazed into his.

"You don't know what I'm saying, do you? You live in another world. And yet we get along so well. Even though you're a dunce."

Kollberg sniffed eagerly at his hand. He put his hand in the pocket of his khaki trousers and took out a long-forgotten dog biscuit. Kollberg didn't know why he was getting a reward, but he gobbled it up and wagged his tail gratefully.

"The worst thing is that I'll never know why," he murmured. "What really happened between them? What did Halldis say or do to frighten him? Both of them are dead now, and we'll never know. But we don't know anything about most things in the world. How strange that we accept that fact. As if we were waiting, all our lives, for something further in the future, something totally different that will be comprehensible. But you, you dunce," he looked down at the dog, "you're just waiting for your next meal."

As he turned his back on the cemetery and walked home, he felt an ache deep inside.

———

Skarre looked cheerful. Showered and tanned.

"What's going on?" Sejer stared at him.

"Nothing. Just feeling good, that's all."

"I see," he said. "Have you heard from the lab? Did they get a match on the fingerprints?"

"Errki's prints were everywhere inside the house. He even touched the mirror. The prints on the hoe are more problematic, but they're working on them."

"Did you write up the interrogation last night?"

"Here you go, boss." He handed Sejer some documents in a plastic folder and bit his lip. "What's going to happen to the boy?"

"Not much. Garpe confirmed that it was an accident. Most likely he'll get to remain at Guttebakken, and by all accounts that seems the best solution. He's certainly been through enough lately. What he needs is some peace, some stability. I'm going out to see him now. He's probably not in very good shape, but I have this tiny hope that he might have found out something about Errki that Garpe missed. Maybe he can offer some explanation."

Skarre gave him a long look. "Is that likely? He's just a boy who's terrified out of his wits."

"Children are observant," Sejer said stubbornly.

"Not really. They just notice different things than grown-ups."

"And that could be useful to us."

Skarre frowned. "There's something going on. What is it?"

"What do you mean?"

"It seems as though you can't accept what happened. And that's not like you."

"I'm just curious," Sejer replied brusquely.

"You look tired."

"I was itching all over last night!" And with that dramatic piece of information, Sejer disappeared into his office.

"Your name is Morten Garpe?"

"That's right."

"But you call yourself Morgan?"

"My friends, if I had any, would call me Morgan."

"You don't have any friends? So why do you call yourself Morgan?"

"It sounds a lot cooler, don't you think?"

Skarre's notes neglected to mention that at this point they both laughed.

"So, Morten, you're all alone in the world?"

"I'm short on buddies. I have only one, and he's in prison. Plus a sister in Oslo."

"He's in prison?"

"For armed robbery. I drove the getaway car. He didn't tell the police about me. The money was for him."

"So he's had his hooks into you for a long time, is that right?"

"Yes."

"And you wanted to put an end to it?"

"I suppose I'm going to get such a long sentence that it doesn't matter anymore."

"You're right. It doesn't. We'll talk about the robbery later. Tell me about Errki."

Skarre indicated that Morgan paused for a long time before he spoke.

"He told me everything about his mother and what happened to her. Errki and I are both Scorpios. He was born a week after me. The best and the worst people are Scorpios, did you know that?"

"No. What do you mean by telling you everything?"

Sejer lifted his eyes from the report and thought about the experts who for years, and with great cunning, had tried to coax the truth out of Errki. This man seemed to have succeeded in a matter of hours.

"Did he seem to remember anything about the murder of Halldis Horn?"

"Not much. He said that she screamed and threatened him. He had a faraway look in his eyes when he thought about it."

"Did he tell you that he killed her? Did he say that in so many words?"

"No. He looked at me with those strange eyes of his and said, 'Things just happen.'"

"Did he seem like a violent person?"

"You saw my nose before they bandaged it. It's going to look really pretty when it grows back. Not that it makes any difference. I actually don't care. The only thing that makes me happy is the thought of Tommy's ugly mug when I bang on the wall from my cell next door, and he realizes there isn't going to be any money."

"His name is Tommy?"

"Tommy Rein."

"Is that so?! What did you and Errki talk about during the hours you spent together?"

"I can't really remember it all. He said so many weird things. We talked a lot about death. Have you thought about that? That we're actually going to die? I see people dying around me, but I can't comprehend that it's ever going to happen to me. I tried to imagine it today, several times. But it's like some trick mathematical equation I just can't get my head around. Do you get it?"

"Get what?"

"The fact that you're going to die?"

"Yes, I do."

"Then I suppose there's something wrong with me."

"Don't worry, it will sink in sooner or later. I know lots of people older than you who haven't faced up to it yet. Where did Errki get the gun?"

"I asked him about that. He muttered something strange, like if your neighbor wishes for a cow, God will send you an ox."

"How drunk was he toward the end?"

"Not nearly as drunk as I was, but he was really unsteady on his feet."

"What did Errki and Kannick say to each other?"

"Not much of anything. They were watching each other like dogs. Kannick was scared out of his mind. He hardly even dared look at Errki."

"Did Errki seem threatening toward the boy?"

"I don't think so. We treated him well, we didn't harm him in any way, we were just drunk. By the time Kannick showed up, the seas were high, to use a figure of speech. The strange thing was that after a while it seemed as if the boy rather enjoyed being there. He settled down. In some way, we belonged together, the three of us. Nobody felt like doing anything. We were just waiting for you."

"What was Kannick's reaction when you discovered that Errki was dead?"

"He panicked. Begged and pleaded with me to help him."

"Help him do what?"

"Convince you that it was an accident."

"Was it an accident?"

"Definitely. He was aiming at the door. He didn't know that we were inside, or that Errki was going to walk through the door at that very moment."

"I see. What else?"

"What do you mean?"

"Did he make any suggestions about running away or trying to hide the body?"

"No, no. Absolutely not. I persuaded him not to."

"So he did suggest something like that?"

"Eh, no, not really. He didn't know what he was saying. He was in a state of panic. And that's not so strange, is it? Lucky for him that he's only twelve and still a minor."

CHAPTER 22

Sejer sank behind the wheel and slammed the door shut. Even though he had not slept well, he suddenly felt inexplicably clearheaded. He had a strange feeling that this was the decisive moment. He could feel it. Time stood still. He stared out the car window, trying to find something outside that would explain this sensation. He felt petrified, couldn't move. It wasn't unpleasant, just unfamiliar. He looked at his hands on the steering wheel. At every single hair on the back of his hands, at the fine lines across his knuckles. At the white fingernails, clean and even. At his watch and the little gold crown on the watch face. He met his own eyes in the rearview mirror. His face looked older than he remembered, but tremendously alert. The honking of a horn roused him. He put the car in gear and drove across the square, past the rows of parked cars.

The boy was standing up straight, his left foot pointed out, his right foot pointed forward. He raised his head and lifted his chin. His arms hung loosely at his sides. He took a long, deep breath, and then slowly exhaled. He turned his head to the left, cautiously, almost surreptitiously. Not hurried, but gently, very gently. He squinted and looked at the gold circle thirty yards away, noting how it grew sharper. Again he took a breath, a deep one, and held it. His enormous chest expanded, and at the same

263

moment he raised the bow. He drew, anchored, and took aim. Saw the little red dot touch the bottom edge of the target. He wanted a ten right now. He was good enough to do it, at those perfect moments when everything clicked. The arrow flew from the bow. The string thrummed and then, in a gesture that was as elegant as it was practiced, he lowered the bow just as the arrow plunged into the bull's-eye with a sharp thwack. He expelled the air from his lungs and felt in his quiver for another arrow without moving his eyes, without shifting his feet. Nocked the arrow into the string. He wanted three tens. If he was lucky, the second arrow would land next to the first one with a clattering sound. Again he inhaled and closed his eyes. Then opened them and stared at the target and the red feathers of the first arrow that were visible in the center of the gold circle.

He heard a noise, but tried to ignore it. A good archer doesn't allow any distractions, he continues without losing concentration. The noise got louder and stronger. He didn't like it. He wanted to complete the series of three arrows. It was a car. Arrow number two flew from the string. Eight points. He grunted with annoyance and turned his head. A police car drove into the courtyard.

Kannick lowered his bow and stood motionless. It was Sejer. He had probably just come to say hello, to ask him how he was doing, and whether he had slept OK. He was nice. Nothing to be scared of. Kannick smiled.

"Good morning, Kannick."

Sejer was not smiling. He looked very serious. Not friendly, like last time, but as if he were worried about something. He turned to look at the target.

"You got a ten," he said.

"Yes," said Kannick proudly.

"Is that hard?" He gave the shiny bow an inquisitive look, without changing his expression.

"Yes, it's hard. I've been working at it for over a year. I would have got another ten, but you arrived and distracted me."

"I beg your pardon." Sejer looked the boy in the eye with a grave expression. "We took your bow away from you. Yet here you are, practicing. How do you explain that?"

Kannick looked at the ground. "It's Christian's. He let me borrow it."

"But I thought you weren't allowed to shoot without supervision?"

"Margunn is in the bathroom. I have to practice for the national championships," he said sullenly.

"I realize that, but I'm still going to have to talk to Margunn." Sejer nodded, first toward the building and then toward the target with its bull's-eye made of reinforced cardboard. This was the boy's only passion, and here he was about to take it away from him. He hated this. At the same time, something was ticking inside him, like a bomb just before it explodes. He felt his heart beating faster. It might not mean anything, but then again it might mean everything, this tiny detail that he saw. He tried to control himself.

"But I can shoot out here in the open, can't I?" Kannick asked, his voice both pleading and sulky. "Just not up in the woods, right? If I'm going to have a chance at the championship, I've got to train every day until the last minute."

"And when is the tournament?"

Sejer didn't recognize his own voice. It sounded hoarse and raw.

"In four weeks."

Kannick was still standing with his feet in shooting position. Wearing black moccasins. Size 9. They had leather soles, and so no zigzag pattern underneath, like sneakers had. Usually twelve-year-old boys wore sneakers. It surprised Sejer a bit that he was wearing moccasins. They looked like dress shoes, and didn't really go with the cutoff jeans that were serving as shorts. He kept on fighting the strange sensation that was rising inside of him.

"Did you sleep well last night?" he asked kindly.

Kannick listened in confusion. The policeman's voice was gentle, but his eyes were cold as slate.

"I slept like a rock," he said bravely. His own lie made him dizzy. Too much had happened. He had woken up when Margunn came in to change Philip's sheets, and he'd had to struggle to keep his breathing calm and regular. At the same time he was afraid to fall asleep again. He had a bad dream that kept bothering him.

"I didn't sleep well," Sejer said flatly.

"Oh?" said Kannick, growing more and more uneasy. He wasn't used to having grown-ups confide in him. But this man was different.

"Would you shoot an arrow while I watch?" he asked.

Kannick hesitated. "All right. But now I'm not in the rhythm, and that means I may not make a good shot."

"I'm just curious," Sejer said quietly. "I've never seen anyone shoot an arrow from close up."

He watched Kannick. The whole procedure—finding his concentration, raising the bow, taking aim, and shooting—was a series of aesthetic movements, even when carried out by this mountain of a boy. The bow pulled together the shapeless figure in a fascinating way. Kannick shot a nine and then lowered the bow.

Sejer glanced up at the building and then at the boy.

"You wear gloves when you shoot?" he said, nodding at his hands.

"Archer's gloves," Kannick said. "Otherwise the string would flay open your fingertips. Some people use a leather brace, but I prefer gloves. Actually, you're only supposed to wear one, on the hand that pulls back the string. But for the sake of symmetry I wear both gloves, and it works fine. You know," he added desperately, "every archer has his own style. Christian blinks once, right before he shoots."

"They're special," Sejer said, staring at the gloves. "They only have three fingers?"

"You only use three fingers to draw the string and let go. The thumb and little finger aren't needed."

"I see."

"These are spare gloves that haven't been used much. That's why they seem stiff," Kannick explained. "But they'll get softer after a while."

"They're new?" Sejer's eyes narrowed. "Why are they new?"

"Why?" Kannick was getting jumpy. "Well, because, I threw out the old ones."

"Oh, I see."

Sejer fixed his eyes on the boy. Kannick looked down at his hands, at the three fingers inside the thin leather. Thin straps connected them to a narrow strip around his wrist, fastened with Velcro.

"Why did you throw them out?"

"Why?" Kannick felt more and more agitated. "Why not? They were old and worn out."

"Is that right?" Sejer was breathing hard through his nose. "And where did you throw them out?"

"Where? I don't remember."

He was squirming and sweating. It was so damn hot. The other boys had gone swimming with Thorleif and Inga, but he hadn't wanted to go along. He felt miserable in a swimsuit, and he needed to practice. Somewhere out there was a trophy waiting for him. For the first time in his life he was going to beat everyone else. Why hadn't Margunn come back? What was happening?

"Where did you throw them, Kannick?"

"In the incinerator."

He started shifting his feet uneasily.

"You moved your feet."

"Damn it!"

"You lied to me, Kannick. You said that you saw Errki up there."

"But I did! I saw him!"

"Errki saw you. That's not the same thing."

Sejer had to struggle to keep his voice calm. "I'm going to tell you one thing. I believe you when you say that Errki's death was an accident. Morgan confirmed that."

For a moment Kannick looked relieved.

"But I doubt that you have any remorse about it."

"What do you mean?" Kannick asked anxiously.

"Now that Errki's dead, he can't tell any tales. You got the jump on him. That's why you reported your story to Gurvin. Before Errki managed to say you were the one who did it, you rushed off to say it was him. Nobody would believe Errki, the lunatic."

At that moment Margunn came toward them. She gave the two of them an uncertain look and cleared her throat nervously. "Is something wrong?"

Sejer nodded. Margunn grew pale.

"Kannick," she said finally, as if to fill the terrible silence with something, even though it wasn't necessary. "You're not allowed to wear those moccasins; they're for Karsten's Confirmation. Where did you put your sneakers?"

The bow sank. Kannick's heart contracted violently and pumped a rush of hot blood into his face. The future had arrived.

———

This is what might have happened. Kannick was up in the woods with his bow. He shot a crow and was about to go home, when he had the idea to go over and see Halldis. Maybe he saw her working on her lawn, with her back to the door. He slipped inside and found the wallet in the bread box. Maybe he was lucky, or maybe he knew that's where she kept it. He tiptoed out again. To his horror, he saw that she was standing on the steps with the hoe in her hands. Kannick, the boy who usually acted before thinking, panicked. He tore the hoe out of her hands, and maybe they struggled for a few minutes before she lost her grip and the weapon was his. He lifted it up and struck. He was wearing his archery gloves and left only slight prints. Halldis collapsed. He ran across the lawn, stopping for a moment at the well to look back. Suddenly he caught sight of the dark figure between the trees. He knew he had been seen. He raced off down the road, but dropped the wallet. Errki went over to the house and saw Halldis. Apparently he went into the kitchen, pottered around in disbelief, touching the doors and windowsills, and leaving tracks from his sneakers. On the road he found the wallet that Kannick had dropped in fright. He stuffed it in his pocket and continued on, overwhelmed by the horror that had occurred, heading toward town and human company. Kannick ran to Officer Gurvin and reported Halldis's death. He had seen someone up there—how convenient. The madman Errki. What had Morgan said?

They were watching each other like dogs.

Sejer took his cell phone out of his jacket pocket and punched in a number.

Skarre answered. "What's going on?"

He looked around. "Not much."

He glanced out of the car window at the hazy woods. If only he could dive straight into the sea. Get out of this dusty heat.

"Did anyone call?" he asked lightly.

Skarre was silent. Over the last twenty-four hours he'd begun to have his suspicions.

"Define 'anyone.'"

"Good Lord, anyone at all."

"Nobody called," Skarre said at last.

"OK."

They were both silent for a moment.

"Has something happened?" Skarre asked.

"Errki wasn't the one who killed Halldis."

"Oh, great. That's all I needed to hear right now. So we'll have to start from scratch. Tell me something else, I'm in no mood for jokes."

"I'm not joking. It wasn't him."

"Right, boss!"

There was dead silence. Skarre thought about it for a long time.

"All right," he said at last. "I think I'm starting to understand what you're getting at. A girl called the station. A cashier from Briggen's Grocery. She'd thought of something vitally important that I absolutely had to know."

"Tell me what she said."

"One of the children from Guttebakken had gone up to Halldis's farm several times with Oddemann Briggen to help him out. Can you guess who it was?"

"Kannick," Sejer said.

"Yes. He used to get paid in chocolate. He might have known where she kept her wallet."

Sejer nodded.

"By the way, someone was here."

"Define 'someone.'"

"Dr. Struel."

"Is that so? What did she want?"

"I have no idea. She asked for some paper and an envelope so she could leave you a message. It's on your desk."

Sejer started the engine. His thoughts were whirling.

"Jacob," he said, with a gleeful tone. "You know what this means, don't you?"

"Now what are you talking about?"

"You're going to have to take that dive."

"Yes, well, I suppose I am."

There was a long pause.

"But having said that, I don't approve of betting. It doesn't matter to me one way or the other. I won't lose any respect for you if you decide not to do it."

"But your respect for me won't exactly increase, either, will it?"

"I have the greatest respect for you already."

"Of course I'll jump."

"Your faith is strong, isn't it?"

"I'm sure this won't be the first time that I really put it to the test, but I suppose it's about time I did."

Sejer opened the door to his office and went in. A white envelope was lying on his desk, on top of the blotter, which was a world map. It lay in the middle of the Mediterranean, like a boat with white sails. He picked up the envelope and slipped a finger under the flap. His hands shook as he pulled out the piece of paper.

Skarre came barging in. He stopped abruptly at the sight of his boss standing there, shaking, with a piece of paper in his hand.

"I beg your pardon," he said, embarrassed. "What's going on?"

Turn the page to begin the first chapter
of Karin Fossum's new novel,

WHEN THE DEVIL

HOLDS THE CANDLE

the next Inspector Sejer mystery.

Available at bookstores everywhere.

CHAPTER 1

The courthouse. September 4, 4 P.M.

Jacob Skarre glanced at his watch. His shift was over. He slipped a book out of his jacket pocket and read the poem on the first page. It's like virtual reality, he thought. Poof!—and you're in a completely different landscape. The door to the corridor stood open, and suddenly he was aware that someone was watching him, someone just beyond the range of his excellent peripheral vision. A vibration, light as a feather, barely perceptible, finally reached him. He closed the book.

"Can I help you?"

The woman didn't move, just stood there staring at him with an odd expression. Skarre looked at her tense face and thought she seemed familiar. She was no longer young, maybe about sixty, and wore a coat and dark boots. There was a scarf around her neck, just visible; he could see it above her collar. Its pattern offered a sharp contrast to what she most likely possessed in the way of speed and elegance: racehorses with jockeys in colorful silks against a dark blue background. She had a wide, heavy face, elongated by a prominent chin. Her eyebrows were dark and had grown almost together. She was clutching a handbag against her stomach. Most noticeable of all was her gaze. Her eyes were blazing in that pale face. They fixed him with a tremendous force. Then he remembered who she reminded him of. What an odd coincidence, he thought, as he waited for her to speak. He sat there as if riveted by the silence. Any minute now, she was going to say something momentous.

"It has to do with a missing person," she said.

Her voice was rough. A rusty tool creaking into motion after long idleness. Behind her white forehead burned a fire. Skarre could see it flickering in her irises. He was trying not to make assumptions, but obviously she was possessed. Gradually it dawned on him what sort of person he was dealing with. In his mind he rehearsed the day's reports, but he could not recall whether any patients had been listed as missing from the psychiatric institutes in the district. She was breathing heavily, as if it had cost her considerable effort to come here. But she had made up her mind, driven by something. Skarre wondered how she had got past the reception area and Mrs. Brenningen's eagle eye.

"Who is missing?" he asked in a friendly voice.

She kept staring at him. He met her gaze with the same force, curious to see if she would flinch. Her expression turned to one of confusion.

"I know where he is."

Skarre was startled. "You know where he is? So he's not missing?"

"He probably won't live much longer," she said. Her thin lips began to quiver.

"Whom are we talking about?" Skarre said. He hazarded a guess: "Do you mean your husband?"

"Yes. My husband."

She nodded resolutely, stood there, straight-backed and unmoving, her handbag still pressed to her stomach. Skarre leaned back in his chair.

"Your husband is sick, and you're worried about him. Is he old?"

It was an inappropriate question. Life is life, as long as a person is alive and means something, maybe everything, to another human being. He immediately regretted having asked, picked up his pen from the desk, and began twirling it between his fingers.

"He's like a child," she said sadly.

He was surprised at her response. What was she talking about? The man was sick, possibly dying. And senile, it occurred to him. Regressing to his childhood. At the same time Skarre had a strange feeling that she was trying to tell him something else. Her coat was threadbare at the lapels, and the middle button had been sewn on rather badly, creating a fold in the fabric. Why am I noticing these things? he wondered.

"Do you live far from here?" He glanced at his watch. Perhaps she could afford a taxi.

She squared her shoulders. "Prins Oscars Gate 17." She enunciated the street name with crisp consonants. "I didn't mean to bother you," she said.

Skarre stood up. "Do you need help getting home?"

She was still staring into his eyes. As if there were something she wanted to take away with her. A glow, a memory of something very much alive. Skarre had a weird sensation, the sort of thing that happens only rarely, when the body reacts instinctively. He lowered his gaze and saw that the short blond hairs on his arms were standing on end. At the same moment, the woman turned around and walked slowly to the door. She took short, awkward steps, as if she were trying to hide something. He went back to his chair. It was 4:03 P.M. For his own amusement, he scribbled a few notes on his pad.

"A woman of about sixty arrives at the office at 4 P.M. She seems confused. Says her husband is missing, that he doesn't have long to live. Wearing a brown coat with a blue scarf at her neck. Brown handbag, black boots. Possibly mentally ill. Left after a few minutes. Refused offer of help to get home."

He sat there, turning her visit over in his mind. She was probably just a lost soul; there were so many of them nowadays. After *a while he folded the piece of paper and stuck it into his shirt pocket. The incident didn't belong in his daily report.*

———

HAS ANYONE SEEN ANDREAS? That was the headline in the town's largest newspaper, set in bold type. That's the way newspapers express themselves, using an informal tone to address us directly, as if we were on a first-name basis and have known each other a long time. We're supposed to break down the barriers of formality and use a straightforward, youthful tone in this fresh, onward-storming society. So even though very few people actually knew him or used his first name, let's just cut right to the chase and ask: Has anyone seen Andreas?

And the picture of him. A nice-looking boy of eighteen, with a thin face and unruly hair. I say "nice-looking"; I'm generous enough to admit that. So handsome that things came easily to him. He strutted around with that handsome face and took things for granted. It's a familiar pattern, but it does no one any good to look like that. Handsome in a timeless, classic way. A charming boy. It costs me a bit to use that word, but all the same . . . charming.

On the afternoon of September 1, he left his house on Cappelens Gate. He said nothing about where he was off to. Where are you going? Out. That's the kind of answer you give at that age. A sort of infinite guardedness. You think you're so exceptional. And his mother didn't have the sense to press him. Maybe she used his obstinacy as fuel for her martyrdom. Her son was growing away from her, and she hated it. But it's really a matter of respect. She should have taught the boy always to reply in a polite and precise manner. I'm going out, well, with someone. We're thinking of going into town. I'll be home before midnight. Surely that's not too much to ask, is it? But she had failed, as have so many others. That's what happens when you

278

invest all your energy in yourself, your own life, your own sorrow. I know what I'm talking about. And the sorrow was going to get worse. He never came home.

Yes, I've seen Andreas. I can see him whenever I like. A lot of people are going to be surprised when he's finally found. And of course they'll speculate, they'll guess, and write up reports, carry on discussions, and fill numerous files. Everyone with his own theory. And all wrong, of course. People howl with many voices. In the midst of that din I've lived in silence for almost sixty years. My name is Irma. Now I'm the one who's doing the talking. I won't take much time, and I'm not saying that I have a monopoly on the truth. But what you're reading now is my version.

A childhood memory comes back to me. I can summon it whenever I like. I'm standing out on the porch with one hand on the doorknob. It's silent inside, but I know that they're there. I open the door very quietly and walk into the kitchen. Mother is standing at the counter, peeling the skin from a boiled mackerel. I can still smell cloying, unpleasant odor. She shifts her heavy body a little, indicating vaguely that she has noticed my presence. Father is busy over by the window. He's pressing putty into the cracks in the frame to keep the draft out. It's an old house. The putty is white and soft like clay, with a dry, chalklike smell. My two sisters are sitting at the kitchen table, both busy with books and papers. I remember how the sunlight became pale, almost nauseating, in the green kitchen. I'm maybe six years old. Instinctively I'm afraid to make any noise. I stand there, all alone, and stare at them. They're all busy with something. I feel very useless, almost in the way, as if I'd been born too late. I'd often think I might have been an accident. There are two years between my sisters; I came along eight years later. What could have made my mother want another child after such a long time? But the idea that I might have been unwanted makes me miserable. I've had it for so long, it's a well-worn idea

This memory is so real that I can still feel the hem of my dress tickling my knee. I'm standing in the yellowish green light again and noticing how alone I am. No one says hello. I'm the youngest. Not doing anything important. I don't mean that at the time my father should have stopped what he was doing, maybe lifted me up and tossed me in the air. I was too heavy for him. He had rheumatism, and I was big and chubby, with bones like a horse. That's what Mother used to say. Like a horse. It was just Irma who had come in. Nothing to make a fuss about. Their heads turning imperceptibly, in case it was someone important, and then discovering that it was only Irma. We were here first, their looks said.

Their indifference took my breath away. I had the same feeling then that I had when I persuaded Mother to tell me about when I was born. She'd shrugged at the question, but admitted that it had happened in the middle of the night, during a terrible storm. Thunder and a fierce wind. That made me happy— to think that I had arrived in the world with a crash and a roar. But then she had added, with a dry laugh, that the whole thing was over in a matter of minutes. You slid right out like a kitten, she'd said, and my happiness had drained away.

Now I waited, my knees locked, my feet planted on the floor. I'd been gone for quite a while, after all. Anything could have happened. We lived near the sea, didn't we? Ships from other countries regularly docked in the harbor. Sailors swarmed through the streets, staring at anyone over the age of ten. Well, I was six, but sturdy as a horse, as I mentioned. Or I could have been lying with a broken leg or arm on the pavement near Gartnerhall, where we often played on the flat roof. Later, three Alsatians stood guard up there, but before that happened we used to play on that roof, and I might have fallen over the edge. Or I could have been crushed under the wheels of a large truck. Not even my big bones would have survived. But they were never worried. Not about things like that. About other things, yes. If

I was holding an apple: Had someone given it to me? I hadn't pinched it, had I? No? Well, had I thanked them nicely? Had they asked me to say hello to my mother and father?

My brain was churning as I tried to think up some kind of task. Some way that I could become part of what I felt they shared. Not that they turned me away, just that they didn't invite me in. I'll tell you one thing: those four people shared an aura. It was strong and clear, and reddish-brown, and it hardly flickered at all, the way it does for the rest of us. It was wrapped around them as tightly as a barrel hoop, and I was on the outside, enveloped in a colorless fog. The solution was to do something. The person who is doing something cannot be overlooked, but I couldn't think of anything. I didn't have any homework; I hadn't started school. That's why I just stood there, staring. At the boiled mackerel, at all the books lying around. At Father, who was working carefully and quietly. If only he'd given me a piece of that white putty! Just to roll between my fingers.

For a paralyzing second I was struck by something that I think is important, important because it helps explain both to myself and to you, who are reading this, how it could happen—I mean, the whole thing with Andreas. I suddenly became aware of the tremendous set of rules governing that room. In the silence, in the hands that were working, in the closed faces, there was a set of rules that I must submit to and follow to the letter. I stood in the silence of the kitchen and felt those rules descend on me like a cage from the ceiling. And it struck me with enormous force: within that set of rules I was invulnerable! If I stayed within that clear framework of diligence and propriety, no one could touch me. That *within* meant I could be around people without offending them, without causing anybody to look askance at me; it meant feeling a sense of peace because I was like everyone else. Because I thought the same way. And then in my mind I saw a narrow street with high walls: this was to be my life. And a terrible sadness overwhelmed me. Until that moment

I might have believed in freedom, the way children do; children believe that anything is possible. But I made a decision, even though I was so young and might not have entirely understood it then. I obeyed a primeval instinct for survival. I didn't want to be alone. I decided that I'd rather be like them and follow the rules. But something departed from me at that instant—it rose up and flew off and vanished forever. That's why I remember the moment so clearly. There in the kitchen, in the yellow-green light, at the age of six, I lost my freedom.

That silent, well-mannered child. In Christmas and birthday pictures I'm sitting on my mother's knee and looking at the camera with a pious smile. Now I have an iron jaw that shoots pain up into my temples. How could things have ended up this way? No doubt there are many different reasons, and some of what happened can be put down to pure coincidence, the fact that our paths crossed on one particular evening. But what about the actual crime? The impulse itself, where does that come from? When does murder occur? In such and such a place, at such and such a moment in time? In this case, I can share the blame with circumstance. The fact that he stepped into my path, that he was the sort of person he was. Because with him I was no longer Irma: I was Irma with Andreas. And that was not the same as Irma with Ingemar, or Irma with Runi. Chemistry, you know. Each time, a new formula is created. Irma and Andreas destroyed each other. Is that true?

Does it emerge over a period of years? Does a crime lie dormant in the body's individual coding? Is murder a result of a long, inevitable process? From now on, I will have to view my life in the light of the horrible thing that happened, and to view that horrible thing in the light of what has been my life. That is what everyone around me will do. They'll look into my past life for something that might explain whatever part of it can be explained. The rest will be left to float in a gray sea of theories.

But to return to the past: I stood, in the silence of the kitchen, and my wordless presence made the silence shrill. Before, it had felt beautiful, but now they couldn't stand it any more. Mother turned around and crossed the room, bent down and sniffed at my hair.

"Your hair needs washing," she said. "It smells."

For a moment I considered going to fetch my art supplies. Instead, I left the kitchen, went out to the garden, climbed over the fence, walked past the abandoned smithy and into the woods. Among the spruce trees there was a pleasant gray-green darkness. I was wearing brown sandals, and on the dry path I came across an anthill. I poked at it with a twig, gleeful at the chaos I was able to create, a catastrophe in that well-ordered society that might take weeks to repair. The desire to destroy! The joyous sense of power as I scraped inside that anthill with the twig. It felt good. I looked around for something to feed them. A dead mouse, something like that. Then I could stand there and watch while they devoured it. They would drop everything, forget the catastrophe: having something to devour would come first, I was sure of that. But I didn't find anything, so I kept on walking. I came to a derelict farmhouse, sat down on the front steps, and thought about the story of the people who had lived there, Gustav and Inger and their twelve children: Uno, Sekunda, Trevor, Firmin, Femmer, Sexus, Syver, Otto, Nils, Tidemann, Ellef, and Tollef. It was incomprehensible, yet true, and all of them were dead now.

Yes. The God that I don't believe in knows that I've seen Andreas. I think back to that terrifying moment when I felt it coming—the desire to destroy him. At the same instant I saw my own face reflected in a windowpane. And I remember the feeling, a sweet pressure, like warm oil running through my body. The certainty that this was evil. My face in the bluish glass: the hideous, evil person you become when the Devil holds the candle.